Cordelia opened the large paneled doors and entered the room, pausing to admire the endless rows of books that lay before her.

"Do you smell that, Lydia? It's the smell of knowledge," she murmured, drawing in a deep breath. She took in the heady scent of leather and parchment, of old ink and dusty shelves, and enjoyed the sensation greatly.

"It is also," said a voice from the depths of the burgundy couch facing the south window, "the smell of a family who cares little for such things as education, literature, or the finer aspects of art, other than what can be obtained as a symbol of status and prestige."

Cordelia froze in midstep. That voice. *Oh dear. Not him. Not here.*

It couldn't be. It simply couldn't. This was absurd.

She peered over the top of the couch and gasped. There, with his head on a pillow and his long legs stretched out before him, was Rhys Aubrey.

He rose leisurely and bowed, surreptitiously pushing a lock of wayward dark hair from his face. "Mrs. Falconer, so good to see you again."

That Falconer Woman

by

Patti Wigington

This is a work of fiction. Names, characters, places, and incidents are either the product of the author's imagination or are used fictitiously, and any resemblance to actual persons living or dead, business establishments, events, or locales, is entirely coincidental.

That Falconer Woman

Contact Information: info@thewildrosepress.com

Cover Art by *Debbie Taylor*

The Wild Rose Press, Inc.
PO Box 708
Adams Basin, NY 14410-0708
Visit us at www.thewildrosepress.com

Publishing History
First Tea Rose Edition, 2021
Trade Paperback ISBN 978-1-5092-3474-5
Digital ISBN 978-1-5092-3475-2

Published in the United States of America

Dedication

For my grandparents,
whose home library taught me
that love and magic can be found anywhere

Chapter One

Ophelia Dean was to be married, and it was her full intention for the wedding to be so expensive and lavish that the best people in society would whisper of it with envy for years to come.

"Well, Ophelia," her elder sister Cordelia said pleasantly, shortly after the engagement was announced to the rest of the Dean family, "you've done rather well for yourself. You've provided Mother with something she can lord over all of the other ladies in Chesham and the rest of Wycombe Heath, made your brothers happy by becoming Brompton's problem instead of theirs, and managed to find a man who will do exactly as you tell him for the rest of your natural lives. Nicely done, I must say. I heartily congratulate you."

Ophelia made a face, the sort of face that the governess had always threatened might just stick but had as yet failed to do, and put down her embroidery. Sewing floral designs in the tiniest of stitches, all of which were expected to be neat and even, was terribly boring. Ophelia was well-bred and proper, though, and would never have been so unpleasant as to make such an observation out loud to anyone but her closest friends.

"Oh, do stop it, Cordie. Brompton is a perfectly decent sort, and I want to marry him, even if he is just a trifle on the dull side. Not everyone can be as exciting as you perhaps would like. He is from an old family with a good name. He is pleasing to look at—other than the one odd upper tooth. I'm sure you've noticed it?—but he does have excellent manners and ten thousand pounds a year, so I'll thank you to be happy for me today and not belittle the fine gentleman that I intend to have for my husband."

"Wealth isn't everything, dear," Cordelia said, raising one eyebrow slightly. "Falconer had nothing at all when I married him, you may recall, and yet we still managed to have a wonderful marriage before he died. A man's income and family name do not, in my opinion, have any bearing on his ability to satisfy and please a wife."

Her younger sister blushed prettily, as befitted a young unmarried lady of her station. "Cordie, please, you mustn't speak of such things." Ophelia glanced nervously at their mother, who was draped across a settee near the hearth, fanning herself and huffing indelicately as she fidgeted with the lacing of her stays. "Mother says it's in poor taste for any of us to mention Falconer at all, really. It's bad enough he was a footman and Irish, but then scampering off to America to live with wild Indians…It's still quite scandalous, and I can't have you flaunting such a sordid relationship when old Lady Brompton is about. She'll refuse to receive you, and then I shan't be able to have you come to visit Fairfield Hall when I marry Henry."

Cordelia leaned closer to her sister and patted her hand. "Ophelia, do you know something? Lady Brompton is a vicious harpy, and I do not especially care what she thinks of me. I was fortunate enough to marry a passionate and lusty man, and I have plenty of money, my own land, and a lovely daughter who is the absolute light of my life, so there's nothing that old, hideous dragon can do to me that will matter one bit. A pox upon Lady Brompton, I say."

Ophelia gasped, feeling a bit faint. Cordie had always done and said what she wanted, even as a child, and then when she had run off with Falconer, everyone had found it very shocking. They'd all rather deliberately forgotten about her except to whisper about her bad behavior in her absence. Now, some fifteen years later, she was back from some wild place far away in America and hadn't changed very much at all.

Certainly, Cordelia was far wealthier now than she had been when she eloped with Father's footman, but her manners were just as scandalous as ever. She cared not a whit whether she was accepted by good society. She often refused to put on a bonnet when out in the sun (which Ophelia knew would cause freckles, a malady that nice people did not get) and she used bad words, like "pox" and "lusty." Ophelia simply could not understand how the two of them could be from the same family.

Cordelia, indifferent as ever to Ophelia's astonished expression, rose abruptly and went to the sideboard to pour another cup of tea. Ten years older than her sister, Cordelia had been off having adventures with Tom Falconer while her younger siblings were still in the schoolroom. And now she was back in Chesham, right where she'd started so long ago, with a bit more money than it was in good taste for a lady to discuss.

She also had in her possession a fourteen-year-old daughter, and the title to a great deal of land in a place called Virginia, which was practically on the other side of the world; she'd had to point at a spot on a globe to show her brothers where she had lived. She also—although this had been noticed only by the most perceptive member of her family, her brother Mercutio, who had shared the observation with Ophelia—wore a small, tasteful mourning brooch with her late husband's rust-colored hair woven into it. To Ophelia's great shock and their mother's absolute horror, Cordelia favored dresses that exposed a bit more décolletage than was appropriate in a widow of three and thirty, and certainly more than could be comfortable in the chilly fall air.

Brompton appeared at Cordelia's shoulder, as she peered out the window. "May I now call you sister?"

She laughed and took his arm. Brompton *was* a decent sort, even if he was foolish enough to agree to marry Ophelia. "You may indeed. I've always thought of you as a brother, you know. Ever since the day you pushed me into the pond."

"Well, I did catch that turtle fair and square. Wasn't quite right of you to take it away, was it?" He stepped back, a somber expression on his face. "I must tell you, having to ask your brothers for their permission was one of the most difficult things I've done in my life. I can never tell them apart, so I was forced to speak to both of them at the same time. They spent a full two hours enumerating her charms, telling me childhood stories, and consuming copious amounts of brandy. I am unashamed to admit it was rather terrifying. You must know, Cordie, that *your* approval means a great deal to me. I know we are friends, but do I have your blessing in marrying Ophelia?" he asked softly.

She patted his arm. “Brompton, you have my blessing if for no other reason than for taking her off my family’s hands.” At his crestfallen expression, she hastily continued. “But, as well, you have my blessing because I know she loves you and that you love her. Yes, my dear, I believe you two will truly make one another happy, and for that I am grateful.”

He smiled with delight, and Cordelia saw, not for the first time, why Ophelia was so in love with him. Henry Brompton was a very simple man who wore every one of his emotions on his face, and there was neither artifice nor pretense about him. When he spoke of Ophelia, his eyes lit in the same way that Cordelia had seen in Falconer’s for so many years. It was the honest and genuine look of a man most truly in love. To be sure, Mr. Henry Brompton would spend the rest of his life trying to make Ophelia Dean happy. She only hoped he was up to the task; it was not one she would have wished upon many men at all, particularly not one of whom she was so fond.

With any luck, her sister would be as fortunate in the marriage bed as she, Cordelia, had been. Falconer had been a giving and passionate lover, and the two of them had fit together perfectly in every way, emotionally and physically. How she missed feeling him next to her in the night. She snuck a glance over at Ophelia, looking demure and prim, and decided that her sister was as yet untouched by Brompton, or any other man, for that matter.

“Cordelia,” her mother called from the floral settee. She breathlessly patted a cushion beside her. “Cordelia, do come sit!”

Because Ophelia was off distracting herself with a

plate of sweets and whispering in the ear of their brother Tybalt, Cordelia had no choice but to obey. She often wished that with motherhood came with the privilege of avoiding one's own parent, but sadly, that had not been the case since her recent return to the country of her birth. She arranged herself properly on the settee so that Mother would have no need to correct her posture.

"Oh, Cordelia," Mrs. Dean began, "is this not the most exciting news? Ophelia and Mr. Brompton to be married at last! I am most overcome—Dear, sit up. You are slouching again and it does not suit you at all—and there will simply be too much to do! A wedding right after Christmas, but before the London Season begins, can you imagine? Too much to do!" she repeated, tapping Cordelia with her fan for emphasis. "Now, I know you are just recently arrived back from America—and you should be grateful, very grateful indeed, that we've agreed to receive you, on account of the way you disgraced your poor dead father and I, what with all that footman business—but there are a few things I feel I must advise you upon now that your sister is officially to marry Mr. Brompton."

She stopped briefly for air, and Cordelia pounced at the opportunity, aware that there might not be another for some time. "Mother," she said, "I do understand that Father was disappointed in me, as were you, and for that I have apologized to you both repeatedly. However, you must remember that Father did write to me before his death, expressing his wish for reconciliation and forgiving me my trespasses. If he could find no fault with me, I see no reason why anyone else should be able to. Do remember that all that footman business was actually my marriage, legally solemnized and binding in the eyes of both the church and a court of law."

"Yes. Well," continued Agatha Dean, "you do know that members of the *ton* have a long memory, particularly when it comes to scandal. Darling, you eloped with a footman. It's just not done. Well, perhaps one sees that sort of thing in dairymaids or butchers' daughters and the like, but certainly not with young ladies of good family." She fanned herself rapidly. "And an Irishman, at that! A red-headed Irish footman! What on earth could you have been thinking? We had that nice Augustus Littleberry picked out for you, you know, and him with hopes of a clergyman's living! Not a great fortune, admittedly, but a stable position, and he could even become a vicar someday with the right patronage. He's a younger son, but his father is quite respectable. At the very least, we might have selected you a nice soldier, wouldn't that have been lovely? Getting married to a man in regimentals?"

Cordelia sighed. She had been back in England just a few weeks now, and so far no one had bothered to discuss The Great Unpleasantness of 1803 with her, because nice people simply did not talk about such things. Now, however, it was clear that even fifteen years later, her mother was prepared to make a very large issue of the event indeed. Really, it had only been a matter of time.

"Mother," Cordelia said firmly, "I could never have married Augustus Littleberry, and you know that quite well. We would not have suited one another at all, despite his respectable living. We would not have suited, even if he were a duke with thousands of pounds a year, if I am to be completely truthful. I would have made him most unhappy within just hours of our wedding, and he would have driven me to commit homicide in a matter of days."

"He's a reverend now, had you heard? Has a nice comfortable living in Wycombe Heath, thanks to the good graces of Lady Brompton, and no wife to share it with. I believe he'd be quite a catch for a lady who could see the benefits of marrying a man of the cloth." Her mother eyed Cordelia thoughtfully. "Your footman's been dead for five years now…Perhaps you might be ready to consider another attachment? Perhaps even more children?"

"Mother!" Cordelia whispered. "Stop it this instant. My footman, as you called him, had a name. His name was Tom Falconer, and although I know it pains you to hear this, I loved him a great deal and he was my husband and the father of your grandchild. Please, I wish to hear no more about you marrying me off to Augustus Littleberry, reverend or not. I would also like to preemptively ask you not to foist me off on some unfortunate retired soldier who would have no idea what he was getting himself into."

Although she dared not speak it aloud, another reason Cordelia could never have been happy with Mr. Littleberry was that, quite frankly, she cringed at the mere thought of seeing him without his clothes. In his youth, he'd been a man who indulged greatly in food and wine, leading a sedentary lifestyle and not putting a great deal of effort into physical exercise or his own hygiene. She didn't have an objection to large men in general, but the sheer lack of care that he took to maintain his health…She doubted that his constitution or her opinion of him could have improved significantly in the past fifteen years. She leaned toward the hearth, adding more wood to the fire, although her mother insisted upon ringing for a servant to come take care of it. The room was beginning to chill, despite the blaze.

There was a burst of laughter from the other side of the room. Her brothers were mercilessly tormenting poor Brompton, having a good joke at his expense.

"Mother, excuse me, I must go rescue Ophelia's beloved. Heaven knows he's too gentle-natured to extricate himself." Without waiting for a reply, Cordelia joined the men. "Oh, Brompton, what on earth are my brothers saying to you? Something thoroughly awful, I'm certain."

In the past, the twins had managed to convince the gullible Brompton to give his favorite horse to a roving tinker and made him lose an entire year's worth of his fortune at a gaming table. Once, they'd even persuaded him that Lord Sackville's largest hound, Hercules, had attained such a prodigious size by being fed a steady diet of live goats and small peasant children.

Brompton smiled pleasantly. "Why, they tell me that I must hold a house party at Fairfield Hall to celebrate my engagement to Miss Dean. Doesn't that sound like a wonderful idea?"

Cordelia eyed Tybalt suspiciously, for whenever there was mischief, he was nearly always the ringleader. A house party seemed remarkably harmless, and therefore completely out of character for her brother. "It does, as a matter of fact. Tybalt, what else are you up to?"

He smiled, giving a look that had melted the heart and resolve of many a Chesham dairymaid. "Why,

Cordie, we simply think it would be lovely to spend a week or two at Fairfield—the hunting is rumored to be splendid, isn't it, Brompton?—and naturally, a small Christmas party and even a dance to celebrate would be the perfect way of honoring Brompton's engagement to our sister."

"Indeed," chimed in Mercutio. He was a perfect replica of his brother, in reverse. They appeared as mirror images—where Tybalt's sandy hair fell to the left, Mercutio's always seemed to drift to the right. Tybalt had a dimple on his right cheek, and Mercutio a matching one on the opposite side. "Wouldn't a holiday party be splendid? And Brompton says he's got new books in his library."

Cordelia blinked. "I must confess, Henry, I am puzzled by your sudden interest in literature. We have known each other some twenty years, and to my knowledge you have never willingly opened a book."

He caught her look and had the decency to look abashed. "Not for me," he admitted. "I know Ophelia loves to read, so I've added a few volumes I thought might be of interest to her. There's some nice poetry and some new books of sermons. And some Shakespeare! Your mother suggested I add Shakespeare."

"Mm. I'm sure she did," Cordelia said, suddenly wishing to be away from all the excitement of Ophelia's newly announced betrothal. "Well, Brompton, you settle the details, and I am certain my entire family will be happy to attend. Please excuse me. I must go check on Lydia."

Lydia Falconer was, as her mother expected, in the stable. Cordelia's father, Alderman William Dean, had purchased a pair of lovely chestnut mares, Gemma and Juno, shortly before he passed away, and Lydia adored them. Accustomed to sitting a horse since the age of five, Lydia had inherited her own father's love of the animals, as well as his skill in handling them. When Cordelia found her, she was feeding Juno apples and stroking the mare's nose. Puffs of steam enveloped Lydia's hands as the horse exhaled.

Lydia, a bit long-legged and coltish herself, smiled at her mother. "This one. If I could choose any horse at all to ride, it would be Juno. She is lovely, is she not?"

Cordelia nodded. "She is indeed. Your father would have been proud to see you ride her, to be sure."

"I miss him a great deal," Lydia said into Juno's mane.

"As do I. However, it's been five years now, and I feel he would have wanted us to put aside our mourning and live our lives. Besides, your grandmother asked me to return home."

"She told you she was ill and that she was dying," Lydia said with a faintly accusatory tone. "She's not ill at all."

Cordelia sniffed. "Well, my mother has spent a good deal of her life being ill when it suited her best. You might think she would be accustomed to it by now, but I believe she must have truly been convinced that she was at death's door, in order for her to write and invite me back to Chesham."

Lydia frowned. "She didn't like my father, did she?"

"It's not a question of her liking your father, dear. It's a matter of your father being a footman, and poor, and Irish. I know that means nothing to you, because in

America such things make no difference, but here…Well, here it caused a bit of a scandal. I was a well-respected girl from a good family, and I did the unthinkable." Cordelia ruffled her daughter's auburn hair, so like Tom Falconer's. "I followed my heart, despite the uproar it caused."

Lydia took up a brush and began to run it over the mare's soft coat. "Why did it matter that Father was a footman? Was he not good enough for your family?"

"Not according to Chesham society, no, or London's. But your father was a good enough man for me, and I loved him very much. We had ten wonderful years together." Cordelia pulled her daughter close and kissed her forehead. "Don't you ever let anyone make you feel that you're unworthy, my darling. You live your life as you wish, no matter what they tell you to do."

"That's what you did," Lydia said knowingly.

"Yes."

"And if I should run off with one of Grandmother's footmen?"

"Then," Cordelia said with a smile, "I should hope he's as honorable as your father was and treats you as well as your father treated me. Handsome would be of benefit as well. I should also want him to be wise enough to listen when you suggest he invest in a tobacco plantation, so that you will be well set if he happens to die too young."

Chapter Two

The home of Mrs. Agatha Dean, a good-sized house called Coltsford, was the largest in the village of Chesham, although certainly nowhere near as grand as the home of their neighbors Lord and Lady Sackville, or that of the Brompton family seat. Coltsford was in a great uproar for much of November, owing to the need of the mistress to mobilize a veritable army of servants and staff for the sole purpose of making and packing dresses in which she and her daughters and granddaughter might attend a winter party at Fairfield Hall. A milliner was brought in from Little Chepping, as well as two dressmakers commandeered from the Sackville household, much to the chagrin of Lady Sackville, along with a lace maker and three seamstresses.

Cordelia was perfectly happy to wear the dresses she had brought with her from America. Daily, she tried to escape her mother's plans and frequently foiled them by hiding out of doors dressed in old skirts and a plain woolen cloak.

Agatha Dean would have none of it. "I will not have it said that any daughter of mine appears in public looking as though she were some colonial backwoodsman's wife, or worse, some traveling vagabond tinker! No, I will not, and so despite your notions that what you are wearing here in Chesham is fashionable or acceptable, I beg to differ indeed. We will have you dressed like a proper English lady once again soon. Really, I cannot imagine what you were thinking, looking like a washerwoman or worse when you arrived here. And poor Lydia! How on earth can we have her come out in society if she is dressed as though she's just climbed out of a barn?"

"Mother. That will do," Cordelia said. "If you insist upon putting new dresses on me, and on my daughter, I shall bear it, if for no other reason than to keep the peace between us. But Lydia is fourteen, and you shall not—I repeat, you shall not—even discuss her coming out in society for another four years. I won't have it."

Agatha shrugged. "You may insist all you like, but girls are coming out younger and younger. You were out at sixteen—for all the good it did us, with you running off a year later—and Ophelia has been out since she was fifteen, although of course we all suspected she'd end up making a match with Mr. Brompton eventually. My dear, if you hope to make a good marriage for Lydia—"

Cordelia rose. "That is quite enough. Mother, there will be no more talk of marriage for my daughter—or for myself, in the event you might be planning to arrange things with the Reverend Augustus Littleberry the moment my back is turned—for many years to come. You've got Ophelia's wedding plans to keep you busy for the next two months, and once that is over, you may spend even more time visiting with her at Fairfield Hall and asking her when she'll begin having babies to keep you occupied."

Agatha was properly shocked. "I would never be so

indecorous!"

Tybalt piped up from across the room. "Of course you would, Mother."

"I would never, and I don't know why you must make such a horrible joke and say such a thing." Agatha pouted. "At any rate, the dressmakers will be ready for you any time, and I promise you, once you've rid yourself of those dreary cotton and homespun things you've been wearing, you'll feel like a proper English lady once more."

Cordelia raised a brow. "I was perfectly content to be an improper American lady, but no one here seems to approve of the notion."

"Oh, do hush! You simply must not say such awful things!" her mother exclaimed, and stormed red-faced from the room, nose in the air.

Tybalt and Mercutio burst into laughter.

"We've really missed you a great deal, Cordie," said Tybalt.

"We have, indeed. It's been very dull without you here. Ophelia is just like Mother, always worrying about what the neighbors might think or say," Mercutio said.

"Yes, well, I've been a bit preoccupied with other things for the past few years." Cordelia helped herself to a cup of tea and a biscuit. "It's rather different in America."

Tybalt nodded. "That's what I'd heard. Sackville told me just the other day that a man can go to America and be anything he wants, no matter his station or birth. Can you imagine? He was rightly appalled by it."

"I'm sure." Cordelia remembered Lord Sackville well. He was about sixty years old, had a nose that ran incessantly, and could not keep his hands to himself. Many years ago, he had cornered her in the garden and tried to slip his meaty paw into her bodice. She had stomped on his foot, jabbed him in the neck with her elbow, and then managed to avoid ever being alone with him again. Sackville was also of the opinion, like many of his station, that the working class should remain working class, and those who owned land should never dirty their hands by toiling away at menial labor.

Mercutio spoke up. "How did Falconer do it? Leave you with so much money, I mean? He was a footman, for goodness' sake."

Cordelia sipped her tea. "Darlings, Mother would be horrified to hear us discuss anything so impolite as money and income. Do come closer, and I'll be happy to tell you all about it."

The twins leaped over the couch to pile beside her, long legs tangled about each other.

"Well," she began, "here's the thing of it. When we left, Tom had a few pounds tucked away. So did I. We used what we needed to in order to buy passage to Virginia, and with what was left over, we bought a cart and a horse. Then we used the cart and the horse to transport tobacco for the plantation owners, and when we had enough money saved up, we bought land of our own and planted tobacco."

They stared at her, astonished. "And that was it?" they asked in unison, incredulous looks on their faces.

"That was it. The tobacco market boomed, and we made lots of money from it."

Tybalt frowned. "How much is lots?"

"*Lots.*" She laughed softly. "Enough that I don't

have to marry again unless I choose to. We don't need to discuss actual numbers, but suffice it to say I'm quite well off."

"Dear God!" exclaimed Mercutio. "And you sold the land when you came back to Chesham? What a pretty profit that must have made you!"

Cordelia shook her head. "No, I still own it. It seemed foolish to sell a profitable tobacco operation, so I hired a manager to look after things in my absence. Nice young man named McGregor, family background in tobacco farming and as honest as the day is long. Each quarter, he'll deposit the farm's earnings in a bank, and I can live quite comfortably off the interest, if I manage my finances wisely."

Tybalt blinked. "That's the most amazing thing I've ever heard. Merc, have you ever heard of such a thing?"

"I have not. Not at all."

"It's called work, my dears, and I do know that's a concept completely foreign to both of you, unless it's the chore of lifting a mug or raising a chambermaid's skirts."

Tybalt choked on his tea, and Cordelia patted him helpfully on the back. "There, darling, I'm sure you'll be fine. So, you see, while Mother may be trying to marry me off again, this time to someone respectable and dull, I will not be playing along with her. I'm sure you both understand."

They nodded. Indeed, Tybalt and Mercutio Dean had been the focus of their mother's matchmaking efforts for a year or so now, and at every society event, she insisted upon parading them past an endless array of horsey-faced heiresses. Tybalt, being some twenty minutes older than his twin, had inherited Alderman Dean's assets upon their father's death two years ago, but Mercutio was left provided for as well. Thus, both of them were, in society's eyes, decent matrimonial material. Although they had no titles, the brothers Dean were considered fairly good society and cut very dashing figures indeed, so most people were willing to overlook the existence of two or possibly three discreetly placed natural children in the vicinity of Chesham and Wycombe Heath.

Despite their mostly impeccable qualifications as potential husbands, neither was prepared to settle down with a young lady who was not to their liking. The twins preferred to spend their evenings at the fashionable clubs of London and came back to Chesham only when their mother ordered it or when they ran out of money at the gambling tables. Each had vowed—although they would never have admitted it to their surviving parent—that they would do as their elder sister had done and marry someone they genuinely loved, rather than a girl who was homely and dull and rich. The problem was that the sort of women Tybalt and Mercutio enjoyed spending time with were not, by any stretch of the imagination, part of polite society.

"How is it for the ladies in Virginia?" Mercutio asked, a thoughtful look on his face.

Cordelia frowned. "Whatever do you mean?"

"I mean," he said, sitting up and pushing Tybalt's legs aside, "if a lady was…not a lady here in England, could she become one? Could she go to Virginia, and perhaps be seen as respectable?"

Tybalt scowled at his brother. "Are you thinking of Bessie Venables?"

"I am, and don't you mock her. She's a nice girl. Very giving."

"Clearly, as she's given you a pair of by-blows already."

Mercutio hit Tybalt in the nose, and soon Cordelia found herself pinned between a pair of pummeling, punching, cursing brothers.

"Stop it!" she hissed. "What would Mother say if she saw you behaving like this?" She separated them forcibly, not unlike she had done when they were small children. "Tybalt, there's no need to be cruel, and it's not as though you don't have at least one side-slip of your own, according to what the servants tell me—and yes, certainly they whisper about it, so you mustn't look so surprised. Please, do stop being hateful. And Mercutio, to answer your question, in Virginia, your worth and status is determined by who you are and what you do, not by who you once were or what your name is or the things you've done in the past." She paused for a moment, remembering Falconer. "That's why it no longer mattered that my husband was a poor Irish footman or that I was the disgraced daughter of a moderately good family. It didn't signify a bit."

Mercutio nodded, tucking away this bit of information.

Oh dear. Perhaps Cordelia had opened up a door that was better left closed.

****

Fairfield Hall lay some twenty-two miles from the Dean home in Chesham proper and sat in a park of almost four thousand acres northwest of Wycombe Heath and south of the village of Brompton itself. Brompton was a quiet little place, nestled in the rolling hills, with an unassuming population of six hundred souls, most of whom found their employment in some fashion relating to Fairfield Hall and its upkeep.

Built at the time of the Reformation, Fairfield Hall had somewhere around twenty bedrooms—no one was precisely certain of the exact number—located in its two fine wings, a ballroom on the second floor, a gallery of portraits and sculptures, and a library which was dusted daily but rarely visited. A dedicated army of servants tended the gardens regularly, although no one in the family could be bothered to do much besides gaze in passing at the lovely work the groundskeepers had done.

A staff of thirty house servants, from footmen to maids to kitchen girls, worked diligently to maintain the utmost degree of hospitality and comfort for Harriet Brompton and her son, Henry. Lady Brompton's husband, a viscount, had conveniently died many years ago, leaving her with the entire estate entailed upon Henry, who was, fortunately for him, an only child. When the young gentleman reached his majority, he quite charitably allowed Harriet to stay on at Fairfield Hall in perpetuity, this decision due in some degree to his own affable good nature, and in part because Henry Brompton was quite terrified of his mother. He was by no stretch of the imagination the only one to feel this way.

Harriet Brompton ruled Fairfield Hall with an iron fist clad in a satin glove, and it was not uncommon for the household staff to change on a monthly—and sometimes weekly—basis, depending on the whims of Lady Brompton. She was merciless and unforgiving, and every servant, from the housekeeper to the butler to the lowest scullery maid, knew that one mistake, even the simplest of errors, could cost them not only their employment at Fairfield Hall, but possibly even prevent them from ever working in the county again. A footman who displayed dirt on his stockings was subject to the same swift retribution as a kitchen girl who dropped the soup, and all terminations of employment were meted out promptly with no regard to contract or length of prior service.

Thus, when Henry Brompton announced that he would be asking Miss Ophelia Dean to do him the honor of becoming his wife, there was a great deal of consternation among the staff at Fairfield Hall. Would Henry's new bride be as demanding as his mother? Katie, the scullery maid, had heard from Mrs. Chibbs in the kitchen that Miss Dean was actually quite pleasant, if a bit of a social climber, and that she would likely be a firm but fair mistress. Davy, however, who worked in the stables, said that his brother Jamie, who worked as a groom for the Deans, thought Miss Dean might be too mild. Perhaps she would be afraid to speak up around old Lady Brompton, and so things might become far worse before they got better.

Harriet Brompton herself had a considerable collection of opinions on Ophelia Dean and her family. Certainly, the Deans were of an old name, having come down to the county several generations ago, but still…there was something a bit less than respectable about them. Alderman Dean had been a generally unexcitable sort of man who was easy to ignore. He'd had a reputation as being pleasant enough, although beneath Harriet's notice, and had never sullied his hands with labor, but the children! Clearly, they had inherited some genetic predisposition to wild behavior, probably some throwback to a less than acceptable attachment in the family tree, which was distantly connected to the Boleyns and therefore not quite as nice as it ought to have been.

Those horrible twins were well-known for their love of gambling and drink. There was a rumor that one of them had been involved in a duel in London, although there was no definitive proof, just hushed gossip, and stories persisted about their involvement with women of questionable virtue. The oldest sister, Cordelia, had created an even greater scandal by eloping with a footman in her father's employ, and as if that hadn't been awful enough, now she was back to lord her bad behavior and her half-Irish daughter over everyone.

Harriet was disappointed at her son's intention of marrying into such a family and would have been far happier if that little milksop Ophelia had turned Henry down, but of course there was no chance of such a thing taking place. Ophelia had set her cap for Henry when they were children, when the Deans had lived near the village of Brompton, before removing to Chesham just a year or two before Cordelia's scandal.

Ophelia might have been tolerable enough, perhaps, for Harriet's nephew Thomas Heyward, who also lived at Fairfield Hall and was a younger son with no hope of inheriting much of anything, but the girl was not suitable for Henry, whose lineage could be traced much further back than that of the upstart Deans. And yet Henry insisted on marrying the girl, which Harriet suspected might be because Ophelia herself—who was getting a bit past her prime for marriage, truth be told, at three and twenty—had told Henry they should be wed.

Dear Henry never had much gumption, and likely it never crossed his mind to protest when Ophelia entrapped him, Harriet was certain.

And now, Henry had come home from Chesham not only with the distressing announcement of his impending nuptials but also bleating about some house party that was to take place in just a few weeks, right before Christmas. So Fairfield Hall was thrown into great disarray and Lady Brompton along with it, as she barked out orders at servants and her son alike.

"Henry! How could you? You know how I feel about this attachment. Ophelia Dean is a moderately pleasant enough girl, to be sure, but her family is prone to scandalous behavior. I won't prohibit you from marrying her—after all, you are nine and twenty years old, and it is indeed time you found a wife and started having children, even if it is with someone of questionable blood—but I do wish we could do this quietly and discreetly. A simple wedding, here at Fairfield Hall, without a great deal of fanfare or trumpets, would suit well enough, would it not?" Harriet cooed, as she was wont to do when speaking with Henry and hoping to change his mind. "I'm sure Agatha would find it pleasing."

"Mother," Henry began, "it's already done. I've invited them all to spend a fortnight, the entire family. And there's to be a small engagement ball in Ophelia's honor, so of course they shall be attending, as well as a few other families of note. The Sackvilles have already accepted, and the Dunlea-Boggins girls, and I've sent a note round to—"

"Not that Falconer woman, as well?"

"Mother, Cordie is delightful, you'll see. And her daughter is charming."

Harriet scowled. "I do not feel we should be receiving the bastard daughter of a footman, Henry, in Fairfield Hall. It's not done, not by decent people."

"The girl is no bastard, Mother. Cordie married Falconer when they ran off. Say what you like, the child—and Lydia's her name; you might wish to make a note of it—is legitimate, and I won't have you insulting either of them. Cordelia's come back to Chesham to make a new start for herself and the girl."

"Very well," Harriet said with a heavy sigh, fanning herself dramatically. She would acquiesce to Henry's unreasonable demands for now and then speak as she liked once the Deans—and that disreputable Falconer person and her offspring—arrived.

Henry smiled happily at his mother's cooperation and left the parlor.

"Aunt Brompton," said Thomas Heyward from across the table, "perhaps you might consider the potential benefits of Henry's invitation to Ophelia and her family."

She scowled a thundercloud at him. She had, as usual, nearly forgotten he was there. "Nephew, I am certain there can be no benefit whatsoever to having those people at Fairfield Hall, unless I wished to greatly aggravate myself by the sheer fact of their presence."

"No, no," Heyward said, leaning forward and helping himself to another kipper. "Think of this as an opportunity to do something good for someone less fortunate than yourself. An act of charity, if you will."

Harriet's eyes narrowed. "Whatever can you mean,

Thomas?"

He glanced up. "Miss Dean's family is clearly unsuitable for Henry. However, he's made it apparent that he means to marry her no matter what. That means you can either live with a connection to a less-than-reputable family, or you can find a way to improve their reputation, which will naturally reflect well upon you and your benevolent manner, should you choose to condescend to such an exercise."

"Go on." She squinted as she peered down the table at him, intrigued. She honestly had never credited Heyward with talent for much beyond looking decorative in a drawing room.

"The older sister. What's her name, Cordelia? Obviously there's some sort of scandal related to her first marriage…"

"If it was a marriage at all, of which I have my doubts," cut in Harriet.

"So take the opportunity to find her a new, more reputable husband. She's a widow, and she's at least thirty. I should think she must be eager to remarry at this point. There must be some eligible men, of not overly high station but of respectable positions, who would have her, even at her age."

There was a long silence, while Harriet shrewdly sized up her nephew. "And just who, Thomas, would you suggest? Yourself, perhaps?"

He shrugged. "I don't know, as I haven't seen her. She's still of childbearing age, and Henry says she's not unattractive. Perhaps find her a nice widower who already has a few children she can look after? Regardless, if not me, then what about Reverend Whatsis, the soft podgy one, that she was meant to marry back before she ran off?"

"Littleberry?" Harriet asked. "Augustus Littleberry! Of course. I'd rather forgotten about him, although I'm sure I'm not the first to do so. Hm. He's still unmarried, which is not a great surprise. My son has already invited him to perform the wedding. He's financially stable, but not overly wealthy, since it wouldn't do for a man of the church to be indulged with too much money. I've given him a decent living here in the parish, with a few hundred pounds a year, and he's certainly respectable enough. He's rather sedentary, and there are some issues with his hygiene, but I suppose that cannot be helped. Do you know, Thomas, I think you may have a wonderful idea. If we were to encourage a suitable match for Cordelia, it could be slightly more bearable to have her connected to the family. And certainly, marrying a curate would improve her standing quite a bit." Harriet was impressed with Heyward, for once. "I shall send word to Reverend Littleberry immediately. I doubt that he would decline an invitation for an extended stay here at Fairfield Hall."

Really, no one with any sense at all would do so, and Harriet Brompton knew it.

****

On the third day of December, the family of Mrs. Agatha Dean piled into two carriages for the journey to Fairfield Hall. The first carriage contained Mrs. Dean, Ophelia, and a lady's maid, as well as Cordelia and her daughter. The second, slightly smaller, carried five servants and their belongings, and a rented horse-cart was piled high with an impressive collection of trunks, hatboxes, carpetbags, and valises, all carefully packed away, held in place with some degree of creative stacking and no small amount of rope.

Tybalt and Mercutio had flatly refused to travel in or atop either conveyance, and instead rode Gemma and Juno despite the unseasonably cold morning. They dashed ahead in abrupt bursts, racing each other down the road, and then galloped back in a manner that meant they were covering the same general route as everyone else, but doing so three or four times rather than only once.

During a brief—although somewhat chilly—stop for a midday picnic by the river at Little Chepping, Agatha began to sneeze heartily and bemoaned the state of her poor aching lungs and the increasingly cloudy skies. The caravan continued on despite the arrival of an afternoon rain, which soon turned to snow. By the time the party struggled into the village of Brompton at sundown, Cordelia could barely feel the end of her own nose. Although the plan had originally been to make the journey of the last few miles on to Fairfield Hall that evening, they had lost many hours to the poor weather, and one of the carriages had a loose wheel, which greatly distressed Mrs. Dean. Combined with her conviction that she simply must be taking ill, it was decided that they could not go on until the morning.

"We shall have to stay the night here in Brompton," Agatha announced, shaking her head and blowing her nose prodigiously. "I will not ride ten miles in the snow on a wheel that cannot be trusted, particularly when the roads are so dark and I am clearly so very unwell, no, I absolutely will not."

"It is but three or four miles, Mother, not ten at all," Cordelia pointed out, trying to be gracious but suspecting she might have failed as usual. "Tybalt, go see if you can find someone to replace the wheel for us once the sun rises in the morning, and Mercutio, you have one of the footmen carry a message to Fairfield Hall to let them know we shall be delayed until tomorrow."

Tybalt sent a manservant to the Rose and Crown, the village's only inn, to see if there would be room for all of them. As it happened, there were two rooms free, enough to hold the ladies in the larger and Tybalt and Mercutio in the smaller. The servants were relegated to sleep by the fire in the kitchen, which was a far better situation than having them quartered in the stables as Mrs. Dean initially suggested. After a great deal of fussing and rearranging in the room, which held her mother, sister, and daughter, Cordelia decided she'd had quite enough of feminine companionship for one evening.

"I believe I shall go out for some air," she said, although no one was really listening. Lydia had her nose buried in a novel—something lurid about a kidnapped virgin and a pirate, safely hidden away within the cover of *Mrs. Bamford's Proper Deportment for Young Ladies of Station* so as to avoid upsetting Agatha. Meanwhile, Mrs. Dean and Ophelia were bickering over who was to sleep nearest the washstand and who by the door. Cordelia sighed, took up her wrap, and descended the stairs.

The innkeeper, a solidly built man whose name was Wilkins, greeted her as she entered the common room. "Good evening, missus. Might I get you something to eat? There's cold mutton stew left over from supper, and I've got fresh-baked bread and some fine hard cheese. Ain't much, but it's good and hearty and should warm the soul on a night such as this," he said, pulling out a seat for her near the large fireplace. The room was dry and cozy, despite the open space.

"That would be lovely, thank you, Wilkins."

"My pleasure, missus. You just sit right here by the fire, and I'll send my Annie out with a tray in just a moment for you."

Cordelia adjusted a bit so that her toes would be toward the flames. Agatha had forced her to wear a pair of good satin shoes rather than her leather walking boots, and naturally they had gotten soaked through the moment she exited the carriage straight into the largest puddle in the entire village of Brompton.

"Watch yourself," said a low voice behind her. "That wood's still green, and it's been spitting out embers all evening."

Practically on cue, there was an ominous popping sound from the hearth, and Cordelia quickly pulled her feet back, tucking them safely beneath the folds of her wrap. "Thank you," she said, looking up. "Your advice was indeed timely, Mr…?"

"Rhys Aubrey."

Cordelia rose and extended a hand. She was tall for a woman, and the same height as many men of her acquaintance, but she only stood to Aubrey's nose. His black eyes glittered down at her in the firelight. "Mrs. Cordelia Falconer," she said boldly, adding a polite nod as an afterthought.

He raised a dark eyebrow at her. "This, I must say, is a first. A respectable lady alone in the Rose and Crown and introducing herself to me without a chaperone."

She took a step back. "I beg your pardon, Mr. Aubrey. I simply wished to thank you for pointing out the dangers of the fireplace."

"No, no, Mrs. Falconer," he said, a look of genuine concern on his face. "It is I who must beg your pardon. I meant no offense—I simply meant that it is refreshing to meet a lady who doesn't appear to be bound by society's constraints. I do apologize if my words sounded critical, but I assure you they were not intended as such in any way."

Cordelia peered at him in the flickering light. Although he was a bit disheveled, he seemed respectable enough. She could tell by the cut of his clothes that he was no tinker or servant.

He regarded her directly, an amused glint in his eye.

"I thank you, Mr. Aubrey. And of course now I find that it is I who must apologize yet again—I found offense where none was intended, and I can only offer the defense of a long day's ride in a carriage spent in the company of my family, which would make anyone feel out of sorts." She glanced around, saw no one else in the common room but the two of them, and made an abrupt decision. "Please. Won't you join me for supper? It won't be much, with the hour so late, but I would truly enjoy the company."

Aubrey blinked owlishly and offered a slight bow. "It would be an honor, although I feel we should perhaps wait for the arrival of Mr. Falconer, so as not to be found guilty of any impropriety."

"Oh. I see." She took a deep breath. "No, there is no Mr. Falconer anymore. I am a widow and have been so for these past five years. Although," she mused, "I believe my family might suspect me of impropriety whether he still lived or not."

He nodded and appeared to flush a bit in the dim light. "Again, my apologies, this time for making assumptions and saying things that might cause you distress. I am very sorry for your loss, Mrs. Falconer."

Before Cordelia could reply, young Annie Wilkins arrived with a tray of bread and cheese, followed shortly by two bowls of hearty mutton stew, and Cordelia and Aubrey ate in companionable silence, the meal punctuated only by the crackling of the flames. She glanced his way on occasion and decided that he was far more handsome than she had originally thought, if a bit unconventional-looking. While not classically beautiful for a man, and certainly not possessing what most society ladies would consider a fine countenance, there was something rugged and primitive about him—like the Romany travelers she'd sometimes seen on the moors during her childhood—that caught her attention. Moreover, she was certain that he was surreptitiously inspecting her as well, although neither of them was indecorous enough to comment on it.

Finally, she leaned back, full of bread and stew, and sighed contentedly. "Thank you, Mr. Aubrey. You have no idea how delightful it is to eat a meal without someone chattering at you constantly, and yet still saying nothing of significance at all."

He laughed lightly and leaned in closer. His faint scent of horse and woodsmoke intrigued her. "You mentioned you were traveling with your family, and yet you tell me you are a widow," he said, his voice low and musical. There was a hint of promise in his voice, a tone she had become fond of during her marriage to

Falconer.

"I did, indeed. Our party is a rather large one, with several servants, my mother, sister, two brothers, my daughter, and a partridge in a pear tree. We are headed for Fairfield Hall. Do you know it?"

Aubrey nodded. "As a matter of fact, I have heard of the place."

"My sister is to marry Henry Brompton, and I have somehow found myself whisked off to spend two weeks at his family's home, against my better judgment, and to enjoy an engagement ball with the cream of country society." She wrinkled her nose.

Aubrey laughed heartily. "I see your opinion of country society is much the same as mine, Mrs. Falconer."

"In truth," she confessed, "I've lived much of my life outside the boundaries of the *ton*, to my mother's great disappointment." Cordelia paused, suddenly aware that she may have said too much to this man, this total stranger who—for reasons unexplained—made her want to tell her deepest secrets. "Forgive me," she said softly. "I should not presume to discuss things of such a personal nature."

His gaze bored into her, and Cordelia flushed with warmth. Had the room not been so dimly lit, certainly, he would have seen her cheeks turning pink.

"You are accustomed to speaking your mind," he said. It was not a question.

It had been a long time since a man had observed her so directly, making her body respond as though her skin were afire. What was it about this Aubrey that set her pulse racing, and turned her to molten liquid inside? She did not know him at all, had never heard of him. He could well be a mere itinerant merchant or—judging by his roguish appearance—a highwayman of the wealthier sort and could be of no real consequence to her.

And yet, when he took her hand and raised it to his lips, she nearly burst into flames right then and there.

"Please." She could not pull her eyes away from him. "You mustn't."

"Of course not," he said, his voice hoarse, although he did not release her. "It would be improper of me to take such liberties. Particularly with a lady I have just met."

She stared up at him, studying a glint of candlelight reflected in his dark catlike eyes, the sharp angle of his cheekbones, the hint of stubble on his jaw. How she would like this stranger to take all sorts of liberties indeed. Her skin grew hotter and her pulse began to pound at her own wicked ideas. What on earth was she thinking? If her mother were to walk in right now, chaos would break loose, and Cordelia would find herself on the receiving end of a shrill lecture on the evils of wanton behavior. She shuddered at the thought—it was a lecture she had already heard, more than once, since returning to her mother's home.

There was a polite cough from the doorway, as Annie Wilkins approached with a fresh pot of tea and deposited it on the table before scurrying away. Cordelia declined another cup, sensing that it was very late indeed, and rose reluctantly from her seat.

"Mr. Aubrey, it has indeed been a great pleasure to meet you. Thank you for passing the evening with me." *Oh dear, I do wish to see him again.* "Might you perhaps join me—and my family, of course—in the morning for breakfast?"

He took her hand, gently this time, and bowed lightly. "No, I believe I shall be on my way tonight. Much to my great regret."

"Tonight! But it is snowing quite heavily, and surely the road will be difficult to travel in the dark," she protested.

Aubrey smiled down at her, and Cordelia melted once more. Part of her wished him to stay, wished so very much that the evening would never end. Something about this man burned into her, lighting a fire, setting her heart racing and making her soul spring to life in a way she hadn't felt in five years.

"My horse is a good one, and I am not troubled by a bit of inconvenience," he said. "I have passed the evening with a good meal, a warm fire, and extremely pleasant company, and cannot ask for any more than that." His dark eyes traveled down her body, slowly, appreciatively, before he raised them to meet hers again. "Unless, of course, there might be reason for me to delay my departure until dawn."

Cordelia took a deep breath. "I suspect, Mr. Aubrey, that the snow will make it very difficult for you to get far along the road tonight, no matter how good your horse might be," she said. "Of course, my family seems to have taken all of the available rooms, so were you to stay at the inn this evening, you might find yourself sleeping in the stables. With your horse," she finished.

"Indeed I might, at that." His eyes searched hers, offering questions and promise all at once. "I'm certainly no stranger to spending the night in such circumstances. In fact, I would think that if one were prone to restlessness in the night, one might find comfort amidst the quiet of a good warm stable." He raised her hand once more and brought it to his mouth, his lips hot and hard against her fingers.

With that, he let her go and vanished through the door, disappearing into the darkness.

Chapter Three

Agatha Dean snored loudly in the bed nearest the window. She was a heavy-set woman to begin with who led a remarkably sedentary lifestyle and had a fondness for sweets. Thus, it was necessary for her to sleep with a great deal of padding propping up her barrel-shaped body in order to facilitate ease of breathing in the night. Here at the inn, she had several pillows beneath her; they were not plump like the ones she had at Coltsford but thin and lumpy. Instead of being raised up, she had rather sunken into the middle of them, like a stone dropped into a pudding. The sound now emerging from Agatha created a noise so deep in its tones that the entire room vibrated with every exhalation.

"Dear God in heaven," whispered Cordelia. "Is there nothing to be done?"

Lydia scowled in the darkness, the only light being provided by her mother's candlestick. "I do not believe so, Mother, other than holding a pillow over Grandmama's face. I have considered it, but Aunt Ophelia tells me that would be inadvisable because it would delay our journey even further, so the only reasonable alternative is to put one over my own head in hopes of drowning out the sound. You'll note that *she* has no trouble sleeping through this cacophony."

Ophelia herself slept in the second bed, snoring daintily and thoroughly oblivious to the sounds of her mother across the room. Lydia had refused to share with either of them and so was curled up on a chair, having built herself a nest of blankets and cloaks near the fireplace.

"I'm sorry, darling," said Cordelia, and she truly was. The room was practically rattling. "We'll just have to make the best of it. It's only for the one night. If I roll her over, perhaps it will muffle the noise a bit." She gave Agatha a hearty shove, and the result was as expected. Agatha burrowed deeper into her pile of pillows, and the loud, vibrant snorts waned to a dull thunder. Cordelia kissed her daughter goodnight and climbed into bed next to Ophelia.

She could not sleep.

All she could think about was Rhys Aubrey. He had made it very clear—he had, hadn't he?—that he would welcome a visit from her in the night. And oh, how she wanted him. Her body had responded to his look, to his touch, almost immediately. But how could she? How could she go meet a man—a stranger—in the dead of night? What might people think? What would they say?

Respectable, nice ladies from good families did not do such things. Not at all.

And yet a part of her—the part of her that had lain dormant so long, the part that was still the young Cordelia who had once slipped through a window in the moonlight and run off into the unknown with a handsome footman—that part of her longed to be touched, to be held, to be loved again. And if she did something so reckless, so dangerous, so scandalous—unlike last time, no one would ever know. After all, he was a stranger, and she would never see him again.

Cordelia lay there, tossing and turning, for the better part of three hours. Her sister and mother snored rhythmically, and Lydia was burrowed deep into her blankets by the slowly dying fire. When the town clock in Brompton chimed two, she could take no more. She rose quietly, pulled her robe over her chemise, and grabbed a wool cloak as well. She slipped out of the room in her bare feet, holding her walking boots in her hands.

No one at the Rose and Crown was stirring. In the kitchen, the servants slept on pallets near the hearth, and not a soul took note of her movements. Without a sound, she pulled on the soft leather boots. If anyone saw her, or asked her what she was about, she would simply say she was en route to the privy. True, she had a chamber pot, but she could plead some sort of female malady, and it was unlikely anyone—other than her own mother—would be so rude as to question her further.

Her heart pounding, Cordelia eased the door open and stepped outside.

The storm had passed for now, leaving a silvery sky above, with the moon not quite a quarter full, and the night was cold and crisp. Stars twinkled overhead, and wet snow glittered on the ground, coming up past Cordelia's ankles as she made her way onto the path. It had been a very long time—years, likely—since she'd been outside at night alone. The stables lay dark some twenty yards behind the inn, and a horse—Aubrey's mare, perhaps?—nickered softly within. She paused for a moment. Was she making a terrible mistake? And if she was, did she really care anymore? She had been alone for so very long, and the thought of being touched by him…

At any rate, he was an itinerant stranger, and she would never see the man after tonight, so even if she went through with this, there was no way anyone would ever learn of her indiscretion. And perhaps he wasn't even here at all. Maybe he had traveled on, as he'd originally planned. That would certainly put an end to any lapse in judgment she might demonstrate.

Cordelia took a deep breath and walked to the stables. She didn't look back as the heavy oak door closed behind her. Her cloak trailed in her wake, blurring her footprints, and as she approached the wide double doors leading to the barn, she turned for a last glance at the inn. No candles or lanterns flickered beyond the windows. There was nothing but silence and darkness within.

Cordelia reached out, and just as she was about to raise the latch, it lifted on its own and the door swung open. She stepped back, startled.

"You came."

She could only see him in the shadows, but his voice was low and clear, and she could smell the scent of woodsmoke from his shirt. Cordelia nodded, afraid to speak, as he reached out a hand. If she took it, she would never force herself to go back to her own bed.

She slipped her fingers into his, and he pulled her into the stables.

As soon as the door closed, his mouth was on her, and she responded hungrily as his tongue probed between her lips. A soft moan escaped her throat, and she shuddered as he tasted her.

Aubrey's hands slid up into the chignon pinned above her head. "Cordelia," he whispered. "Let me take your hair down."

She nodded, unable to speak.

His hands, rough and firm, tugged gently at the pins holding her hair in place, and suddenly it fell free, tumbling down around her shoulders in a golden cascade. "By God, you're beautiful," he murmured into the soft curve of her neck.

Cordelia clutched him to her, his hot breath on her skin as he gently slid the top of her chemise aside. She twined her fingers into his dark curls, and her body reacted to him immediately. "Mr. Aubrey," she said with a soft gasp.

"I think perhaps you could call me Rhys. I believe circumstances make it acceptable." Before she could argue about what to call him, he slid a hand beneath her and scooped her up in his arms. "Not here in the doorway," he said.

All she could do was nod, because his lips were on hers once again, plundering ravenously as he carried her to the small tack room at the back of the stable where his belongings were stored.

Once there, he set her on her feet and stepped back to look at her in the dim light of a single candle. In a flash, he had unclasped her cloak and tossed it to the floor. "Cordelia," he whispered almost reverently and plunged his fingers into her hair once more. His hand returned to the neckline of her chemise, and before she knew it, he was caressing her breast.

She moaned softly as his mouth fastened upon her nipple.

Together, they slid to the narrow pallet covered with a thin wool blanket. Aubrey kicked her soft cloak up from the floor, caught it in one hand, and spread it beneath them, never giving up his hold on her. He pulled back for just a moment, releasing her. "Let me look at you," he said. It was practically a growl.

Her pulse quickened. Boldly, she met his eyes, and a small twitch of a smile appeared on her generous lips. "Mr. Aubrey—Rhys," she corrected herself, laughing softly. "I do hope you like what you see."

"My God, woman. You are glorious." He slid his arms around her once more.

Before he could move any further, she pushed him back, wrapped a leg around him, and was suddenly straddling his lap, effectively pinning him to the pallet. He strained against her, hard, and she was pleased that he didn't protest the abrupt shift in their positions. She smiled down at him, fully aware of his arousal.

"Dear God," he groaned.

She paused a moment. What was he doing? "Mr. Aubrey? Are you…counting?"

Aubrey suppressed a laugh. "Do not judge me too hastily, Cordelia. This was a rather unexpected turn of events, and I've found that counting to ten momentarily will keep me from embarrassing either of us."

She giggled, despite herself. "Fair enough. Carry on. Let me know when you reach ten, and I shall continue."

With Aubrey counting silently beneath her, Cordelia was enjoying herself immensely. She was no shrinking society virgin, clueless about the ways of desire and passion, nor was she some untouched spinster living in perpetual fear of male body parts. She liked a man who knew what he wanted, and more importantly, she liked a man who took pleasure in giving her what *she* wanted.

And right now, the only thing she wanted was Rhys Aubrey, the consequences be damned. If she'd had any doubts before, they'd vanished the moment he'd begun tasting her.

The hardness in Aubrey's trousers pressed against her pleasantly, and she shifted lightly against him, causing him to gasp even louder. "Mr. Aubrey," she whispered, "I believe you must have reached ten by now. Would it be too forward of me if I were to simply remove my chemise? I believe it will be in the way."

Aubrey made an unintelligible sound into her neck.

She reached down, caught the lace hem of her nightgown, and swept it over her head. She was completely and unabashedly naked in front of him.

"That's it," he said. "It is entirely possible I will die right herc and now, but I am consoled by knowing that if I do, I shall die a very happy man."

"May I remove this as well?" she asked politely, tugging lightly at the drawstrings of his collar. She suspected that Aubrey was used to being the one who did the seducing, and now, here she was, sitting on his lap, thoroughly nude, and asking permission to take off his clothing.

It was very clear to her that he didn't mind it one bit.

"You may, indeed," he said hoarsely.

She pulled the soft linen shirt over his head and sat back to admire him. His chest was solid and tanned, like a man's would be when he worked outside often. Cordelia smiled as she admired the view and ran a hand lightly down his firm skin. She leaned forward to kiss him again, hard and hot, her breasts tingling as she pressed them against the dark hair on his chest.

Suddenly his hands were pulling her back, and his mouth found her nipple once more. His tongue swirled lightly over it, and Cordelia closed her eyes, groaning softly as he clamped his lips around the tender skin, sucking and tasting her.

Her entire body was on fire, and the heat was pooling rapidly downward. She slid a hand to the top of his trousers. “These must go,” she said into his hair.

“I agree,” he said, his breath ragged.

Her fingers deftly opened the button that was the only thing keeping him contained. Before he could say anything else, her hand had reached down even lower and was encircling him.

“Mmmrpph.”

“Indeed,” Cordelia whispered. He was, she was certain, the perfect size, and she ran her fingertips lightly across the velvety smooth skin of his cock. “Lovely.” Though she didn’t think it could be possible, he hardened even more at her touch, and she lifted herself slightly to push the remaining interfering bits of clothing out of the way.

Aubrey had no idea how he managed it, what with his hands and face buried in Cordelia, but somehow he kicked his boots off, and they landed with a distant thud. Before he knew it, she had pushed his trousers down, and they ended up flung into a corner near a sack of feed. “Cordelia,” he groaned. It was getting more and more difficult to keep things under control, and just when he thought he could stand it no longer, she rose up and enveloped him completely.

There had been many impressive events in Rhys Aubrey’s thirty-nine years, but none would ever be as memorable as the moment in which Cordelia Falconer impaled herself upon his cock.

She threw her head back and sighed loudly, a shudder reverberating through her entire body and carrying over through his as well. “Mr. Aubrey,” she whispered, sliding up ever so slowly.

“It’s Rhys. It really must be, at this point. Oh, dear God, woman.”

“Rhys,” she continued, moving up and down upon him, “I do hope you’ll forgive my wanton behavior.”

“Mmmhmmph. Gladly.” He was having trouble concentrating but had the presence of mind to forgive her, if that was what she wanted. He’d have gladly given her every one of his worldly goods and all of his property, as well as the sun and every star in the universe, had she asked at that moment. “Oh, Cordelia, you are so beautiful,” he said hoarsely, and meant it.

What little there was of the moonlight shone in through the cracks in the wall above them, and Cordelia’s body was bathed in a soft silver glow. He had never seen anything quite like her before, golden hair flowing out behind her like a river of honey, as she continued to straddle him. Her movements quickened, and he was lost in the heat of her. His fingers entwined with hers as she arched her spine and leaned back, and he felt himself drive even deeper inside her.

Aubrey buried his face between her breasts, tasting her soft, warm skin, and released her hands so he could clutch her around the waist. “Cordelia,” he murmured, “you are the most magnificent thing I’ve ever seen.”

Her only response was a low, throaty moan, which pushed him nearly to the brink. How, he wondered fleetingly, had he become so fortunate as to encounter a woman like this? How had he found himself in a moonlit stable at a roadside inn, making love to a strange woman—not a prostitute, not some frisky dairymaid, but a stunningly beautiful lady of high station—who made him feel so complete?

"Mr. Aubrey," she whispered. Her eyes widened as she rode him harder, faster.

His hand slid up into her hair, pulling her head back and baring her neck to him, so that he could taste her again as his tongue slid up into the delicate curve beneath her ear. "It's Rhys. Say it."

"Rhys," Cordelia said, although by now it was more of a whimper. "Dear God, Rhys."

"Say it again," he told her, his lips hot on her neck. "I want to hear you say my name."

"Rhys," she moaned, moving up and down upon the hardness of him as he used his mouth on her. "Rhys."

"Cordelia," he growled once more, raising her up and sliding her back firmly, plunging into her over and over again, faster and harder each time.

She called out again, and a second time, and by the time she cried his name the last time, she was practically weeping with joy. He watched as her face changed in the moonlight, reveling in her pleasure as the world exploded. Her body contracted and shuddered, tightening exquisitely around him as she reached her peak.

He gave himself over to her completely and thoroughly, clutching his hands in her golden mane, burying his face in her throat as she arched her back, and emptying himself within her.

He inhaled the soft lavender scent of her hair and skin as Cordelia slumped forward, her head upon his chest, heart pounding against him. She remained there like that for a long while, and he didn't want her to move. Ever. Cordelia Falconer was the most exciting woman he'd met in his entire life, and he'd known it within moments of meeting her by the fire. Now, she lay sated and drowsy atop him. This was madness in every sense of the word.

After an eternity, she shifted slightly. "I must return to my room before I am missed."

His arms reflexively tightened around her. "Stay. Just a bit longer."

Cordelia shook her head. "I cannot. I…thank you. For a lovely evening."

Aubrey laughed softly, a low rumble. He lazily traced his fingers along her breast, feeling her skin erupt in goosebumps as she shuddered once more. "It was my pleasure."

She smiled at him in the dim light. "And mine as well. I do hope, Mr. Aubrey, that this shall remain…Well, one must be discreet, mustn't one?"

Back to *Mr. Aubrey*. Not *Rhys*. "Indeed, one must. You may be assured, Mrs. Falconer, I am the epitome of discretion in all things. I give you my word."

She kissed him. Not hard and rough as it had been moments before, but softly, tenderly. "I thank you for that." She slid off him and began gathering her chemise and cloak.

He watched silently as she put them on, and then twisted her hair back up into its respectable chignon.

"I must leave," she said again.

He walked her to the door, and pulled it open a crack. "Wait," he ordered. Aubrey glanced out and saw no one. "If you go straight back, you should be safe enough."

She stood on tiptoe and kissed him once more. "Thank you once more, Mr. Aubrey. For everything."

"You are most welcome."

"It is…" She hesitated. "It is a great pity we shall not see one another again." With that, she slipped out of the barn and raced down the path to the inn.

He watched her go, the moonlight catching her hair and turning it silver. "Oh, Cordelia," he murmured. "Don't be too certain of that."

****

The next morning brought more gray and foreboding skies. A brisk wind blew in from the north, and the snow had frozen in the night. The entire Dean party descended on the inn's common room to eat before setting out again for Fairfield Hall, and Cordelia did her best not to draw any attention to herself whatsoever. She was rather certain that the moment she made the smallest movement, everyone would know what a brazen bit of muslin she was.

Every once in a while, though, she touched her lips, still swollen from Aubrey's unyielding mouth, and smiled to herself. He would be well on his way by now, of course, off to wherever it was that itinerant travelers went when they left Brompton. London, perhaps. Or south to the docks of Portsmouth. Wherever it was, it was far away from this village, and that suited Cordelia just fine. She was certain of it. He was gone, and it was over, a thrilling experience to tuck away in the corner of her memory and draw out only in those moments when she was lonely.

She had crept back into bed as the church bell struck four chimes, narrowly missing Annie Wilkins, who had gotten up to light the fires. Once back in her room, she was squashed between Ophelia and the wall, yet even the deep tenor tones of her mother's prodigious snoring several feet away could not keep her awake.

Lydia was stiff and grumpy this morning from sleeping in the chair, and Mrs. Dean complained because she believed it her responsibility and privilege to do so. In the time it took for her lady's maid to lace her stays, Mrs. Dean managed to find fault with the size of the rooms, the quantity of available chamber pots, and the lack of sufficient blankets for warmth.

"Mother, we managed to put four women in a room designed for two. You should be pleased that we did not all end up on the floor under the beds," Cordelia pointed out, stretching and yawning. Despite her mere three hours of sleep, she was feeling quite refreshed indeed. She hoped that the glow she felt on the inside would not be noticed or commented on by the others.

"Truly, they should have more rooms here," Agatha said. "Whoever heard of an inn with just two bedrooms to let? I declare I never did hear of such a thing."

"Many inns in Virginia have just two rooms," Lydia said helpfully. "If you need more, the innkeep gives you a spot on a table in the common room."

"That would not have done at all," argued Mrs. Dean. "Can you imagine me sleeping upon a table in here? Now, Tybalt and Mercutio…"

"Have slept on, under, and between our share of tables indeed," interrupted Tybalt, who appeared considerably the worse for wear.

"What on earth happened to you?" Cordelia

whispered. "You look awful."

"I shared a room with Merc, you'll recall, and he kept me up all night bemoaning his love for Bessie Venables," he said, loading a plate with ham and apples.

Cordelia frowned. "You look far worse than you should from merely listening to Mercutio moan about Bessie all night."

"I couldn't bear it, so I came down and requisitioned a firkin of Wilkins' finest ale. We drank it all. Merc stopped moaning, and I eventually fell asleep just before sunrise."

Ophelia, the only member of the group who wasn't cranky and out of sorts, said, "How lovely today shall be! I cannot wait to see Fairfield Hall again! Oh, Cordie, do you remember when we played there as children? And to think, soon I shall be the mistress of the entire house!"

Cordelia stifled an unladylike snort. "You may well indeed, at least in name. Although, for you to truly be the mistress of Fairfield Hall, old Harriet Brompton must first die, and believe you me, she has no intention of doing so for at least another hundred and fifty years. She'll outlive all of us, just out of spite."

"What an awful thing to say! Why, Cordelia, once Henry and I are married, then I will naturally take my place as mistress of the house. Lady Brompton, I am sure, will be generous and charitable and happy to step aside for her new daughter."

Cordelia stared at her sister. "At what point, Ophelia, in our entire acquaintance with that family, has Lady Brompton ever given you cause to think of her as generous and charitable? No, I suspect that you will have the Devil's own time getting your way with her. She may hand you the house keys, but I wager she will be counting the silverware every evening to make sure you've collected it properly and not had it melted down for pin money."

Ophelia pouted but had no time to protest, for at that very moment one of the footmen came in to let them know the wheel was nearly repaired and should be back on the carriage within the hour. Breakfast was hurriedly completed, hair was combed and brushed and tucked into bonnets, lint was hastily removed from cloaks, shoes dusted off—Cordelia was still forbidden to wear her boots and was thankful no one noticed they were damp—and trunks packed once more. Servants were rousted from their spots in the pantry and picked free of dust, and Tybalt and Mercutio, in a foul-tempered ale-soaked fog and tired of waiting for everyone else, saddled up Gemma and Juno for an early start.

Cordelia was once again bundled into the carriage, and for a moment, she truly envied the freedom her brothers had. She herself was an accomplished horsewoman, having spent the first half of her life being trained to ride her father's horses and the second half raising her own with Tom Falconer. She could ride and jump with the best of them and in Virginia had, in fact, won a foxhunt, much to the delight of all the gentlemen present. Here, however, she was rapidly being relegated to the position of an ornamental, if slightly disreputable, accessory, and she did not particularly like it.

She wondered where Aubrey had gone after she'd slipped back to her room last night—or, to be more specific, this morning. He had been tender and passionate, and despite her knowledge that her reputation would be instantly destroyed should anyone learn of her late-night assignation, Cordelia had no regrets whatsoever about meeting him. No one would ever know but her. She closed her eyes, relaxing to the motion of the carriage, and smiled to herself. Perhaps someday she would do something completely scandalous and take a permanent lover. If she did, she hoped he would arouse her as much as Aubrey had done.

He was, she had decided, the sort of man who must thrive on the fringes of what was right and proper and quite likely had no use for society's rules whatsoever. It was rather a shame that she knew nothing about him beyond his name (if in fact Rhys Aubrey even *was* his name; it could easily have been something else altogether), but that could not be helped. In fact, it was probably better this way. She had not indulged her own needs and passions for a very long time, and she had been long overdue.

Her reverie was interrupted by Ophelia's eager chattering. "And there are swans!" she was saying. "Swans! Can you believe it? They live in the pond, and Henry says that they may well be descended from the swans that lived at Hampton Court when Queen Elizabeth reigned! It's very exciting, to think I might be mistress of a pair of swans that have royal blood, is it not?"

Lydia frowned at her aunt, curious. "Swans? What are they for? Can you eat them?"

Ophelia was properly shocked. "Eat them? Of course not! That's not what they're for at all. Can you imagine, eating a swan?"

“What do they do, then?” asked Lydia.

“Do?” Ophelia was perplexed. “Whatever do you mean?”

“You said they’re not for eating, because that is not what they are for. If they are not for eating, what do they do? What is their purpose?” Lydia pressed.

Ophelia gave her a blank look. “Why, they look pretty. They are for decoration, mostly.”

Lydia turned to the window. “That’s the silliest thing I’ve ever heard. Who ever heard of a bird being used for decoration? How must it feel to have no purpose other than to look pretty?”

Ophelia had no response to that, although Cordelia certainly did, but had no time to express it—perhaps for the better—because suddenly the grounds of Fairfield Hall opened up before them. It was precisely as Cordelia remembered it. Some things never changed, and if the end of the world were to arrive this very day, only small exotic insects and Fairfield Hall would remain, withstanding all nature of disaster and the ravages of time.

The carriages followed the long snow-covered lane up to the front of the house, and as they arrived near the door, Henry Brompton came tumbling out of the house, looking—as always—a bit rumpled, as though he had slept in the clothes he was wearing. Another young man of about thirty, who bore similar features to Henry but carried himself in a manner that was significantly more put together, accompanied him. Brompton introduced him as his cousin, Thomas Heyward, and Mrs. Dean fussed a great deal over both of them, to the extent that finally Cordelia had to silence her so that someone else could get a word in edgewise.

“And where is Lady Brompton this morning?” she asked, not because she especially wanted to see the woman, but because an encounter was surely inevitable. Certainly, delaying it would only make things more uncomfortable.

Henry brightened. “Oh! Mother was feeling unwell—nothing serious, of course—and should be down by midday. Never fret, though—she’s given me leave to show all of you a tour of Fairfield Hall. After all, you must become acquainted with the place where your dearest Ophelia shall soon be mistress!” He took Ophelia’s arm and proudly escorted her through the front door, leaving Cordelia and the rest of the family standing in the chilly morning air, up to their ankles in freshly fallen snow.

“Well,” said Heyward after an awkward silence. “Mrs. Falconer, would you be my guest?”

She smiled. “As much as I would be delighted to wander the halls of Fairfield, you may not know that I have in fact seen the house before. Ophelia and I played here on occasion as children. Alderman Dean was a friend of Henry’s late father.” Heyward seemed a bit disappointed, so she quickly spoke again. “I’m sure my mother would love to see what has changed, however, would you not, Mother?”

Mrs. Dean latched onto Thomas Heyward, linking an arm around his. “I would indeed! Oh, I do remember the art gallery was very fine. Tell me, Mr. Heyward, is it still full of all those marble sculptures? I never did approve of the nudes, you know. It’s not really appropriate to have that sort of thing in one’s home, is it? Of course, I suppose if you call it art, then it’s a bit more acceptable to display, despite the sheer lewdness of such things."

Cordelia shot Heyward a sympathetic look, mouthed a silent apology, and sent her mother off with him to join the tour of Fairfield Hall. It would keep them occupied for hours, and out of her hair. "Come, Lydia," she said. "Let us forego making proper noises of approval of your aunt's new home and instead attempt to find your uncles. There is no telling what they may have gotten up to, but I'm certain it will be much more interesting than walking about admiring the draperies and voicing our disapproval of sculptures."

Lydia gazed about her as she followed her mother. "Mr. Brompton is very rich, then, isn't he?"

"Yes, or at least, he will be some day. He is the sole heir, but I believe his mother still controls the purse strings," Cordclia admitted. "Their family is far wealthier than the Deans ever were, so naturally Ophelia is quite thrilled about marrying him. And your grandmother, of course, is thrilled for her."

"This is the biggest house I've ever seen," Lydia announced, "even bigger than the governor's mansion in Virginia."

"It is, indeed." Cordelia's home in Virginia was a large farmhouse, smaller in size than Agatha Dean's home but significantly more practical. The governor's mansion, which was a half day's ride away, was regularly opened up for garden parties, and Cordelia and Tom Falconer had taken Lydia on occasion during her childhood. "Fairfield Hall has a great many rooms of no use whatsoever, tended by many people whose sole livelihood it is to make certain those rooms continue to be clean and available for their perpetual lack of purpose."

They fell behind the others, and after everyone had disappeared, Cordelia said to her daughter, "Now, if we spend any time here at all, there is one room in particular I am certain you will love as much as I do. Brompton's father was an avid reader, as was your grandfather, and took the time to fill the library with wonderful and fantastic things to read. Although I suspect Lady Brompton and Henry have never bothered themselves with such frivolous activities, the library here at Fairfield is a thing of great joy for me."

"Mr. Brompton said he'd gotten a collection of Shakespeare for Olivia," said Lydia.

"Yes, well, that was quite thoughtful of him, was it not?" Cordelia really didn't have the heart to tell Brompton that his family's library already held a very rare illustrated edition of Shakespeare's works, rumored to have been printed over a hundred years ago. It wasn't as though he would ever notice, since he spent no time at all in the room. "It's just around this corner," Cordelia said, guiding her daughter to the left. She opened the large paneled doors and entered the room, pausing to admire the endless rows of books that lay before her.

"Do you smell that, Lydia? It's the smell of knowledge," she murmured, drawing in a deep breath. She took in the heady scent of leather and parchment, of old ink and dusty shelves, and enjoyed the sensation greatly.

"It is also," said a voice from the depths of the burgundy couch facing the south window, "the smell of a family who cares little for such things as education, literature, or the finer aspects of art, other than what can be obtained as a symbol of status and prestige."

Cordelia froze in midstep. That voice. *Oh dear. Not him. Not here.*

It couldn't be. It simply couldn't. This was absurd.

She peered over the top of the couch and gasped. There, with his head on a pillow and his long legs stretched out before him, was Rhys Aubrey.

He rose leisurely and bowed, surreptitiously pushing a lock of wayward dark hair from his face. "Mrs. Falconer, so good to see you again."

Chapter Four

"Oh! Mr. Aubrey!" Cordelia flushed, and her heart began to race. She fought the urge to flee the library like a madwoman. What was he doing here? "Please forgive my rudeness. I was unaware—*very much* unaware—that you intended to be a guest at Fairfield Hall." She sounded faintly accusatory.

"I'm not certain you asked. In fact, I'm positive you did not," he said, taking her hand to his mouth, brushing his lips gently across her fingers. "It is, of course, a great pleasure to see you once more."

She glanced up, and his dark eyes pierced her soul completely. There was a polite cough beside her; Lydia was awaiting a proper introduction. "Oh! Lydia. Yes. Mr. Aubrey, may I present to you my daughter, Miss Lydia Falconer."

Lydia, to her credit, bobbed a curtsey but did not lower her eyes, saying, "I am most delighted to make your acquaintance, Mr. Aubrey. I have not heard you spoken of before. Do you and my mother know one another well?"

Cordelia blinked, caught off guard, but Aubrey merely nodded. "Our acquaintance is a very recent one. We met briefly last evening at the Rose and Crown, at Brompton. Your mother told me she was on her way here to Fairfield Hall, and I most neglectfully did not mention that I too was en route to visit the Brompton family. I do beg your forgiveness for the oversight, Mrs. Falconer."

He gracefully smoothed a wrinkle out of his claret velvet coat, and she was struck by the memory of his hands on her skin.

Here, in the morning light of the library, he looked even more delicious than he had in the darkness of the stables. But how on earth had he come to be here? "Well," she said finally, wishing to be anywhere at all but Fairfield Hall. "We are most sorry to bother you. I shall leave you to your rest."

"No bother at all. I'm sorry to say this library seems to be a generally unnoticed room." His mouth twitched, trying to suppress a smile and failing miserably. "Are you a devotee of Shakespeare, Mrs. Falconer?"

"Somewhat. My father was. Hence, the names of all four of his children."

"Perhaps at some point during your stay here at Fairfield, you and I might enjoy the pleasures of the Bard's work together."

"Perhaps you need to get back to your nap, Mr. Aubrey. You look weary," Cordelia said, trying not to sound shrewish. She folded her arms across her chest, drumming her fingers irritably.

Aubrey grinned from ear to ear, appearing quite the gentleman rogue. "As a matter of fact, I slept quite well last night."

She scowled at him. "That is of no consequence to me or, more importantly, to anyone else."

With a shrug, Aubrey plucked a worn leather tome from the shelf. Lydia had wandered across the room to examine a stack of books left open on a table. "On the contrary," he said, his voice low, "it is of very great consequence. Since you left me in the early hours before sunrise, I have not been able to erase you from my mind."

Cordelia glanced over at Lydia, who was immersed in the pages of a large atlas. "Mr. Aubrey," she said softly, "certainly you must understand that what happened last night was something which a gentleman would never reveal about a lady who had, perhaps, lapsed a bit in her judgment."

"Is that what it was? A lapse in judgment?" His dark eyes flashed, making him appear just a bit dangerous.

Maybe her notion of Aubrey as highwayman hadn't been so far off the mark.

"Please, sir," she whispered, praying Lydia could not hear. "It is better left unspoken of. I do not know what brings you to Fairfield Hall, but I must ask you for the utmost discretion regarding…certain events."

"You came to me." It was not an accusation, but a simple statement of fact.

Cordelia closed her eyes. "I did not think I would see you again."

Aubrey raised an eyebrow. "Well, that certainly makes things awkward."

"Mother," called Lydia, bouncing with excitement, "do come see! I've found Virginia on this map! How very far away it seems!"

Pulling away, Cordelia joined her daughter, but not before hearing Aubrey say softly, "We shall be discussing this further, Mrs. Falconer, you can be certain."

****

"Cordelia! My dear, you would not believe some of the wonderful things Mr. Brompton has done to Fairfield Hall since we last visited!" exclaimed Mrs. Dean as Cordelia joined the gathering in the drawing room. "Why, did you know he has had wardrobes built into some of the bedrooms? Built in! Right into the walls. Can you imagine such a thing? There's no need at all for a cupboard or chest if everything is just built right in! The clothing simply hangs on rails, can you imagine that? It's very exciting, and I've no doubt it must have been very expensive indeed. Won't it be lovely for Ophelia to be able to hang things right up and close a door?"

"I'm sure it will be," Cordelia said. Ophelia had never hung up a dress of her own in her life, Cordelia was quite certain. According to her sister, that was what maids were for.

Mrs. Dean sat up and peered over Cordelia's shoulder. "Now, who is that? I do not believe we have been introduced."

Somehow, from the tingling sensation on the back of her neck, she knew it would be him. She turned, and as she suspected, there was Aubrey, sauntering through the doorway as though he owned Fairfield Hall and everything inside it.

"Mother, that is Mr. Aubrey."

Aubrey immediately bowed low in front of Agatha. "Mrs. Dean. Such a pleasure to finally meet you. Rhys Aubrey. I'm a friend of Henry Brompton's."

Mrs. Dean scowled a bit at the intrusion. "Aubrey? What sort of a name is that? Is it Irish?"

"Mother!" Cordelia was horrified. "I am so sorry, Mr. Aubrey…"

"It is of no consequence, Mrs. Falconer," he said, offering a feral sort of grin to Agatha Dean. "To answer your question, Madame, it is a name not uncommon in Yorkshire, from whence my family hails."

"Yorkshire! Whatever sort of business can a Yorkshireman have here in Brompton? And surely you must not really be from Yorkshire, as you speak very well, and never in my life have I met anyone from Yorkshire that I could understand, for it's practically a foreign tongue. Are you certain you are from Yorkshire? I do not believe it!"

Cordelia closed her eyes and wished, not for the first time, that a large hole might appear in the floor and swallow her. In the absence of such an occurrence, perhaps one could be conjured up to devour her mother instead.

"Mrs. Dean," Brompton said, coming to the rescue, "Mr. Aubrey is an old school friend of mine, and we recently renewed our acquaintance while in London. I invited him to join the party these next few weeks so that he could enjoy the hunting here at Fairfield and of course meet my dear bride-to-be. I promise you, he's quite well educated, reasonably good-tempered, and doesn't bite very often."

Mrs. Dean's eyes narrowed a bit. "Hm. Perhaps. Frankly, I'm surprised your mother would encourage such a connection." She spoke as though Aubrey were not even in the room.

"Mother, please," Cordelia whispered.

Agatha, once scolded, lost interest. "Speaking of which, where *is* your good mother, Mr. Brompton?"

"She'll be joining us for nuncheon in a short while, I'm sure. Perhaps you and the ladies would like to freshen up a bit before we eat?"

Cordelia shot an apologetic glance at Aubrey, but he paid no mind, being engrossed in a whispered conversation with Thomas Heyward. She hoped her mother would stop being so rude, but then it had not yet happened in over thirty years, so Cordelia supposed a visit to Fairfield Hall now was unlikely to bring about any new changes.

Once upstairs, she and Lydia changed out of their traveling dresses. "Mother, why is Grandmother so discourteous to Mr. Aubrey? He seems pleasant enough."

"He's very pleasant, you are correct, and your grandmother is taking advantage of her status as an old cranky woman of good family in order to belittle him simply because she can. Most men would find her troublesome, to be sure, and be intimidated beyond reason by her cuts. Aubrey, however, doesn't appear to pay much attention to her at all."

Lydia frowned. "She doesn't particularly like anyone who's not of good society, does she?"

Cordelia pulled a pair of fresh stockings from her trunk. "Your grandmother is a relic from a dying age, darling. She has no use for people without money or land, and even less use for those she believes to be socially inferior—which is essentially everyone. I don't know Aubrey's history or background, but he could be rich as Croesus, and it wouldn't signify. Mother won't have anything to do with him because she's gotten it into her head that she must suddenly dislike anyone from Yorkshire."

"She thought he was Irish," Lydia said, bouncing onto the large feather bed and wiggling amongst the fluffy pillows. "Is it because of my father? I don't think she likes me very much either."

Cordelia sat down beside her. "Darling, my mother will never forgive your father for taking me away, nor me for falling in love with him. She may, however, given some time, forgive you for having been born. She'll warm to you eventually, I'm sure, although your greatest flaw is that you're far more like me than you are Ophelia. If you were more superficial, and could just learn to bat your eyes and blush demurely, your grandmother would have all sorts of grand plans for you," she teased.

Lydia fluttered her lashes and simpered. "Oh, gracious, I'm ever so thrilled to be in a house with so many chamber pots! They are so expensive! I do believe they must be plated with gold and simply cannot *wait* to sit upon one!"

Cordelia fell to the bed beside her, hooting with laughter.

****

The midday repast was served in the smaller of Fairfield Hall's two dining rooms, which was typically used by the Bromptons for simple, more intimate family meals. The larger dining hall, which seated some sixty people, was only used when entertaining or when Lady Brompton wished to make a guest feel inferior by placing them alone at the far end of the long table.

Cordelia took the seat nearest Thomas Heyward, who graciously pulled her chair out, and helped herself to a platter of mackerel adorned with mint and fennel. Lydia sat on her other side, and Aubrey slid into a chair directly across. The twins had positioned themselves so that they could mercilessly tease Henry Brompton, but far enough away from his mother that she could not hit them with the soup tureen should the whim strike her.

Harriet Brompton, as the daughter of a duke and the widow of a viscount, was normally very strict on matters of precedence, but she had enough common sense to make an exception this day, knowing it would not be wise to seat Mrs. Dean too far away. After all, their children were to marry one another in less than a month, and matters of the wedding must be sorted out. Besides, Agatha Dean would raise a great deal of fuss if she were to be placed at table beneath Thomas Heyward—the younger son of a mere knight—or worse yet, Rhys Aubrey, whose ancestry was anyone's guess. Harriet noted with pleasure that Agatha didn't seem to object to the Falconer woman and her daughter being put at the far end. Perhaps she could find some common ground with Mrs. Dean after all. Once the other guests arrived, place cards would certainly be needed to keep everyone where they belonged.

Cordelia kept a watchful eye on her mother and Lady Brompton at the opposite end of the table. The two of them were plotting and discussing, while Ophelia occasionally got to put a word in. Poor Henry Brompton, sitting beside his mother and across from his bride-to-be, mostly just nodded his head in agreement at appropriate moments. Cordelia blinked, startled. Mr. Heyward was speaking to her, and she'd been completely oblivious.

"I beg your pardon?" She dabbed a bit of sauce from the corner of her mouth.

"I asked if you would be interested in seeing the horses this afternoon. My aunt Brompton has a new stallion, as you may be aware. I've been told you're quite knowledgeable about horses."

Cordelia nodded. "While I would never presume to claim myself an expert on the subject, I do have some understanding of what makes a horse a good one or a bad. I'm a tolerably good rider as well, I'm pleased to say."

Lydia interrupted. "Mother, you're far more than tolerably good. Mr. Heyward, did you know my mother won a jumping competition just last summer? And she was quite adept at the fox hunts in Virginia," she said with pride.

"Lydia," Cordelia said quietly. "I am sure no one wishes to—"

"Good for you, Mrs. Falconer!" Heyward exclaimed. "In that case, perhaps you might accompany me on a ride once we've finished eating? Fairfield's horses do quite well in the snow. And you as well, Miss Falconer, if you would like to join us?"

Lydia perked up. "I should like that very much, Mr. Heyward, thank you."

Cordelia considered Heyward's suggestion for a moment. She hadn't ridden since returning to England, and she missed her horses. She had a lovely mare in Virginia, Seraphine, of whom she was very fond. It would be good for her, she decided, to get back on a horse. It could take her mind off the problem of Rhys Aubrey's presence at Fairfield Hall. Perhaps more importantly, it would get her out of doors for the afternoon, and away from her own mother and Henry's. "I agree," she said, "that would be delightful. Thank you for the invitation."

Aubrey was staring at her with bemused interest.

He would look a fine figure indeed on horseback,

she thought briefly, before pushing the idea away. No, she told herself, she had no further interest in Mr. Aubrey. None.

If she said it enough, perhaps she might come to believe it.

"Mr. Aubrey, would you care to ride with us this afternoon?" Heyward asked. "If you and your horse aren't too tired from your ride this morning?"

Aubrey smiled, catlike. "No, thank you, Heyward. Although it takes more than one ride to wear me out, I believe I'll let Mrs. Falconer enjoy your company by herself."

Before she could scowl at Aubrey or fling a mackerel at his forehead, Henry Brompton leaned toward her and tapped her arm. "Cordelia, might I ask you to meet me for a few moments in the library? I must consult with you about a matter of some discretion," he said quietly. He inclined his head slightly toward Ophelia, and Cordelia took the hint.

"Of course," she said. Most likely, Henry wished to ask her advice as to the style of wedding ring Ophelia would like. She would have to tell him the truth—that her sister would not care a whit about the design or style of the ring, so long as it was large and ostentatious and properly represented the Brompton wealth. Perhaps something with jewels in a dozen different colors, sizes, and shapes.

Once finished with her meal, Cordelia excused herself, suggesting to Heyward that they meet at the stables in an hour's time, to which he cheerfully agreed.

Aubrey's eyes were upon her as she slipped out of the dining room but she simply strode past him without acknowledgment, her head held high. While there was absolutely nothing she could do about his presence here, she wasn't obligated to talk to him. He really had spoken very little to her during the meal, and she couldn't bring herself to look at him without feeling very warm. If she were fortunate, and the stars aligned, he would vanish in the night once more, and the problem would neatly resolve itself.

It was not long before Brompton joined her in the library.

"Henry," she said, greeting him with a smile. Despite his elevation to the rank of viscount since his father's death, she couldn't bear to call him by anything but his Christian name. "I am so happy for you and Ophelia. You said you wished to speak with me about a matter of some delicacy?"

"Yes," he said, tugging at his waistcoat. "Cordelia, do sit down. If you don't mind."

She perched on the divan and waited for him to speak. Instead of doing so, Brompton merely fidgeted about, anxious and fussy. Finally, she said, "Why, Henry, whatever is this about? Do you need assistance in choosing a ring for my sister?"

He blinked. "No, oh no, that's not really it. I mean, I suppose I should ask you for assistance, because I can't very well marry her without a ring, and I have no idea of what ladies really like in the matter of jewelry. We've got some family pieces I should like to give to her, if she likes them well enough. But no, I must speak with you about something else. And please, Cordelia, I must ask you not to be angry with me, because we are old friends and you are like a sister to me."

She frowned. "I've found that when someone begins a conversation by asking me not to be angry with them, inevitably it is on a topic I find shall indeed make me angry with them. Whatever is the matter, then, Henry?"

He sat beside her, and took her hands in his. "I must ask—oh, dear. This is troublesome. You see, my mother…she has some concerns."

"Concerns? About Ophelia?" Cordelia instantly leapt to her sister's defense. "My sister is a wonderful young lady, Henry, and despite that I occasionally find fault with her proper ways and her desire for constant approval by the *ton*, she loves you very much and would never do anything to bring scandal or unhappiness to you or your family."

"Oh yes, yes," he said hurriedly, "I know that, and I believe my mother knows it too, despite your father only having been a knight, while mine was a viscount, and his father before him an earl. No, her concerns are not about Ophelia, not really, but more about…well…erm, some other members of your family."

Cordelia's gaze narrowed, and her left eyelid twitched. "Do go on, Henry," she said, unnaturally cool.

Henry inched back slightly on the seat, putting a bit more distance between them just to be safe. "You see, my mother feels that because of some of the…Well, I'll just come right out with it, Cordie. You yourself caused a scandal, and neither of your brothers has made much of an effort to maintain a good reputation in the county. My mother is not certain that your presence, or that of your brothers, at the wedding is really desirable at this time."

Cordelia pondered, for a moment, how Henry

might react if she picked up the heavy globe and dashed it against the back of his head. It might, perhaps, put something of a damper on his wedding plans. "Is that so?"

"Now, don't be angry," he said, seeing her black look. He patted her hand. "It's a simple thing, really. Mother would like to invite a small but select group of guests, the cream of the *ton*, you see. Since your family is moderately respectable even though your grandfather made his money in trade, Mother thought perchance you would like to still visit with us for the next two weeks, and then simply depart for Chesham before the ceremony itself takes place. Would you mind very much speaking to Tybalt and Mercutio about the matter?"

"Is Ophelia aware of this request?" Cordelia's voice was measured and precise, which frightened Henry more than a little. He had expected her to strangle him with his own cravat immediately upon his delivery of the news. A calm Cordelia could not possibly be a sign of good things to come.

"She is, and she agrees that it might be best for only your mother to be in attendance at the wedding." He gazed at a small spot on the rose-covered damask settee. Anything was better than eye contact with Cordelia right now.

Cordelia was so furious she could barely contain herself. She rose with dignity and gazed coolly at Henry, peering loftily down at him. "Henry, I must offer you my sincere apologies. I always believed you were too good for my sister. Now I see that I was wrong. The two of you were clearly made for one another. I do hope you'll be happy together, for certainly, it is unlikely anyone else could ever live up to the standards you have set for yourselves."

Henry smiled up at her. "Well, then. I must confess I am immensely relieved. This went far better than I'd expected it might. I was rather afraid you'd throw something at me. So you'll speak to your brothers, then?"

"Oh yes," she said. "I most certainly will, *Lord Brompton*." Still stunned, she spoke no more and stepped out into the hallway, leaving Henry behind and alone with his shallow thoughts. As she closed the door, she collided into a tall footman, knocking the two of them off balance. He was young, about twenty. "Do watch where you're going," she said, far more sharply than she had intended, as she regained her footing.

He bobbed his head. "Yes, milady, my apologies."

She stopped in her tracks and sighed. "No, I apologize. I came barging through the door and then chastised you for being in the way, when you could not have known I was about to come out. I should not have spoken to you so severely. The fault is entirely mine."

He bowed slightly. "Will there be anything else, milady?"

"No. That is all—what is your name?"

"Grimm, milady. Owen Grimm, first footman."

"Grimm. That will be all. Thank you." She dismissed him with a wave of her hand, although not unkindly, and he continued on down the hall. Grimm was young enough to look dashing in his forest green uniform with the Brompton crest, yet seasoned enough not to bat an eye when she had scolded him, nor when she had apologized. A good servant indeed, trained to be all but invisible and to never question the words or actions of those above him in the social hierarchy.

There was a commotion from the dining room, and Cordelia nearly went in to see what sort of fuss her brothers were causing, but her heart just wasn't in it. *Oh, for pity's sake. Let them sort things out themselves.* She had no wish to see Ophelia or their mother, and she certainly did not want to deal with Lady Brompton. It would take very little provocation for her to cheerfully jab a serving fork straight into the woman's eye.

How could Henry be so cruel? Despite their friendship, despite her support of him in his courtship of Ophelia, Henry was at his very core no better than his mother, concerned only with the appearance of propriety. Cordelia was well aware that she had once damaged her reputation and her family's with her own scandalous behavior—but that was half a lifetime ago, when she was just seventeen. She had atoned for her mistakes and apologized to the people she'd hurt the most—her parents—and been, as far as she knew, forgiven. And yet now her mother and sister and Henry were agreeing with Lady Brompton that she should not be seen at the wedding.

With her mother and Ophelia, she could not help feeling unsurprised; they had always been far more concerned with appearance than anything else. Henry, though—Henry was the worst betrayal of all. And now she must tell her brothers that they were considered too low to be seen at a Fairfield Hall wedding. She wondered if they should all just return home immediately and be done with the entire matter.

"Mrs. Falconer, you look unwell. Is there something amiss?" Aubrey had emerged from the dining room and was watching her.

Why did he make her feel as though she were completely disrobed? “No,” she said, flustered. “Yes. I mean, I don’t know.” She smoothed her skirts and regained her composure. “I am well enough as I can be, given the present circumstances. Thank you, Mr. Aubrey, for asking.”

He frowned. “I don’t believe you.”

“I beg your pardon?”

“I don’t believe you are well at all,” he said, genuine concern on his face. “Forgive me for being forward, but your face is pale, and your hands are shaking. I believe you have completely shredded that bit of lace in your hands.”

Sure enough, the delicate handkerchief she’d been holding was in tatters. Cordelia took a deep breath. “I suspect you and I are a great deal alike. I cannot fool you, can I, Mr. Aubrey?”

He waited, not saying a word, and in a moment it all came pouring out.

She quietly told him what Henry had said and that Lady Brompton was an awful woman, an opinion with which he wholeheartedly concurred, and her own mother not much better. To make matters worse, now she, Cordelia, must spend the next two weeks pretending to be cheerful when in fact half her family had rejected her, and the other half was considered too disreputable to be acknowledged by polite society.

“And what will your brothers say when you tell them this news?” he asked, his voice gentle. Taking her by the elbow, he guided her to the billiard room, currently unoccupied, and shut the door.

She shrugged hopelessly. “They’ll be angry, of course, especially Tybalt, because he’s the man of the family now that Father is gone, and he's expected to marry well. How is he to do that when our own mother won't even stand up for him to old Lady Brompton? Poor Mercutio will be upset too, more hurt than anything, but really no one ever listens to him much because he's the younger of them. And Lydia! She's had a hard enough time of things, leaving the only home she's ever had and coming here where she didn't know anyone…Perhaps I should have stayed in Virginia." Cordelia swiped a hand across her eyes furiously.

"Please," Aubrey said softly. "Please don't. I know you're unhappy…"

"I'm not unhappy, I'm angry," she corrected him. She grabbed a red ball from the billiard table and began tossing it lightly from hand to hand. "I knew I should not have come back. Even after fifteen years in America, I still thought of England as my home, and I now recognize that I was wrong to do so. This is not my home. It is simply the place where I used to live."

Aubrey took the ball from her hand and placed it on the table with the others. He removed a cue from the rack on the wall. "Do you play?"

"What?" She stared at him.

"Billiards. Do you play?"

Incredulous, she shook her head. "No. I never…ladies don't play billiards."

He laughed lightly, although with no malice. "Of course not. But you are a lady who generally defies convention if it pleases you to do so, and I thought that at some point in your illustrious life, your brothers or perhaps even your late husband might have taught you."

She sighed. “They didn’t. What shall I do, Mr. Aubrey?”

Aubrey blinked, surprised. “About your family?”

“No,” she said. “About billiards. How, exactly, does one play the game?”

Chapter Five

By the time Cordelia went to collect Lydia and head to the stables, she had calmed down a bit. She was still angry, but playing billiards—or rather, attempting to play—with Aubrey had given her some focus, a sense of something to do rather than seething over a problem. He hadn't talked much, hadn't pestered her or even mentioned their encounter in the stables. Instead, he'd just allowed her the opportunity to hit balls with a stick—sometimes with far more force than needed, and once leaving a large scrape on the table's fabric, to her great satisfaction. He'd let her air her frustration at Brompton's slight, not attempting to solve the problem but merely listen, which was just what she'd needed. Aubrey had been a very good sport, despite her poor company, which was why she felt a little bad about leaving him to go riding with Heyward.

She anticipated Heyward would want to talk as they rode, and certainly, she was not wrong in her estimation, although it was more of a monologue than a true conversation. He was incredibly polite, paying her many compliments on her riding, her attire, the way she sat a horse, her good judgment in selecting the finest of Lady Brompton's mares, and her good manners. He confided that he was delighted to be in Cordelia's company, despite his aunt's misgivings about her. He praised her fortitude in raising Lydia alone for the past five years without the wisdom of a husband to guide her and commended her bravery for traveling aboard a ship with only a child for company. At one point, he even hinted that a break in the weather, which included the temporary appearance of the sun, might be attributed in no small part to the efforts of Cordelia Falconer.

"If I may beg your pardon, Mr. Heyward," she interrupted when he paused in his exaltations for a breath of air. "Do you know, it seems that the snow on the ground makes this a lovely day for listening to the birds. I believe if we try to travel as quietly as possible, we might perhaps hear some of them singing to us."

"Of course," he exclaimed. "We shall be silent as the grave, and when we do hear them sing, it will be a great pleasure indeed!"

Lydia, who was riding along with them, giggled a bit at Heyward's vociferous enthusiasm but quickly turned the laugh into a dainty and ladylike cough when Cordelia poked her on the leg with a riding crop.

Heyward was good to his word and managed to maintain a reasonable amount of silence as they rode. Occasionally he burst out in raptures of joy at the sight of a particular shrub or tree, but for the most part he was quiet enough that Cordelia could be alone with her thoughts, however distressing they may be. It was not long before the cold weather became uncomfortable, and they eventually returned to the stables, where the grooms were waiting to take the horses. By this time, Cordelia had formed some semblance of a plan.

"Lydia, run along and warm up, and then we shall dress for dinner. You'll want to look presentable," Cordelia said with a wry smile. She turned to Thomas Heyward. "Thank you, Mr. Heyward. It was a pleasure to ride with you this afternoon."

"It is I who must thank you for such enjoyable company," he said, bowing lightly as he handed the reins to a stable boy. He grinned at her, with a look that likely melted the hearts of lonely women all over London. "Might I presume upon you for yet one more thing?"

All Cordelia wanted was to soak in a nice warm bath for a few moments and drink some hot cider before she was forced to endure the formal evening meal with Henry and the rest of them. "Yes, Mr. Heyward, what is it?"

"At the grand engagement ball tomorrow evening, might I have the honor of a dance or two?"

She smiled back at him. He was harmless enough and quite charming when it struck his fancy; it certainly wasn't his fault he was part of the Brompton family. She of all people knew there was nothing to be done about unfortunate ancestry. "Of course you may, Mr. Heyward. I'm sorry, I must go speak with my brothers about a matter of family importance, and then make ready for dinner."

He graciously excused her, and she hurried up to the house. Once in her room, she had the maid fill a tub, and Cordelia slid into the hot water with a sigh. Her farmhouse in Virginia was built near an artesian spring, and warm water had been available year-round to anyone willing to go outside with a bucket. At one point, Tom Falconer had discussed finding a way to pipe the water into the house—he'd been clever that way—but he had died before his plans materialized.

She soaked in the copper tub and memories of Tom crept in unexpectedly. She missed him, although after five years it was more sadness for what they might have had, rather than the sharp, stabbing pain of first loss. When it had first happened, the hurt was heartbreakingly brutal. Only Lydia had kept her from spending the days in her bed sobbing; she had gotten up each day because her daughter needed her, and after five years, the ache had subsided to a dull emptiness. Cordelia had learned to live without Tom and to be thankful for the ten years she'd spent with him. She had even, after a time, managed to forgive him for making her a widow at twenty-seven.

As she scrubbed her skin with bayberry soap, her thoughts drifted away from her old life and the past. It was high time she began making plans for the present and future. Cordelia had never taken a lover before her night with Aubrey—other than, of course, the footman who had eventually become her husband and the father of her child, but she knew other women who had done so. It wasn't quite talked about in polite society, but occasionally after a few too many glasses of claret, a lady might accidentally let a secret slip out to her close friends. It seemed a very practical and sensible thing to do—after all, a woman had certain needs that only the passion of a man in the bedchamber could satisfy.

It was never discussed in the open, but she was certain she couldn't be the only woman who enjoyed the act of making love. She knew her mother's advice regarding the matter was to close one's eyes, lie still, and hope it ended quickly, but she had never seen lovemaking as a chore. No, she had enjoyed it tremendously—much to Tom Falconer's delight, and to her own.

Five years was a long time to be virtuous, and she

had enjoyed Aubrey's touch a very great deal. She was keenly aware that he had enjoyed the experience as well. But she knew nothing about him, despite their intimacy in the stable. He could, for all she knew, be a thoroughly disreputable man. What if he was a criminal? Or worse, had a *wife* tucked away off in Yorkshire?

Eventually the water cooled down, and she quickly dressed in front of the fire. She could have called the maid in to help, but Cordelia was a woman of simple tastes. She had no need for assistance in putting on her own clothing; she was perfectly capable of doing it herself. If she needed something tied or laced that she could not reach, then Lydia was right next door. Ophelia was across the hall and Mrs. Dean beside her, but Cordelia would rather be seen at dinner wearing a feed sack than ask either of them for help with anything if possible.

Once she was in her evening dress and a comfortable short wrap, she rang the bell for a servant, and the young footman who responded was the one she'd run into earlier in the day, right after Henry had dropped his hateful, hurtful request upon her. "Yes, milady, you rang?" he asked without any hint of recognition.

"Yes, Grimm, is it? Would you please find my brothers and send them up? They're likely somewhere that whisky is to be found."

"Certainly, milady. I believe I know exactly where they are. I shall deliver the message immediately."

"Thank you. And Grimm?"

"Yes'm." His face was expressionless.

"I apologize once again for my rudeness this

afternoon."

"As you say, milady. Will that be all?"

With a sigh, she sent him off to find Mercutio and Tybalt. They arrived after a quarter hour or so, rumpled and damp, and had, judging from their merriment and revelry, been drinking continuously since around breakfast time. Mercutio had a pair of goblets in one hand and a half-empty decanter of claret in the other, which he raised to her as a greeting.

"Cordie!" Tybalt exclaimed. "We've been out on the lawn playing ninepins, but there's too much snow on the ground for the ball to roll, so we were throwing it instead. And then we got wet and cold—You know, it's snowing again? It seems as though that's all it's done since we left home—and so we brought everything inside. Brompton was horrified to see us tossing balls about the gallery."

"Sit, you two," she ordered. "Right now." Startled by her abrupt tone, to which they were unaccustomed in their good-natured sister, they obeyed instantly.

"What is it, Cordie? We were just having a bit of fun," said Mercutio. "We didn't break anything."

"Well, it's time to stop having fun. We've all spent so much time indulging ourselves that we've been banned from Ophelia's wedding to *Lord* Brompton," she snapped.

"What?" the twins exploded in unison.

Patiently, she relayed the nature of her conversation with Henry. By the time she was finished, all three of them were ready to down a bottle of Fairfield Hall's finest claret. Mercutio wordlessly passed her the decanter.

"And that," Cordelia said, "is what Mother and

Ophelia and Lady Brompton have decided, and so we shall be asked to make ourselves scarce prior to the ceremony. It appears we are good enough to attend the engagement ball tomorrow night and the rest of the prewedding festivities, but beyond that…Well. There you are. I'm a disgraceful trollop, and you're a pair of gambling drunks. I'm not entirely sure which is a more unpleasant label, but I don't suppose it matters."

Tybalt and Mercutio were, for once, silent.

"So you see," she concluded, "we must come to an agreement, the three of us. Mother will do as Lady Brompton tells her, because she wishes to gain her approval. Ophelia will do as Mother says, simply because she's Ophelia, and Brompton will do whatever anyone at all instructs him to do because he hasn't the good sense or the gumption to refuse."

"Then it is Lady Brompton we must convince that we are worthy of attending our sister's wedding," finished Mercutio.

"Precisely. However, the last thing I wish to do is fawn over her—she has Mother and Ophelia to do that, and goodness knows she's a horrible person besides. She can't be reasoned with like a normal person, because she's made up her mind already. I would suggest a different, more subtle approach, but we must all three of us agree to it in order for it to work."

They looked at one another, a pair of handsome—if thoroughly inebriated—bookends, and then shifted their attention to her, nodding their sandy blond heads together. "Tell us."

"You two must behave yourselves."

There was silence. Tybalt spoke first. "Behave ourselves? I'm not certain what you mean, Cordie."

"Of course you aren't, because you haven't behaved a day in your life, either of you. I mean," she said, "that you will cease any and all public displays of drunkenness. You will immediately pay off any pending gambling debts, and by immediately, I mean before sundown tomorrow. You will stop spending time in the company of women of questionable virtue—Mercutio, stop." She held up a hand, cutting him off before he could speak. "I know you hold Bessie Venables in high esteem, and you may continue to do so. But for the next two weeks, at least, you must not mention her in front of anyone but Tybalt and myself. In addition, you will both refrain from any sort of activities which might give Lady Brompton further cause to find us disreputable. You will stop playing ninepins in the house and flirting with scullery maids, and you will take up nice respectable hobbies like reading books and discussing horses and expressing sincere interest in the proper management of our family estate."

Tybalt scowled. "What of you? You're on good behavior already, and she still finds you scandalous, from what you've told us. You can't very well pretend you never ran off with Falconer or hide Lydia away in the attics."

She took a deep breath. "Well, I don't plan to elope with any more footmen, having done that once already, so I shall therefore endeavor to be more proper, as our station allows. According to Lady Brompton and Mother, this may be done by finding a suitable attachment to restore my reputation."

"An attachment?" Mercutio sputtered. "You don't need a husband, you told us so!"

"Hush," she said. "Of course I don't need one, nor do I want one. However, what I do need and want is for Lady Brompton and Mother to think that I *hope* to marry again. I don't plan to actually *do* it. It's merely the *appearance* of propriety that's important in this case."

Tybalt examined his fingernails. "You have two weeks to convince Lady Brompton that you've found someone you might marry, then. If she believes there's an understanding between yourself and a respectable gentleman, and that Merc and I have reformed our wicked ways, then perhaps she will rethink her position on our attendance at the wedding."

"Correct, although I'm still not convinced that Ophelia deserves to have us there." Cordelia sat down. She had given this a good deal of consideration, and as much as she hated the idea, there really was no alternative. It was almost ridiculously simple, but she could think of no other solution.

Mercutio frowned at her curiously. "Who, exactly, do you have in mind?"

"Pardon?"

"For your future attachment. There's a limited number of gentlemen available here right now, although to be certain, there will be more after tomorrow night's ball," he mused.

"Oh. Yes," she said. "I hadn't really thought that far into things."

"Well," said Tybalt, pouring himself a drink, "there's Heyward. He seems a good sort. Not going to inherit much, but respectable and friendly. The chambermaids think he's handsome, if a bit bland and unexciting."

"Likes to hunt and ride," Mercutio commented. "Says he's got a couple of fine hounds."

Cordelia shook her head. She didn't especially care about Heyward's fondness for sport, although that clearly was a major concern to her brothers. Not only that, he would probably be shocked by her plan. On the other hand, Heyward might find it amusing to fool his Aunt Brompton, for whom he seemed to harbor a subtle dislike.

"What about Aubrey?" Tybalt suggested. "Rather mysterious, no one knows much about him, but he's definitely a gentleman."

Oh dear. She really could not bring herself to consider Aubrey, not when she had thrown herself at him at the inn, like some common serving wench. Besides, Aubrey was an enigma. Might he be willing to play along with her deception if she asked him to? He would probably laugh at the very suggestion.

"There's one other option," Tybalt said, "and likely your best wager." He glanced at Mercutio, who nodded.

"But you won't like it at all," Merc said.

Cordelia sniffed. "I don't like *any* of it at all. Who on earth is there besides Mr. Aubrey and Mr. Heyward?"

"Erm." Tybalt cleared his throat. "You don't know, then?"

"No. Whom are we discussing?"

Merc shifted in his chair. "Do you remember Augustus Littleberry? He arrived just this past hour."

It was all Cordelia could do not to drop her glass of claret straight into her lap. "Augustus Littleberry? Dear Lord, however did he end up here?"

"Apparently Henry—or more likely Lady

Brompton—has asked him to perform the ceremony. He's been invited to stay here at Fairfield Hall for the next two weeks like the rest of us. He's got a living that the old dragon gave him, you know."

"Yes, yes. I know. Mother made a point of telling me. I simply…forgot. He's staying here? In the house?"

Tybalt nodded.

"I am certain," she said, "that the Reverend Mr. Littleberry's presence is no coincidence." After all, their mother had been anything but subtle in pointing out that Mr. Littleberry was as yet unmarried. Had she somehow convinced Lady Brompton that some matchmaking could be done between the two of them? "No, Mr. Littleberry is out of the question. He would never go along with such a scheme, considering how things turned out the last time. And besides, I could never…I do not find his countenance all that pleasing to look at," she said primly.

Tybalt and Mercutio nodded. They were too young to remember the particulars, but they knew—from their mother's regularly delivered tirades—that Mr. Littleberry had intended to speak to Alderman Dean and ask for Cordelia's hand back before all the scandal hit. Then one day she was gone, eloped with an Irish footman, and Littleberry had been left dangling in the breeze.

In all honesty, Cordelia had never encouraged Littleberry's attentions and had not once indicated to him that she would like to become Mrs. Littleberry. He had presumed, without actually speaking to her, that Cordelia might find such an offer to be a great honor, and so had been deeply startled when it turned out she'd gotten on a horse and vanished off to Gretna Green with

Tom Falconer.

"Is it because he's plump?" Tybalt asked.

"Actually, no," Cordelia said truthfully. "It is because of his lack of interest in things such as cleaning his teeth or skin, and the constantly running nose. Oh, and his terrible inability to be even remotely interesting to speak with."

"Well, he's here at Fairfield, so you may as well plan on at least being pleasant to him," Mercutio said. He reached across his brother for the decanter, and then thought better of it, given the nature of the discussion.

Cordelia scowled out the window. The winter sky had turned gray once more, matching her mood, and fat snowflakes swirled outside the window. Despite the early hour, it was nearly dusk. Down below, the swans glided gracefully in circles along the pond in front of the house; had she married Littleberry, she would have had a life much like theirs—a life of reasonable comfort and social standing with no real purpose or direction at all. For the first time in many years, Cordelia really had no idea what to do with herself.

"It's a scandalous thing in itself to ask a man to pretend we have an understanding. What on earth would Mr. Heyward think of me?" she asked.

Her brothers had no answer.

Lydia tapped on the door, ready for dinner, and with a sigh of resolution Cordelia joined the party.

Chapter Six

Dinner was blessedly uneventful. Cordelia managed to sit as far from Augustus Littleberry as possible so there was little to no chance of being forced to speak with him, which pleased her greatly. The years had not been kind to him. His complexion was significantly sallower than it had been the last time she saw him, and he had developed a rather unfortunate tic which caused him to snort loudly on occasion. Each time he dabbed at his nose, he shot furtive, watery glances her way. When she could take no more, Cordelia angled her chair so her back was to him as much as possible, while she chatted with her brothers and Mr. Aubrey and Mr. Heyward.

She went through the motions of polite social interaction, but her heart wasn't in it. At some point in the next two weeks, she would have to pretend a whirlwind engagement—or at least the potential for one—on which she had no intention of following through. Mr. Littleberry was out of the question, as far as Cordelia was concerned. He made strange wet noises, sweated profusely, and every sentence that came out of his mouth was designed strictly to improve his standing with Lady Brompton.

Heyward might be a possibility, now that she contemplated it. He certainly cut a fine figure on a horse, had good manners, and according to her brothers' reports from the chambermaids, there was no hint of scandal about him. Although not nearly as dull as his cousin Brompton, Thomas Heyward was a good solid man who would likely never do much of anything disreputable at all but could always be counted upon to stand about looking handsome when the need arose. He might be horrified by her plan, but if she took the time to learn more about him, she could perhaps find a way it would benefit them both. Then again, if Cordelia was too scandalous to attend a Brompton wedding, she might be too scandalous to be courted by a Brompton nephew. That might present a bit of a problem.

Which left Aubrey, and he was an unknown, an unpredictable factor. Certainly, he aroused sensations in her that had long lain dormant, and heaven knew that her hours with him in the stable had been time very well spent. Equally certain, the smoldering glances he gave her when no one else was looking made her suspect he might wish to repeat the encounter. But desire was one thing; deception and a public sham another. Would Aubrey consent to be part of her charade, or would he simply throw back his head and laugh at such a preposterous idea?

She glanced toward him every once in a while. Often, she didn't think he noticed, but then once she was watching him, he would flick a look in her direction, catching her in the act. The first few times, she let her eyes drift away and pretended she had been watching something else, perhaps contemplating something interesting behind his shoulder, but eventually she gave up trying to fool him. Instead, she returned his slow, casual smile with a polite nod of her head.

He pointedly let his gaze slide down to her bodice and then raised his glass in acknowledgement.

Who was he? she wondered, distracted once more by his blatant behavior. The cut of his perfectly tailored clothes indicated that he was well-off. His shirt and waistcoat were of more than good quality, and the coat he'd worn at the Rose and Crown had likely cost a pretty penny. He'd gone to school with Henry, and that couldn't have been managed unless someone in his family had money and connections.

On the other hand, his black hair was in need of a trim, he didn't appear to have shaved in a day or two, and his costly boots were scuffed at the toes, so clearly he had no valet or manservant to attend him. Of course, she reflected, it may well be that he simply wasn't a man who cared much about appearances—Aubrey wasn't the type to need a valet to tie his cravat, not when he was perfectly capable of doing it himself. They were, apparently, disturbingly similar.

And although he was likely from a good family—for if he was not, he would not have been sitting at Harriet Brompton's table in Fairfield Hall—he struck Cordelia as being unlike any gentleman of her recent acquaintance.

She couldn't remember the last time she had wanted a man so badly.

Rhys Aubrey, damn him, always appeared as though he could read her thoughts. His dark eyes followed her, despite her best efforts to ignore him, and she suspected he might be laughing at her. He was hot and cold—sometimes, like in the library or at the inn at Brompton, he was open and friendly. Other times, he virtually ignored her, as he was doing now, pausing every so often to shoot a barely concealed smile in her general direction.

How would he react if she asked him to pose as her pretend suitor, even were it just for two weeks? Would he laugh and cheerfully agree to be in on the joke, fooling her mother and Lady Brompton convincingly? Or would he dismiss her, pity her, and refuse to participate at all? Worse, given their intimacy, would he turn up his nose, scandalized, and denounce her as a brazen harlot?

Normally, she could read members of the *ton* by their demeanor, but Aubrey was a complete puzzle.

"And so you see," Lydia was saying to Heyward, "once the tobacco has worn out that particular part of the land, we rotate wheat and corn crops through it for the next two years. That helps the soil regain its strength, and in the third year, the tobacco may be planted again in that parcel, and it will flourish."

Heyward nodded. "Fascinating, Miss Falconer. How much land did your family have?"

"We still own it, Mr. Heyward," Cordelia cut in. "It's about three hundred and fifty acres—not much compared to a park like that of Fairfield Hall, to be certain, but easily enough land for us to live well in Virginia."

"Who does the labor?" Aubrey asked. It was the first he'd spoken all evening.

Lydia spoke. "We have hired men who work the fields, and three women who work in the house. Mother tends the gardens herself," she said, obvious pride in her voice.

Lady Brompton spoke from the other end of the table. "Lydia, did you say your mother works in a field?"

Cordelia smiled sweetly. "I tend the family gardens at our home in Virginia, Lady Brompton. I assure you, many of the farm ladies in the area do the same."

Lady Brompton sniffed, clearly thinking such things beneath her, and turned back to her quiet conversation with Ophelia.

"You have hired men," Aubrey said. "No slaves?"

"None," Cordelia said. It had been the one bone of contention between her and Falconer, in regards to the running of the farm, but in the end, she had won. "We pay free men to plant and bring in the harvest. Are you, Mr. Aubrey, familiar with the writings of Mr. William Wilberforce?"

He raised a brow. "I am, indeed, Mrs. Falconer."

"He said, 'You may choose to look the other way, but you can never say again that you did not know.' I have seen men in shackles, Mr. Aubrey, and choose not to live in a manner that would cause me to look the other way to begin with."

"A tobacco farm free of the institution of slavery. Admirable indeed. And where do you stand on the use of indentured servants?" he pressed.

"Mr. Aubrey," she said levelly, "my late husband, as you may have heard, was of Irish birth and of the servant class. He could not, in good conscience, own one of his countrymen for seven years—you do know that most of the indentures are poor Irish, I assume? While indentured servitude may, on paper, be a manner of paying off one's debts, it is a hard and oppressive way for anyone to live. Cheap labor for landowners, to be certain, but not something I ever wished to be a part of, or to profit from."

He raised his glass to her in a mock salute. "To freedom, then."

Everyone toasted, glasses held high, and as she sipped, Cordelia caught Aubrey's gaze. Had the conversation had been a test of sorts?

She wondered if she had passed.

****

The next day, the house was all abuzz with servants preparing Fairfield Hall for the engagement ball. Bright and early they rose, polishing silverware, dusting wood paneling until it shone, and being ordered about by Lady Brompton, whose tone became increasingly shrill as the morning progressed.

Cordelia, who hadn't had any time at all to speak with Ophelia, decided it was time to confront her sister. Ophelia's door was opened by one of the maids, and Cordelia shooed her away, closing the door behind her.

"Cordie! I must have her in here to arrange my hair," she pouted prettily.

"Ophelia, the guests will not be arriving for another five hours, so I believe that even *your* hair will be completely finished by that time. You and I must talk."

Ophelia sat at the vanity table, peering into the mirror. It was one of her favorite pastimes. "Do you think my skin looks too dark? I forgot my bonnet the other day when we walked to church, and I'm worried I might have taken too much sun. I'll be almost as tanned as you—oh! I didn't mean that the way it sounded, Cordie."

"Ophelia," she said without preamble. "Lady Brompton has asked me not to attend your wedding ceremony. And Tybalt and Mercutio as well."

"Yes, I know. I'm sure it will not signify, though—

Mother will be there for me, so even if you and the boys miss it, I shall still have family beside me." She held a pair of teardrop-shaped emerald earrings up to her face, admiring her own reflection.

Cordelia was incredulous. Ophelia, as was typical, was only seeing the situation in how it affected her directly, with no thoughts whatsoever toward the feelings of others. "Ophelia, my dear, had it not occurred to you that your brothers and I would like to see your wedding day?"

Ophelia shrugged as she picked through a box of brightly colored ribbons, tossing the ones she disliked onto the floor. "Well, I suppose that's true, but Lady Brompton says that there will be many people from good families there, and she wouldn't want to give them the wrong impression by receiving you and the boys, because doing so might indicate approval of your past unpleasant behavior."

Cordelia wanted to slap her. "It's *your* wedding, Ophelia, yours and Brompton's. You should have your entire family there with you, not just Mother. You'll never have another wedding. We want to see it, and frankly, the three of us are quite hurt that no one thinks we're proper enough to attend."

Her sister blinked at her. "I don't understand, Cordie. All three of you have done horrible things that could have destroyed my chances for a good match. And now I have one, and you wish to ruin it for me."

"No one wants to ruin anything for you," Cordelia snapped. "We all want you to be devastatingly happy. However, we would also like to come to your wedding, rather than being dismissed by Lady Brompton simply because we might offend her guests with our presence."

Ophelia turned, finally tearing herself away from the mirror, and rose from the floral bench. "Cordie, you ran off with an Irish footman and had a baby. No one even knows if Lydia is legitimate or not. You should be honored that you're even received here at Fairfield."

Cordelia was so astonished she couldn't speak.

"Mercutio," Ophelia continued, "has fathered two natural children with that Bessie Venables, who is the daughter of a blacksmith, for goodness' sake, and who knows how many other brats he might have? Tybalt gambles away his annual allowance in the first few months of each year, and then must live on the good graces of his friends for the remainder." Ophelia had her hands on her hips, scowling at Cordelia. "And this is my family, Cordie, my family from which I cannot separate myself. You and Mercutio and Tybalt, upon whom I had counted to help me have a decent husband and marriage, you're all simply scandalous and have terrible reputations. What will people think of me, and of dear Henry, if you come to the wedding?"

Cordelia was silent for a moment. Finally, she rose and moved to the door. "You are, of course, correct, Ophelia. Whatever would people think of you if you stood up to Lady Brompton and showed her that you loved your siblings, despite their past indiscretions? Whatever indeed would people say?"

She stepped into the hall and clenched her fists, digging her nails into her hands and forcing herself not to cry. In her anger, she suddenly became acutely aware that she was not hurting because of her requested absence from the wedding, not at all. She didn't give a fig for that. No, she was hurt because her own sister, the one person who was in a place to defend her and speak on her behalf, had refused to do so. In fact, Ophelia had genuinely not understood why Cordelia was affronted.

"Very well, then," she murmured. "Perhaps it is not worth the effort of appearing respectable, for now I do know where I stand with the rest of my family."

Wrapped tightly in her own resignation and deep, heartbreaking regret, she went off to find Lydia. After all, the two of them must be presentable for the ball that evening.

****

Guests began arriving at Fairfield Hall at dusk, and the snow had started to fall heavily once more. A line of carriages stretched nearly halfway down the lane to the main road. Each carriage—many emblazoned with crests Cordelia had never seen—approached the front steps and was greeted by a team of footmen in full livery. Ladies clad in the most stylish of gowns stepped out daintily, and Cordelia, watching from her window, knew her simple dress would pale in comparison, but she just couldn't bring herself to work up the enthusiasm that her mother and sister had for fashion.

Her gown was a new one, put together with great haste and skill by Lord Sackville's seamstresses, of plain gray silk trimmed with a smattering of tiny glass beads that glittered when she walked near the candlelight. She wore a bright scarlet shawl with it, and a matching red cap with a gray plume. Her mourning brooch was, for the first time in many years, left behind this evening, tucked into her jewelry box. Perhaps it was indeed time to move forward.

Cordelia was not classically beautiful, but she was aging well, and she knew it. The lines she saw in other women her age were barely visible in her own face, although certainly, grief had added a few that were not there in her youth. She still had all of her teeth, and they were even and white, thanks in no small part to her fastidious attention to daily hygiene. Falconer had always laughed at her, thinking it foolish to scrub out her mouth each day with a small brush and some soda powder, but when other women lost their teeth at five and twenty and hers were still strong and healthy, he admitted she must indeed be on to something. She had no gray hair yet, her breasts remained rounded and firm, and her skin was smooth, albeit a bit darker than was stylish in English ladies, owing to her fondness for the outdoors.

All in all, she credited herself as quite handsome for a widow of three and thirty.

As the ladies and the fine gentlemen alit from their conveyances, she recalled her conversation with Ophelia. Their mother had taken Ophelia's side, as was to be expected. Tybalt and Mercutio could try behaving themselves while at Fairfield Hall, but Cordelia had a feeling that ultimately, it was going to fall to her to impress Lady Brompton.

On the one hand, she owed her sister nothing.

On the other, it was hard to shake the sense of duty, knowing that Ophelia would, if Cordelia cultivated a façade of newfound respectability, instantly find herself propelled through the Bromptons' stratum of the social sphere.

"Mother, shall we go downstairs?" Lydia asked. She was bouncing up and down in excitement and was lovely in a demure gown of pale lavender silk. She was still a bit young to be presented to society, despite Ophelia's insistence that all of the best families let their girls out younger and younger each Season. Lydia, not particularly caring whether she was “out” or not, nor knowing much about what it meant, was perfectly happy to spend the evening socializing with the other girls her age, all of whom would likely make their debuts a year or two hence.

Lydia had never attended anything remotely like a formal private ball. In Virginia, certainly there had been country dances, often held at assembly halls or other public venues, and she had even accompanied her parents to a private dance in Richmond, held in a very large house. The governor himself had been in attendance, her parents had danced until sunrise the next morning, and it had been very exciting indeed. Shortly after that, though, her father died and there had been no more dances or parties to enjoy.

Now they were in England and at a home like Fairfield, no less, and the bedroom Lydia slept in was twice the size of the parlor at their farmhouse in Virginia. There were servants everywhere, lingering silently in corners, ready to do as she asked at a moment’s notice without question. She wondered what it had been like for her mother, growing up with Grandmother and Grandfather Dean. They too had servants, although not nearly as many as the Bromptons did. Grandmother Dean was very proper and concerned with appearances, and Lydia was certain the old woman wished her invisible.

Lydia eagerly followed her mother down the stairs to the hall and was astounded by the sight before her. Perhaps five score gentlemen and ladies were stuffed into the main hall, a sea of elegant bodies in satin and silk, with emeralds and lace everywhere. The crush was magnificent, with the gentlemen politely removing their tall hats and the ladies gliding about in their feather-trimmed caps. Lydia clapped her hands with joy. "Oh, Mother! See how lovely they all are!"

"Indeed," Cordelia said, scanning the crowd for familiar faces. "It is a veritable cornucopia of beauty."

Lydia couldn't tell if her mother was serious or not. "Oh, look!" she exclaimed. "There's Mr. Heyward and Mr. Aubrey! Are they not handsome?"

Cordelia followed Lydia's gaze across the room. Heyward was bowing and bobbing his head to Lord and Lady Sackville, grinning from ear to ear. Aubrey, beside him, appeared bored already. And Lydia was correct, they were very handsome indeed.

Aubrey, in fact, wasn't just handsome; he was magnificent. Several inches taller than most of the men present, he stood out in the crowd. His dark hair, which had been disheveled every time she'd seen him up until now, was trimmed and pulled back into a neat queue, and he wore a jacket of soft fawn velvet. She found herself wondering if he tasted as wonderful as he appeared this evening. She remembered his mouth on hers and her skin flushed, a delicious tingle coursing through her body.

He turned to meet her gaze, as if hearing her thoughts, and nodded. He offered a slow, lazy smile, and in that instant her heart plummeted all the way to her satin-slippered feet.

Suddenly, she wasn't as certain of herself as she'd been moments ago.

"Mother? Are you well?" Lydia whispered. Without waiting for an answer, she tugged Cordelia's hand. "Please, let us join the party! It is so exciting!

I've never seen anything like it."

"Neither have I," Cordelia murmured, so low that Lydia could not really hear her. "Not for a long time."

They reached the bottom step, and Lydia darted into the crowd. She was instantly greeted by a group of girls her own age, fascinated by the American newcomer they'd heard so much about, and they swept her away through the crush, leaving Cordelia alone.

As is common in an assembly so large, she was not alone for long.

Augustus Littleberry appeared next to her, holding two glasses of punch in his sausage-like fingers. "Miss Dean—I do beg your pardon, it is Mrs. Falconer now. Please, can you forgive my error?"

"Of course," she said, accepting the punch politely. She could not very well send him away.

"I am pleased to see you back in our country," he said, huffing a bit and wiping his pink face with the back of his hand. "Does it seem very different to you, after such a long absence?"

"Do you know," she said, "some things change, and yet the things that one hopes to be different seem to remain very much the same."

He studied her quizzically for a moment, and then nodded. "To be certain. Fifteen years is a long time to have been away. I understand you settled in America?"

Cordelia nodded. "Yes. We have a tobacco farm and horses. In Virginia."

"Is that near Boston?"

She smiled, despite herself. He was trying to be friendly, and as she was presently without very many friends at all, decided to make the best of her conversation with Augustus Littleberry. "It is not especially close, but America is a very large place. I believe it might take several days' ride to get to Boston from my home in Bedford County. Things tend to be much farther apart there than they are here," she said, feeling a bit apologetic for the sheer size of her adopted country.

"Well, I for one am glad to see you returned to us and looking so well. Your daughter is lovely, if I may say so?"

"You may indeed," she said with a laugh. She and Mr. Littleberry had always gotten along well enough socially, despite his completely unreturned attentions to her in the past. "She is a wonderful girl. I'm very proud of her."

His face clouded for a moment with genuine concern. "I know you lost your husband some time ago. I must offer my condolences, Mrs. Falconer, although I do hope you'll forgive me if my words cause you painful memories."

She patted his arm. He wasn't a bad man and truly meant to be polite. "Your words are kind, and I greatly appreciate the thought."

Littleberry snuffled and took a sip of his punch. "I am honored to be invited to perform your sister's wedding ceremony. It was rather a surprise when Lady Brompton wrote to me, but I am indeed flattered."

"Yes, I believe I heard you mention something about that during dinner last night." In fact, he had spoken of it several times.

"Well, it is quite an honor," he said, puffing his ample chest up importantly. "The Bromptons are an old and noble family. That Lady Brompton would condescend to allow me—a simple clergyman of no real importance—to perform the ceremony…Well, I can hardly contain my pleasure. Of course, becoming part of the Brompton family speaks volumes about the elevation of your sister as well. She is a fine and respectable young lady, with impeccable manners."

"Indeed." How long would it be before he recalled that she, herself, was not entirely respectable? A means of escape was nearby; her brothers stood near the opposite wall, cornered by a pair of sallow and simpering young ladies. If she had to, she could excuse herself to go rescue them.

Mr. Littleberry chattered on, telling her all about his parish and his cottage and its gardens, its three fireplaces, and its proximity to both the village of Brompton and to Fairfield Hall itself, as well as the fine mincemeat pies his cook prepared. She had tuned him out at some point during an exposition on the values of fresh carrots versus those kept in storage, when a hand lightly brushed her elbow.

She turned, and there was Aubrey.

"Mr. Littleberry," he said, "I must impose upon your good graces and borrow Mrs. Falconer for a time. I have questions on a matter of horses and have it on good authority that she is most knowledgeable about the species." Without waiting for a response, he steered her away, leaving Mr. Littleberry behind with his mouth open, gaping at them like a very large carp.

"Thank you," she whispered, leaning into him as they navigated the crowd. A few people stared at her, likely for the sheer novelty of seeing her back in the area, but most just ignored them both, too wrapped up in their own conversations to pay any notice. "Mr. Littleberry is kind enough, but he does tend to go on once one gives him the slightest hint of encouragement."

He laughed softly. "Yes, I noticed. I waited until you looked as though you were about to expire from boredom, and then felt it was my duty to step in." He guided her through the throng, and they made their way across the room to a far wall, where a group of wizened dowagers sat gossiping near a screen of potted plants.

"Well, Mr. Aubrey, I thank you again," she said. Perhaps she was wrong about him. Maybe he had not been laughing at her at all. "I must say, you're not the sort of man I would expect to be close friends with Henry Brompton. How on earth do you two know one another? Old school friends, was that it?"

Aubrey, standing just inches from her, brushed a bit of something invisible from his sleeve. "Don't you think that by now, at least in private, we might call each other by our Christian names? *Mr. Aubrey* does seem awfully formal, considering—"

"Do not speak of it," she said quickly, flushing once more. Damn the man for making her so utterly rattled. He was always in control of the conversation.

He shrugged. "Suit yourself, my dear Mrs. Falconer. At any rate, regarding Henry—it's a long story, and I won't bore you with the details. We attended school together briefly and lost touch with one another after that. Bumped into him at a club in London not too long ago, and now here I am. But I did not interrupt your conversation with Littleberry to discuss Brompton. I must tell you something, Mrs. Falconer, for it is something that has nagged at me since I first met you at the inn, and I can no longer keep silent, despite my better judgment."

Cordelia peeked over her shoulder to see if anyone was listening, but the dowagers either hadn't noticed her yet or were too busy gossiping about Leticia Dunlea-Boggins' far-too-exposed décolletage. "Mr. Aubrey," she said quietly, "I doubt there's anything you can say to me that is more shocking than the things I've been told by my own family this weekend."

He leaned closer, inhaling the scent of her. "The truth is, Mrs. Falconer, that I'm afraid you'll have made some enemies among the ladies here before the night is done. You are, by far, the most desirable woman in the place."

She heard none of the sounds of the ball, or the music, or the other dancers—there was only his voice.

"I know this is not done in proper society, but we are both well aware that you and I are neither of us proper," he continued. "That is why I wish to make you an offer."

Cordelia's jaw dropped. *He can't possibly be about to propose marriage!* She barely knew him. "Mr. Aubrey," she whispered, "despite the nature of our first meeting, and of course the intimacy of it, we really have only been acquainted a short while…"

"Listen," he said firmly, his hand gently tracing its way along the back of her neck. They were all but hidden from the rest of the crowd, and he was taking advantage of their privacy. "I wish to make you a business proposition."

She burst out laughing at his matter-of-fact tone. "A business proposition? You do continue to surprise me, Mr. Aubrey. Pray, do continue. This I must hear."

Aubrey shifted, nearer still, and she caught a scent of cloves and bayberry soap, as well as something more primitive and male. She closed her eyes and inhaled deeply before regaining her composure.

"You yourself have told me," he said, "that you are in a precarious position. You wish to attend your sister's wedding in two weeks—despite it being clear that you owe her no loyalty at all—and to do this, you must obtain the approval of the Dragon Queen of Fairfield Hall." He shot a glance in Lady Brompton's direction.

Cordelia was intrigued. He'd definitely gotten her attention, and while the conversation was hardly going the way she had anticipated, she wondered if her fortune was about to change.

"Lady Brompton can have no use for me whatsoever, despite my friendship with Henry," he went on, "but she will not disregard the fact that my family is reasonably well off and that we've had land in Yorkshire for longer than the Brompton name has even existed. That makes me, at least on paper, and despite my numerous other failings, the sort of man that good society considers a moderately decent matrimonial prospect."

"Mr. Aubrey," she said, flustered once more. How had he taken the upper hand of the conversation? "While I very much appreciate your sentiments, I must tell you quite certainly that I—"

"Will you stop for just a moment?" he snapped. "I am *not* proposing marriage to you, so you may rest easy. You make it quite clear you are uninterested in such an attachment, and to be frank, at this time I have no desire to enter into a state of wedded bliss myself."

She breathed a small sigh of relief. "If that is the case, then what—"

"You need Lady Brompton to think you respectable, at least upon the surface," he repeated. "I am a single man in possession of a reasonably decent fortune and from a family that can trace its somewhat tenuous ancestry back to one of King Charles's favorite bastards. Despite my status as a younger son, if Lady Brompton were to think you and I had come to an understanding of sorts, it might gain you the leverage you need to attend this wedding of your sister's. After the wedding, we can announce to friends and family that we've chosen to end our engagement. It will most likely be due to some scandal caused by my own boorish behavior, poor upbringing, and overall unacceptable manners."

She stared at him. A group of young ladies scampered past, giggling, and Cordelia observed just long enough to be certain her daughter was not one of them. Had she heard Aubrey correctly? Had he actually just suggested the very sham engagement that she herself had been planning?

"You do not have a response?" he murmured, sipping his claret.

"Forgive me, Mr. Aubrey, I am all astonishment. I did not expect such an…interesting consideration." She frowned a bit, as something else occurred to her. "You did refer to this as a business proposition, did you not? While I clearly gain a small dose of respectability and the opportunity to attend my sister's wedding, what do *you* intend to gain? I have the shadow of scandal in my past and my family has no real standing with the *ton*, so you can hardly suppose to use me as a method of social advancement." She could not mention that she had already granted him the sorts of favors that nice ladies did not bestow upon strangers. It was unlikely he needed reminding.

"Ah." He smiled. "That, Mrs. Falconer, I have not yet decided. I meant what I said earlier, you know. You are by far the most desirable woman in this room. That I say such a thing should come as no surprise to you." His hand was on the back of her neck again, caressing gently.

She was flushing to the point of distraction. Determined not to play his game—at least, not right now, and not on his terms—she stepped away, putting a safe arm's length of distance between them. "Mr. Aubrey, you are an absolute rogue."

"Are you suggesting you regret our previous encounter?" He raised an eyebrow at her, questioning.

She snorted in a most unladylike fashion. "I am not given to regrets, Mr. Aubrey. It is simply not in my nature. However, our encounter, as you call it, at the inn would never have occurred had I suspected I would see you again."

He burst out laughing.

Her eyes widened, horrified at what she had just said. "Hush! Everyone will hear you! Stop it!"

Aubrey turned his laugh into a cough and unsuccessfully tried to stifle his grin. "I do apologize. You are the most amazing—oh, stop, don't look at me that way, Cordelia."

She scowled.

"Mrs. Falconer, you may rest easy. Your secrets are safe with me. I understand that you would never have done such a thing under normal circumstances. You assumed I was a traveler merely passing through."

Cordelia was mortified. "That is not…I didn't

mean…I never do that sort of…"

"No, please. I quite understand you. Although," he mused, "you did not seem troubled by the idea of meeting with me in the billiard room, unchaperoned. Had you not been in such a perfect rage, who knows what might have transpired between us, all alone in there together? I'm rather glad we had a billiard table between us, protecting me from you."

She raised her fan and rapped him sharply on the hand. "Enough."

He shrugged. "Suit yourself. Consider my offer, though. You should be aware that I never say anything I do not mean. Oh, look, here comes young Heyward. He'll be wanting that dance you promised him." With that, he vanished into the crowd before she could say another word.

Heyward bowed formally when he reached her. "Mrs. Falconer, such a pleasure. Shall we?"

"We shall, indeed," she said, but as she took Heyward's arm she couldn't help searching through the sea of bodies for Aubrey. He had disappeared completely.

Heyward was quite a fine dancer, and although Cordelia was out of practice—Virginian dances were not quite like English ones—she managed to avoid embarrassing herself or her partner at all. In fact, she did tolerably well, and when the dance ended she was flushed and laughing. She curtseyed gracefully to Heyward and excused herself, her pulse pounding. The room was warm and sticky with so many people crammed into it, and so she made her way toward the great bottles of elder wine and then, glass in hand, to the terrace. The warmth of the wine—made, of course, from elderberries picked right here at Fairfield Hall—was a departure from the normal party fare of punch, but welcomed as she neared the open doors. The fresh air was jarring, a cold breeze and a few stray bits of snow blowing in from the gardens outside, and the crispness of the evening was a shocking change from the stifling heat of the hall and drawing rooms.

Cordelia stood in the door, sipping daintily, peering out at the gardens. She pulled her wrap closer around her arms, the sensation of goose pimples prickling on her skin. Although there was a faint glimmer of moon and the stars twinkled brightly, the sky seemed blacker than usual. Even the glittering blanket of snow did not illuminate the gardens as much as it should have. Cordelia squinted, wondering if her eyes deceived her. They had not—there was a lantern moving about in the darkness. She moved out onto the freshly-swept flagstone, pulling her shawl even closer. Who on earth could be out roaming around in such cold weather as this? A footman, perhaps? One of the cooks? A young man on his way to a secret tryst with a lady? She smiled a bit, remembering the night she had slipped out of her parents' home to meet Tom Falconer—a chilly night much like this one, with nothing but a small torch to light her way, and a lifetime of love and anticipation to warm her heart.

As the light in the garden grew closer, footsteps approached behind her, and she turned. It was Augustus Littleberry, looking sweaty and pink. "Mrs. Falconer, you must be cautious in the night air. I would be most concerned were you to catch cold out here." His breath puffed out in little clouds.

"Thank you for your consideration, Mr. Littleberry.

After the last dance, I found it dreadfully oppressive inside, so I thought I would risk a chill in order to avoid expiring from the heat. I promise you my constitution is strong enough to not suffer from the cold. In fact, I prefer it," she said with a wink. She turned back to face the gardens once more, but the light had disappeared, and all was still.

He frowned, not entirely sure if she was taking him seriously. "Well, I must encourage you to come back inside. I believe they'll be starting another dance in a moment," he said, a glint of hope in his eyes.

"Ah. Well, Mr. Littleberry, I feel I may still be a bit faint, although it is nothing for anyone to worry about. I shall be back inside momentarily," she assured him, taking a slight step back from his warm breath. "Perhaps when I rejoin the party, you and I can take some refreshment together. I have heard a rumor that there are some magnificent cakes to sample."

"Very well," he said, an expression of deep concern on his round face. "I shall await your arrival eagerly."

"Thank you, Mr. Littleberry," she said, bobbing her head in dismissal. He trundled back inside, huffing and wheezing a bit, and she breathed a sigh of relief. That had been a close call. The last thing she wanted right now was to be cornered into a dance with Augustus Littleberry. If walking to the terrace had exhausted him, goodness knew what a lively country reel might do to the man.

A whisper came from the stone stairs behind her. "Cordie!"

She whirled around, staring into the night. "Ophelia? What are you doing out there? Where are you?"

"Down here."

Cordelia leaned over the terrace's railing, and there was her sister in her fine dress and soft slippers, standing in the snow and looking rumpled.

"Is anyone up there with you?" Ophelia asked. "I saw Mr. Littleberry go inside."

"I'm alone. Come on up," Cordelia whispered. What on earth had gotten into her sister? "Do hurry."

Ophelia tiptoed up the stairs and attempted to smooth her gown. Her slippers were soaked, and she was shivering. "Cordie, please do not say anything of this to Henry or Mother."

Cordelia scowled at her. "Not until you tell me where you were. You poor thing, you're shaking. Do take my shawl. You'll catch your death out here like that. Now, whyever would you be out here scampering about in the dark? Especially," she said, jabbing a finger at Ophelia, "after all I've had to hear from you about my own behavior. Lady Brompton would have your head on a spit if she were to see you right now, looking as though you'd just returned from…well, from God only knows what. We'd all be sent home in an instant."

Ophelia patted her hair down. "It is nothing. I promise, I have done nothing untoward or improper, Cordelia. We must speak no more of it." She took a deep breath and handed Cordelia's shawl back to her. "There. Now, let us return to the party. I am cold and damp, and I don't like it one bit."

Ophelia stepped through the wide terrace doors, vanishing into the crush, and just then, somewhere in the chilly night, someone began to scream.

Chapter Seven

Leticia Dunlea-Boggins was from a good family of respectable name and a substantial amount of wealth, and she was accomplished in all manner of ladylike pursuits. She was adept at the pianoforte, sang reasonably well, comported herself with grace in dancing, and was known to have painted several very pleasant watercolor images of the fruit trees in her father's orchard. She was small and plump, with a button-like nose and blue eyes, an ample bosom, and lovely golden ringlets that crowned her head like a halo.

When she began screaming in the garden, all of Leticia Dunlea-Boggins' good manners evaporated, her ladylike demeanor gone. A look of abject terror gave an unpleasant countenance to her normally pretty face as she ran across the lawn, slipping and sliding in the snow, followed closely by none other than Cordelia's brother Tybalt himself.

Cordelia's first thought was that her family was completely done for, with no question, if Tybalt had attempted taking liberties with Leticia Dunlea-Boggins, who was very clearly at the engagement ball in pursuit of a husband rather than a mere flirtation. Her second thought was that while not all ladies would be flattered by Tybalt's attentions, she had never seen one actually run away from him shrieking and sobbing as though pursued by the hounds of hell. And that meant that there was something very wrong.

"Tybalt? What's happening?"

Her brother caught up with Leticia, taking her hand, and gently shushed the girl's hysterical sobs as she moaned into his coat. He pushed her toward Cordelia. "Get her out of here, and keep her quiet. I must find Brompton immediately. Do you know where he is?"

Cordelia shook her head, alarmed at her brother's frantic behavior. "Inside somewhere. The last I saw him, he was with Mercutio discussing his newest litter of hound pups."

Tybalt did not say another word and instead slipped inside the hall. A few people glanced out at Cordelia, but she ignored them and did her best to get Leticia Dunlea-Boggins under control. She dabbed at the girl's face with her handkerchief, trying to mop up the tears. Leticia snuffled and gasped. "Oh, Mrs. Falconer, it was awful!" she whispered.

Cordelia frowned. "I'm certain that Tybalt meant you no harm, dear."

The younger woman shook her head, puzzled, and wiped her nose, hiccoughing rapidly. "No…not Tybalt. He's such a gentleman," she said, stifling a sob. "It was the footman."

"One of the footmen?" There was no sign of her brother returning yet. "Did one of the footmen harm you?"

Leticia shook her head again and wept even more, sliding weakly to the ground. Cordelia gave up, knowing that she would get no further information from Leticia, at least not until she had regained her composure. She took off her shawl and wrapped it around Leticia's shaking shoulders, muttering a silent prayer of thanks that Ophelia had been thoughtful enough to give it back.

A few ladies and gentlemen had gathered already, standing inside the doors, peering out onto the terrace. Cordelia refused to look at them, would not give them the honor of letting them think it was she who had been howling like a *bean sí* just a few moments ago. She had already moved Leticia out of sight, propping her up against a large potted ornamental in the shadows.

Tybalt appeared then, accompanied by Henry Brompton and Aubrey, and all three of them appeared distressed, ranging from Aubrey's frown to Henry's look of sheer terror. "Cordie," Tybalt said, "take Miss Dunlea-Boggins around to the kitchens, and get her something warm to drink. She's had a fright."

"What's going on?" she hissed. "She said something about a footman."

Tybalt and Brompton ignored her and hastened down the stairs to the lawn. It was Aubrey who paused for a moment when he reached her. "Don't take her through the house," he said, his voice low. "Lead her around the stone path down to the kitchens. You know the way?"

"Yes," she nodded. "What's happened?"

His dark eyes met hers, looking troubled. "Murder."

Cordelia's hand shot to her mouth, and she shook her head. "Not here. At Fairfield Hall?"

Aubrey nodded. "Say nothing to anyone, and keep the girl silent. I shall come find you soon." He bounded down the steps, taking them two at a time, and disappeared into the dark gardens with Tybalt and

Brompton, their footprints materializing like shadowy ghosts in the white snow.

Cordelia took Leticia's elbow and guided her down the stairs. She felt numb. Ophelia had been in the gardens—what if she had narrowly missed an encounter with a murderer? And who was it that was dead? Leticia had mentioned something about a footman. Had she seen one of the Fairfield servants commit a terrible crime?

Worse yet, was the killer still lurking in the shadows?

Hastily, she led Leticia, clearly still in shock, along the stone path around the far side of the house. This was where the servants' quarters were, as well as the kitchens. Leticia noticed nothing; she was far too busy weeping into her hands and making great gulping sounds. The sounds of the ball continued in the rooms above her as she clutched the girl's arm, dragging her along. Apparently, things had returned to normal. Through the open windows ladies laughed, gentlemen boasted loudly, and the string musicians tuned their instruments as they prepared for the next set. Somehow, none of it seemed quite real anymore. The kitchen door was open, and she pushed the girl inside, much to the surprise of Mrs. Chibbs, the cook.

"Hello, dears," Chibbs said, bobbing an automatic curtsey, despite being unaccustomed to well-bred and damp young women stumbling through her door in the evenings. "Is there something I can help you with, missus?"

"Some hot cider for Miss Dunlea-Boggins, if you please," Cordelia said briskly. She moved to the large hearth, where a fat pig rotated on a spit, and rubbed her cold hands together.

"And for you, missus?"

She was suddenly exhausted. "What have you got hidden about that's unladylike and completely inappropriate for someone of my station?"

Chibbs laughed heartily and pulled an earthenware jug from the shelf. "Good for what ails you, milady," she said.

Cordelia and Leticia sat quietly in the corner with their drinks, while the kitchen sprang to life around them. Dinner was scheduled for eleven, and that was a mere two hours away. The long wooden tables were piled high with pots and pans, soup tureens and chopped vegetables. One of the scullery girls stirred a large vat of stew over a fire, and a young boy chopped a wheel of cheese into small blocks. The servants bustled in and out, and at one point the butler popped in on his way to the wine cellar. Chibbs stayed busy ordering her underlings about and was constantly cutting, arranging, seasoning, and tasting the dishes, running the entire operation with military-like logistical precision.

After what seemed like forever, Aubrey poked his head through the door and nodded to Cordelia. "May I speak with you, Mrs. Falconer?"

She glanced down at Leticia Dunlea-Boggins, who was slumped over the table with her head resting on her arms, and wondered briefly what had been in Mrs. Chibbs' warm cider. She patted the girl's blonde curls and stepped into the doorway with Aubrey.

"Tell me what has happened," she ordered.

"It's one of the Bromptons' footmen," he said abruptly. "He's been bludgeoned in the head. I must ask, did you see anything out of the ordinary before

Tybalt and the girl came out of the gardens?"

Against her will, Cordelia gasped, her hands shaking as she steadied herself against the door. This could not be happening. She took a deep breath and steeled her resolve, regaining control. She would not let Rhys Aubrey see her worry, no matter what. "Ophelia. She was…oh, Mr. Aubrey! She may have been in danger as well!"

Aubrey nodded, his mouth set in a firm line. "Indeed. Your brother says that he and Miss Dunlea-Boggins saw your sister exiting the gardens just a few moments before they found the body, near a marble statue of Apollo. Did Miss Dean give you any indication as to what she had been doing out there?"

"No," she said, shivering now that she'd left the warmth of the kitchen's stone walls. Her wrap was still tucked around Leticia Dunlea-Boggins. "No, she wouldn't tell me. She just said it wasn't what it seemed, and that she had done nothing improper." She stepped back, momentarily shocked that such a thing could cross her mind. "Wait. Mr. Aubrey, what are you implying? I shall not, will not allow you to question my sister's reputation."

Aubrey pulled off his coat and dropped it over her shoulders before she could protest. He stared at her, hard. "I'm not implying anything and would never impugn a lady's honor, as you are well aware. But a man is dead in Brompton's gardens, and not by his own hand, nor by accident, nor by simple misfortune. Your sister may have been one of the last people to see him alive, Cordelia. I must speak to her immediately to ascertain what she may have seen."

Without taking her eyes from him, Cordelia called

over her shoulder, "Mrs. Chibbs? Will you have one of the staff deliver a message to my sister?"

They returned to the warmth of the kitchen, and a runner was dispatched, posthaste, to bring Ophelia belowstairs. As Cordelia and Aubrey waited in silence, Tybalt and Brompton arrived. Tybalt shot a glance toward Leticia Dunlea-Boggins, snoring delicately, her mouth open just a bit, the empty cider glass beside her. "Is she recovered?" he asked with a frown.

"As well as can be expected, given the shock she must have had. Never fear, Tybalt," Cordelia said, "she will have a great adventure to tell her friends about when she awakens, and she will once again be the toast of society. If you're smart, you'll not mention that you were walking around the gardens with her—can't have you ruining her reputation along with the rest of ours."

Brompton helped himself to the earthen jug and took a hearty gulp. He looked far more pale than usual in the moonlight. "Cordie, my first footman's been killed, and my fiancée may have been out there with him unchaperoned. This is hardly a moment for frivolity."

Cordelia patted his hand. "You are, of course, correct, Henry. It was inappropriate. I would never try to—Ophelia!"

Her sister was clearly puzzled at being summoned to the kitchen by a servant, particularly when it was just not the sort of thing that normally happened during a large society ball. "Whatever is it, Cordelia? Henry, what are you doing down here?" She peered down her nose at the sleeping Miss Dunlea-Boggins. "And is that Leticia? Good God, is she drunk? What have you done to her, Tybalt?"

Brompton stepped forward and took her hands. “Please, my dear, have a seat. No one has done anything to Miss Dunlea-Boggins, but she’s had a bit of a fright.”

Ophelia blinked. “She doesn’t look frightened; she looks asleep. Or inebriated.”

“Yes, well,” Cordelia interrupted, feeling a bit apologetic. Thank heavens Ophelia was not harmed. “That’s partly my fault. I gave her an awful lot of Mrs. Chibbs’s cider to calm her down. I didn’t realize it was quite so potent.”

Brompton cut in. “At any rate, my dear, there’s been an accident of sorts out in the garden, and—”

“An accident? Has one of the statues fallen? Do you know, Henry, I was just speaking with your mother yesterday about the one of Apollo—or perhaps it’s Aphrodite, I don’t know which of those people are which—that’s over near the roses, and it’s looking quite topple-y. You’ll need to get it fixed. How would it look if it fell into the grass and people saw it just lying there, as though you couldn’t afford to take care of it?”

“Ophelia, stop,” said Cordelia. Clearly her sister was back to her old superficial self, chattering on endlessly about nothing in particular.

“A man was murdered,” Aubrey said abruptly, from his spot in the corner. He was nearly invisible, standing in the shadows.

Ophelia froze, looking about the room, her eyes darting from one of them to the other. “Murdered? I don’t understand.”

Brompton patted her solicitously. “No one of society, my dear, but still, a man was killed tonight. One of my footmen, and I’m very put out.”

A shadow passed over Ophelia's face. "One of the footmen?" she asked.

Tybalt nodded. "Grimm was his name, I believe."

"Owen Grimm?" Cordelia exclaimed. It was the footman she had scolded in the hall, and later apologized to for her outburst. Ophelia had gone white as a sheet. "Ophelia, what is it?"

Tears began to stream down Ophelia's cheeks. "I did go out there," she whispered. "I meant to meet him in the gardens." Seeing the look on Brompton's face, she hastily continued. "It's not like that, Henry. It was nothing inappropriate, he was only a *footman*, you know. I had to speak with him about a matter of some delicacy, but there has been no improper behavior on either of our parts. I was only out there a few moments. You must believe that."

Brompton sat on the bench, stunned. "You were meeting my first footman in the dark gardens during our engagement ball, about a matter of *delicacy*? Ophelia, whatever can you expect me to believe?"

She buried her head in her hands, weeping. "Oh, Henry, you must understand! I was meeting with Grimm in hope of preventing a scandal, not causing one!"

Cordelia instinctively moved closer to her sister, wrapping an arm around her.

Aubrey stepped forward. "Miss Dean," he said firmly, "you're going to have to explain things more specifically. I'm sorry, but this is not the time for evasiveness."

"Leave her alone," Cordelia snapped. "Can't you see she's upset? Everyone is! Why must you badger her so?"

Aubrey took a candle from the iron holder on the kitchen table and lowered it near the floor. “This is why.” He pointed to the hem of Ophelia’s silk dress. There was a dark, ominous stain along the edge, several inches long. “Unless I’m a complete and utter fool—and I like to think I’m not—that, Mrs. Falconer, is blood.”

Cordelia stared in horror at her sister. “Ophelia? You must tell the truth, my dear, right this instant.”

Ophelia shook her head. “I did not kill him, Cordelia, I did not! He was dead when I got to the garden, you must believe it!”

“Ophelia, why did you not tell us?” Cordelia was astonished. Her sister, who had never done, said, or even thought anything scandalous, had been in the garden with a dead footman. Indeed, Lady Brompton would have a great deal to say about this.

The door slammed shut, as Henry Brompton stormed from the kitchen without another word.

Tybalt moved Leticia Dunlea-Boggins over a bit, and she snuffled softly but did not wake. “Out with it. You must see that this looks very bad, Ophelia.”

She shook her head. “It doesn’t matter, does it, Tyb? Henry’s gone, and I’m sure he’s telling his mother all about this, and she’ll make him break our engagement. She will say he can’t marry me, and then no one else will have me. It doesn’t matter at all what I’ve done or not done. It doesn’t matter why.” Ophelia curled her arms around herself and refused to say another word.

Cordelia maneuvered around Aubrey and swiftly made for the back stairs.

“Where are you going?” he called.

"I must find my mother," she said quietly. "Ophelia is right, you know. A man has been murdered, and that will not signify to the *ton* very much, for he was only a footman. What will matter greatly, however, is my sister's presence in the garden with a servant. Somehow, they will manage to make a scandal of her involvement, to whatever degree it might be."

His look pierced through her. "Do you not believe her innocence?"

"Of course I do!" *Damn the man. Did he take pleasure in being intentionally difficult?* "But my faith in her innocence means nothing. I know little of your history, Mr. Aubrey, and do not know how much experience you have had in the past with country society. Truth, sir, means nothing, not to these people. All that is important is the appearance of impropriety, and if Miss Ophelia Dean has such poor upbringing and bad manners as to be unchaperoned at night in a garden with a murdered servant, then that is what they shall latch on to, make no mistake about it."

"I need you to stay here," he said, his voice low. Aubrey glanced past her to the crew of kitchen help. Each of them was far too well trained to speak of anything they had overheard, but eventually word would get out nevertheless. "Stay with Ophelia and your brother. I have something I must attend to, but I will make excuses for all of you."

She blinked. "Something you must attend to? Is it something more significant than a man's death by murder?"

Aubrey gave her an odd look. "It may not be more significant than murder, but that makes it no less important. I must move Grimm's body inside, but then I shall return, Mrs. Falconer. Make no mistake of it."

And with that, Cordelia sat between the dozing Leticia Dunlea-Boggins and silent Ophelia to wait.

Chapter Eight

Providence Adkyns was five and forty years old and cut an impressive figure at just over six feet in height, which he liked to display to his own advantage by wearing a hat that added another seven inches at the top of his head. Adkyns was thin and lanky, and this combined with his dark, bushy muttonchops, his large hooked nose, and a tendency to wear black jackets with sleeves just a bit too short, made him look like a tall, hungry crow.

His family had been in the village of Brompton for many years, since the time when it had been merely a crossroads with a tavern and a gallows pole. If one traced his ancestry back five or six generations, a distant and moderately disreputable connection could be made to the Brompton family itself. It was because of this loose and tenuous grasp at kinship that Providence Adkyns had been, a decade ago, appointed as magistrate for the area.

When a servant rapped on the door of his small but well-appointed country house, telling him he must attend urgently to Fairfield Hall, Adkyns responded as any man of his station would have done—with great speed and alacrity. He had his horse saddled immediately and set out without delay despite the inclement weather. He paused only long enough to tell his wife that he had been summoned by Lady

Brompton, and that whatever the matter was, it must be of great importance for such a person to condescend to calling upon the magistrate rather than quietly handling the issue herself.

When he arrived at Fairfield Hall, he was escorted with no fanfare at all through the servants' entrance and led to the kitchens. It was clear there was a very large party in progress. The sounds of music and laughter were audible from the floor above, and Adkyns noted a significant number of carriages and liveried servants at the front of the house.

Once belowstairs, he was greeted by Mrs. Chibbs, whom he had once wanted to marry, long ago when she was still Alice Telford, and she pointed him toward a table at which sat three very well-dressed ladies. Providence Adkyns used his powers of deduction—always helpful in a magistrate, and something upon which he prided himself—and determined by their appearances that two of the ladies were likely related to one another. A handsome gent sat nearby, and he too had the same honey-golden hair as the women. *Aha*, thought Adkyns, *a family affair*. It was the dark-haired gentleman in the corner with the brilliant eyes and high cheekbones that gave Adkyns pause.

"Are you the magistrate?" Aubrey asked, without bothering to be pleasant, before Adkyns could speak.

"I am, good sir, and I understand there's been some sort of…misunderstanding." Adkyns drew himself up to his full height as Aubrey stepped from the shadows, but realized belatedly that he was still the shorter of the two.

"It is no misunderstanding," Aubrey said, abrupt and formal. "We've a dead footman who was killed out in the garden. I've had him moved into the icehouse for safekeeping, although he certainly can't stay there long. We also have Miss Ophelia Dean, who stumbled across his body. Before she had a chance to report it, however, Mr. Tybalt Dean and his friend"—he indicated Leticia Dunlea-Boggins, who was beginning to stir—"found the corpse as well and came back to the party to tell us of their find."

Adkyns scowled. "And who exactly are you, sir?" This upstart had clearly been asking questions, and Adkyns was more than a little put out. How on earth was he to be taken seriously as an investigator, if someone else had already done the investigating prior to his arrival?

"Rhys Aubrey, late of Derwent Scar, Pen-y-Ghent, Yorkshire."

Adkyns's eyes narrowed. "And what brings you to our quiet country village, Mr. Aubrey?" It was his job to be suspicious of strangers, particularly strangers who looked as though they ought to be traveling with a tinkers' caravan, stealing horses, and deflowering farm girls, rather than sitting as a guest at a respectable home.

Aubrey regarded the magistrate up and down, and the hint of a smile played on his face, but it was promptly suppressed. "I'm visiting my old friend, Mr. Henry Brompton, because he is to formally announce his engagement this evening to Miss Ophelia Dean. Perhaps you'd like to question her as to what she saw?"

Adkyns sniffed. "I'll have to question each of you, as I'm sure you understand, but first I must ascertain that a crime has indeed been committed."

Cordelia spoke up. "I would say, Mr. Adkyns, that

if a man has been bludgeoned to death, that the question is not whether a crime has been committed, but rather who might have done so ghastly a deed."

Providence Adkyns was rapidly realizing that, despite their being in the kitchens, he was in a room full of people who were all of far higher social station than he, and who thus could not be bullied or cowed into doing or saying anything. Normally, he was in complete control of every investigation—few as they had been—but now, this Mr. Aubrey was sneering at him, and the woman, whoever she was, had no interest in controlling her tongue.

"Well, then, let's start by looking at this body. Hmm. Yes," Adkyns said, trying to stay in command.

Tybalt jumped to his feet. "This way, if you please." He led the magistrate through the wine cellar to the small, chilly room beneath the kitchens, where Owen Grimm's body was temporarily stored. Cordelia followed along, accompanied by Aubrey.

"You should remain with your sister," Aubrey murmured in her ear.

"My sister is fine. Mrs. Chibbs will look after her."

He raised a brow at her, holding the door to the icehouse for her. "I defer to your judgment about the matter. After you, Mrs. Falconer. If, that is, you feel your constitution can withstand seeing the footman's corpse?"

Cordelia stopped for a moment, hoping her voice would not betray her anger and fear. "I beg your pardon, Mr. Aubrey," she said softly, "but I might remind you that the sight of a footman's corpse is something with which I am very personally acquainted." She did not know if his shocked expression was due to her forthrightness, or to the recognition of his own thoughtless comment. She pushed by him without another word.

Owen Grimm had been a very good-looking young man in life, almost girlishly pretty. In death, laid out on the sawdust-covered blocks of ice, his body was like a wax statue, and Cordelia shivered a bit. More saddening than his cold face, however, was the damage done to the side of his head and the terrible dark stain that surrounded it. Owen Grimm would never flirt with another chambermaid, nor bow to a nobleman, nor stand by silent and unobtrusive as the world went on around him. He was dead and in a manner that was, to Cordelia, blasphemous and vile.

She hadn't lied to Aubrey—she was all too familiar with death. She'd been the one to find Tom out in the stable, after the horse kicked him. She was the one who sat a vigil with him for three nights as the life drained out of him, but the truth was, the man she knew as Tom Falconer had died the minute that giant hoof connected with his temple, and it was merely a matter of time before his body caught up with his soul.

There was no doubt that both Owen Grimm's soul and his body had thoroughly expired.

Adkyns inspected the large and bloody indentation along Grimm's scalp and apparently reached the same conclusion. He made a great show of examining it, although what he hoped to see Cordelia could not begin to imagine. "Well, then," he proclaimed at long last, "I believe we can ascertain a trauma to the head to be the cause of this man's death."

"Dear God," Cordelia muttered, and Tybalt shushed her.

"Furthermore," Adkyns went on, "we may ascertain that the decedent—whose name we know to be Owen Grimm, first footman of Fairfield Hall—did not die by his own hand. The size and depth of the damage to his person would indicate that perhaps a second party caused this man to die."

Aubrey swiped a hand over his face but could not mask his clear frustration. "Mr. Adkyns. I believe these are two facts we can all of us agree on. Could we, perhaps, move on toward the more pressing question of who exactly killed Grimm?"

"Indeed," said Cordelia, "what if a violent killer is roaming the gardens at this very moment, watching from afar all the ladies and gentlemen? What if, Mr. Adkyns, he has set his murderous eye on Lady Brompton herself and is only waiting for the right opportunity to attack?"

Aubrey raised a brow, and Cordelia turned away.

Certainly, the notion of a crazed maniac sneaking up on Lady Brompton might, in other circumstances, have its benefits, but now was not the best time to consider such things.

Adkyns puttered around some more, poking and prodding at Grimm's body, and Tybalt took the opportunity to confer with Cordelia. "I must go back to the kitchen to check on Ophelia. Mother is still upstairs, and she's bound to notice by now that we've all disappeared. I asked Merc to keep her busy, but eventually she'll make a scene and want to know where everyone has gotten to."

"Yes," she agreed. "Do go. Dinner will be served shortly, so you'll need to find Brompton and make sure he removes the place settings for all of us, except for

Ophelia. He can tell everyone she is unwell and convey to those who ask, that we are attending her. This way, there shall be only a single empty chair to raise anyone's suspicions."

Tybalt disappeared, and once Mr. Adkyns had run out of things to do and notes to make regarding Grimm's body, he did not seem to know how to next proceed.

Aubrey indicated the stairs to the kitchen. "Should you perhaps like to ask some questions of the young ladies?"

Adkyns huffed impatiently. "Of course, Mr. Aubrey, although I am certain you must understand when I say that any investigation—particularly an investigation into a crime so heinous—must be evaluated with a keen eye indeed, and every possible…possibility looked into before it is discounted. I shall exhaust all other options before discussion of such an unpleasant matter with the young ladies."

Cordelia took the stairs hastily, hoping to avoid any more of Mr. Adkyns's observations. Surely a murder was far beyond the scope of anything a country magistrate could be prepared for. The man was clearly out of his realm of expertise, and worse, he was a bumbling fool. A killer was on the loose in the countryside, and so far all Adkyns had discovered was that Owen Grimm was indeed dead and that someone else was responsible for it. If the finding of this information was all that was required to become a magistrate, Cordelia herself was qualified for the job.

Her own experience with crime and law was minimal at best. Once, in Virginia, a man had stolen a horse and been hanged for it, which was the talk of the town for weeks. She had also met two indentured servants transported to America for thievery, and there were rumors at some point that a local landholder had beaten and killed his own cousin, although—much to Cordelia's chagrin—nothing had ever come of it. Here in England, among the gentry, crime was rare, and absolutely never spoken of in polite society.

Certainly, it was understood that a chambermaid might occasionally pilfer a small piece of jewelry to sell, although she wouldn't stay employed long if she made a habit of such behavior. Men racked up gambling debts now and then—certainly Tybalt and Mercutio were not unique in that—but as long as they were gentlemen and paid eventually, such things were generally overlooked. But murder—murder was something else indeed. It might happen in the stews of London, or in a drunken country tavern brawl, but it did not happen at places like Fairfield Hall.

At least not until now.

Why on earth could Ophelia have been meeting Owen Grimm? Her sister had said it was to prevent a scandal, rather than cause one. Ophelia was going to have to start talking soon, whether she liked it or not.

The servants had been busily making certain that dinner, in all its many courses, was properly set out upon the tables upstairs, and so there was a great flurry of activity in the kitchen. Mrs. Chibbs was ordering people about while Ophelia and Leticia sat crying prettily together at the table.

"Come, my dears," Cordelia said. "We have done all we can do, and now we shall leave things to Mr. Adkyns to investigate. Mr. Adkyns, if you need nothing else from us, we shall retire for the evening."

"Will you ladies be returning to the party, Mrs. Falconer?" he asked, squinting at her with his beady eyes.

Cordelia shook her head. "No. My sister has had a terrible shock, as has Miss Dunlea-Boggins. I will get them to my sister's bedroom and attend them for the rest of the evening. Should you need us, please do not hesitate to send someone."

He nodded, peering down his long nose at her, giving no hint as to what he might be thinking.

She turned to her sister. "Come, Ophelia. Let us put you to bed. Miss Dunlea-Boggins, will you not join us? I think perhaps a rest might do you well. We shall take the servants' stairs."

Leticia nodded clumsily. She had recovered from her rapid consumption of Mrs. Chibbs' cider, and now was just a bit wobbly on her feet.

Aubrey stepped in front of Cordelia. "Do not," he said.

"I beg your pardon?"

"You forget that the purpose of this party is to announce Henry's engagement to your sister. Although some of his guests have already left for home, others are staying for dinner. It will look more than a little strange if she remains absent, no matter how unwell she may be feeling. Miss Dean, you must change your clothes, have the maid fix your hair, and then return to the ball as soon as possible."

"But Henry left me here," Ophelia said sadly. "He believes the worst of me, and who can blame him? He thinks I had an...an *assignation* with that servant!"

Aubrey took her hand firmly in his. "Miss Dean, it

does not matter right now what Henry believes or does not believe. What matters is that the two of you put on a happy appearance for his guests. Your absence is conspicuous, all things considered. All of you must be seen at dinner, despite everything that has happened. You too, Miss Dunlea-Boggins. Cordelia, get your sister upstairs and into a clean dress, tidy her hair, and wash her face. Meanwhile, I shall let Brompton know you will join the rest of the party very soon, behaving as though there were nothing at all out of the ordinary."

Ophelia nodded, stifling yet another sob.

Aubrey peered over her head at Cordelia. "Take care of her," he ordered. For once, she did not feel like arguing with him.

****

"Ladies, gentlemen," began Henry Brompton, as dinner wound to a close, "as some of you may have heard, our family has a special and most joyous announcement to make this evening." He raised his glass of Champagne. "I am tonight most honored and humbled to say that Miss Ophelia Dean has agreed to become my wife."

There was polite applause from the three dozen guests gathered at the large dining table, and much congratulatory clinking of glasses. Lord Sackville himself patted Brompton on the back repeatedly, telling him what a good show he had made in selecting Ophelia as his bride-to-be. Harriet Brompton beamed with pleasure, at least on the outside—internally, she was simply fuming.

That awful Ophelia Dean had vanished for a good two hours of the party, and then when she returned she was wearing a different dress, looking flushed and exhausted, as though she had been weeping—or worse. Harriet had her suspicions—after all, she was a woman, and knew how women thought—but could prove nothing. Despite this, her convictions were strong that Ophelia was no better than her trollop of a sister, who went about eloping with servants. Harriet, always perceptive, noticed that her future daughter-in-law seemed far more distracted and anxious than she should be. Any woman in London would have happily traded places with Ophelia, for a chance to marry the Brompton name and money, and here was Miss Dean looking for all the world as though she'd rather be anywhere but Fairfield Hall.

Harriet realized her nephew was talking to her and sniffed at him with impatience. "What is it, Thomas?"

Heyward offered her a replacement glass of Champagne. "Here's to a felicitous match, right, Aunt Brompton?" He tossed back his own glass in one gulp.

"A felicitous match, indeed," she said quietly. "I wonder how long it will take Henry to realize that he has, as I warned him, married beneath him."

"Not long, I would imagine," Heyward murmured. The room was filled with the cream of the county's society…and the Deans. "Look at the rest of her family. It is a spectacle to behold."

Harriet followed his gaze to Agatha Dean, who was sitting beside Lady Sackville and loudly proclaiming her own great joy at being the mother of a girl so loved by a man as rich as Henry Brompton. Tybalt Dean, much farther down the table and yet not far enough away, was a good way into his cups and whispering into the ear of Leticia Dunlea-Boggins, also a bit the worse for wear—there was no telling what the two of them were up to, but things looked bad indeed. Mrs. Falconer had spent much of the evening talking to that horrible Mr. Aubrey—Harriet didn't like him at all, what with him being from Yorkshire and acting as though he was as good as the rest of them, and besides, she'd placed the Falconer woman right next to Reverend Littleberry, who'd found himself shamefully ignored. And the daughter—Lydia, was that her name?—was certainly pretty enough, but that scandalous red hair of hers betrayed her low Irish parentage, and the girl was far too bold and laughed more often than a young lady should in public.

"Henry insists on marrying Miss Dean, Thomas, and there's nothing to be done about it. Her family just skirts the boundaries of what is acceptable and what is not, but I have requested that the only one in attendance at the wedding shall be her mother." She sniffed once more. "The sister and the brothers will only draw attention to themselves. The sooner those people are out of Miss Dean's life, the sooner she can settle into her role as Henry's wife and be rid of her unpleasant associations of the past."

"They've all been acting quite strangely this evening," Heyward commented. "Disappearing and running about as though they were on some sort of treasure hunt."

Later, as everyone began making their way back into the ballroom, Augustus Littleberry approached Harriet, sweating profusely. "Good evening, Lady Brompton. I must once again thank you for allowing me to attend such a wonderful event as this. We don't often have parties of this magnitude around these parts, do we? Simply lovely." He gazed wistfully at Cordelia

Falconer as he spoke.

"Mr. Littleberry, you were, I believe, acquainted with the Dean family some years ago, were you not?"

"Oh, yes," he said, nodding vigorously, not looking at Harriet. "I had hoped, at one point in the distant past, to be far more closely acquainted with a particular member of the family, although as you can see, that did not in fact come to pass. Circumstances, you know, were beyond the control of anyone."

"Perhaps," Heyward suggested, "it is time for you to renew your attentions in that quarter."

Littleberry blinked, astonished at the bold suggestion. "I do not, Mr. Heyward, believe such a thing would be either appropriate or advisable at this time. A reverend's wife must be a pillar of obedience, so that all parishioners will see her as a model of decorum and piety. There may never be any doubt as to the wholesome and chaste nature of her character. No, I believe that any opportunity in that direction has been long gone, as I'm sure you must agree."

Heyward grinned and raised a glass to Littleberry. "Indeed, you are correct, sir. The merry widow is not the sort of person who would set a good example for your parishioners, I am sure…unless you wished to demonstrate an example of how Christian charity may redeem the fallen from previous indiscretions and the poor judgment of their youth."

An odd look flicked across Littleberry's face. "That is so, Mr. Heyward, to be sure. I had not considered it from such a perspective. Perhaps I have some more thought to put into the matter, after all." He bowed politely and made his way back into the crowd, aiming toward Cordelia Falconer.

Lady Brompton sighed heavily. “Oh, badly done, Thomas. Whatever could you have been thinking?”

Heyward winked at his aunt, much to her horror. “Mostly of my own amusement, I confess, Aunt. I do apologize, but I thought it might not be a bad thing to give poor Mr. Littleberry a bit of hope.”

“Oh, pish.” Harriet Brompton snorted as delicately as a lady of her station could. “That woman would no sooner give Littleberry her hand than she would give him the time of day. Look at her. She has spent far too long in the wilds of America. A man like Littleberry will hardly be capable of taming her, and although he may not know it, she certainly does.”

Heyward studied Cordelia. She was clearly distracted by something as she talked quietly with her brother—which twin it was, Thomas could not tell—and although she smiled politely when Littleberry approached her, it was obvious she was not interested in speaking with him. Nearby, Rhys Aubrey was watching Cordelia with undisguised attentiveness. In fact, he behaved in a manner almost proprietary toward her. Heyward was surprised—although he himself was quite drawn to her, he would not have expected her to appeal to a man like Aubrey, who puzzled him more than a bit.

Henry ambled by, overwhelmed by all the congratulations, and took Heyward’s Champagne glass from him. He drained it and promptly took a second from a passing servant. “Good man,” he said, toasting his cousin.

Heyward grinned at him.

“Excuse me,” Harriet said, rising to her feet. “I must go and endure a few more minutes with Mrs. Dean. The things I am forced to tolerate for your happiness, Henry. Do remember all of this when I am old and feeble."

After they had bid her farewell in unison, Thomas turned to Henry. "That Aubrey fellow," he said. "What do you know of him?"

"We went to school together."

Thomas laughed. "I know that part. What I'm trying to figure out is who he actually is."

Henry shrugged. "Younger son of a viscount of some sort, from off on the moors somewhere. We attended school together briefly, although Aubrey was a few years ahead of me. Ran into him in London not long ago and struck up a conversation. He didn't have much else to do, so I invited him up here to Fairfield." He paused. "Is there a problem, Thomas?"

"No, no. I just like to know who people are. Oh dear. Emma Pinsgrave is headed this way. Now I'll be forced to dance with her." Thomas sighed and extended a hand to the toothy young lady who had just approached.

Henry stood back, watching the crowd, acutely aware of the dead footman in the ice room. He wished fervently that the façade could end and this night would soon be over.

Chapter Nine

By half past three in the morning, most of the guests had departed, other than those who were already in residence at Fairfield Hall for the smaller, more intimate house party. Henry Brompton knew he must tell his mother about the footman, and besides, Providence Adkyns was still lurking in the halls belowstairs, making noises about poking around Owen Grimm's rooms and speaking to the staff. Sooner or later, Harriet was going to find out.

Henry called everyone into the sitting room. It had been a long evening indeed, and he wanted nothing more than to go to bed and let someone else take responsibility for Fairfield Hall and everything in it. "I ask your forgiveness for forcing you to stay up a little bit longer," he said. "I do apologize, but I must make everyone aware of something that transpired earlier this evening. Obviously, some of you already know, but the rest of you—"

"Out with it, Henry!" his mother snapped. "I am exhausted and wish to retire, so if you must say something displeasing, then pray do so immediately, that I may get some sleep at last."

"Well, you see, it's just that—"

Aubrey spoke up. "A man is dead. Murdered in the gardens tonight."

There was a collective gasp from Mrs. Dean, Lady

Brompton, and Lydia. Mercutio just shook his head and began liberally pouring claret into glasses, which he passed around.

"The man who was killed was a footman here," Aubrey continued. "Owen Grimm."

Lady Brompton's hand flew to her face, which had gone pale. "Owen Grimm," she whispered. "Are you certain?"

"Quite. The magistrate, Adkyns, is here right now, searching Grimm's room up in the servants' wing for some hint of what might have happened, but I believe it unlikely he will find anything of much importance."

Harriet nodded, an unreadable look on her face. "I would, for once, agree with you, Mr. Aubrey. Good heavens. That poor boy. Who could have imagined?"

Aubrey was surprised. Lady Brompton's reaction was far different than he had anticipated. In fact he was a bit startled that she even knew who Owen Grimm was. "At any rate, he was murdered, and it appears that Miss Dean found him first and was followed shortly by Tybalt and Miss Dunlea-Boggins, who alerted Mr. Brompton and myself."

"I see," said Harriet.

Mrs. Dean whirled to face her youngest daughter. "Shame on you, Ophelia! How could you get mixed up in such a thing? You are very fortunate, you know, that Mr. Brompton still wishes to marry you after this."

Ophelia sobbed quietly into her handkerchief.

"Mother," Cordelia said quietly, "Ophelia has done nothing wrong, and Henry loves her. There can be no scandal at all in that."

"Hush," snapped Mrs. Dean. "I believe we can agree that nice young ladies do not go about in the dark, discovering dead bodies. It is simply not done."

"Regardless," said Aubrey, cutting her off, "Miss Dean did discover one, as did her brother and another perfectly nice young lady. Now, Mr. Adkyns is here to ask questions, and it is important that everyone cooperate with him." He glared directly at Harriet Brompton as he said this last.

She nodded haughtily, the mask of reserve once more in place. "Very well. Henry, you must speak with Waverly and have him contact the footman's mother."

Waverly was Fairfield Hall's majordomo, and all staff members reported to him. Waverly arrived within moments, and Henry instructed him to write a message to send Owen Grimm's kinfolk, as well as to prepare the servants for questioning by Providence Adkyns.

"Now," Aubrey continued, "I would suggest that everyone try to get some sleep. Brompton, you and I can assist Adkyns in whatever manner he needs, but meanwhile we should let the rest of your guests retire for the evening. Any further questions can wait until morning."

Cordelia ignored her mother's protests and hurried Lydia out of the room, leaving Ophelia to contend with Mrs. Dean's scolding. As she took her first step onto the stairs, a deep voice from below stopped her.

"Mrs. Falconer, a word?" It was Aubrey.

"Go on up, Lydia, and change for bed. I shall be with you in a matter of moments."

"Mama, are we safe here, do you think?" Lydia whispered, blue eyes wide.

Cordelia nodded firmly. "We are indeed. I do not believe we are in any danger at all, so long as we are here indoors. You must not fret. Go on, my darling."

She kissed her lightly on the forehead and sent her on her way. "Yes, Mr. Aubrey?"

"May I speak with you privately? I know it's late, but I must have a moment of your time."

She followed him to the library, and he closed the door lightly behind them.

"Please forgive my rudeness, I beg you, but it has been a most eventful evening, and I am tired. What may I help you with?" she asked. She wanted to throw herself into his arms and let him plunder her mouth with his, but this was not the time, not while the shadow of death lingered over the house.

"I'll get right to the point. I am concerned about your sister's involvement in Owen Grimm's death."

Cordelia scowled at him, shocked. "What do you mean by this? My sister knows nothing. She told you, the man was dead when she found him in the gardens."

He nodded. "Indeed, that is what she told us, and I confess it is what I would have believed were it not for one thing." His dark eyes were troubled. "Cordelia, your sister had blood on the hem of her dress. And when Brompton and Tybalt and I went to move Grimm's body, I found this."

Aubrey held out his hand, and in his palm was an emerald drop earring. It was part of the set that Ophelia had been trying on earlier in the evening.

"That means nothing," Cordelia said, her eyes filling. "Perhaps Ophelia lost it when she discovered his body, and it fell as she ran away in shock."

"I did not pick it up from the snow. It was clutched in his hand."

She froze. "In his hand? That cannot be."

"I am sorry, Cordelia, I truly am." Aubrey moved

toward her then, and before she realized it, his finger was tracing its way down her damp cheek. “I am sorry that I must be the one to tell you such bad news,” he said softly, his eyes burning through her like a flame.

Rather than glance away, she met his gaze directly.

“And I am sorry to hear it,” she whispered. She reached up and clutched his hand to her face. They stood silent for what seemed like an eternity, and for a brief moment she wished things were different, wished she could move even closer to Aubrey, and more than anything, wanting to take comfort in the pleasures of his body.

“Cordelia,” he said, his voice low, “can you not understand the agony I am in right now? To be here, close to you like this, and know that you may well end up hating me?”

“I could never,” she murmured into his hand.

“You could, Cordelia. If your sister is charged with killing a man, you’ll hate me for it.”

She took a step back, peering up at him. “I can see right through you, Rhys Aubrey. You wish to protect me, keeping me safe from the public wrath and judgment of Lady Brompton and the other society dragons.”

Aubrey shook his head. “You do not need or want me—or anyone, for that matter—to protect you. You may appear to be in a vulnerable position, but I think you are most capable of taking care of yourself.” He moved forward, closing the gap between them once more. “You smell of rosemary.”

She bowed her head. “I am all alone,” she whispered. “I need you so much.”

That was all it took. Aubrey pulled her close,

enveloping her in his arms, his mouth on hers. She made a soft whimpering sound into his throat as her lips parted, and she felt him shudder in response.

For a brief fleeting moment, Cordelia wondered if the library door was locked and then pushed the thought from her mind. She didn't care what anyone said about her reputation, didn't care about anyone's opinion of her anymore. All that mattered to her now was how badly she needed his hands on her skin, how she needed to feel his mouth tasting every bit of her.

When she'd slipped out to meet him in the stables that night, it had been passionate and heated, but she'd been the one in control. This time, she needed to give herself over to him completely, to let him take the lead, and possess her thoroughly. She pushed her hands into his hair, gasping for breath as he moved his mouth from hers and began to move his way down her neck. "Rhys," she said softly, "I want you so badly."

He paused a moment, his teeth just grazing her earlobe.

She moaned softly and tangled her fingers in his hair. Gripping his dark locks, she pulled him away from her ear, moved his head back, and kissed him hard and fierce. "I want to be yours," she said. "Now. Here."

She met him eagerly as he plundered her mouth with his tongue, exploring and tasting her lips, blazing and hungry. When he pressed himself against her, his hands sliding behind her and lifting her onto the desk in one fluid motion, Cordelia gasped at the sensation of his hardness through his breeches. She hiked up the folds of her dress to wrap her legs around his waist, making a guttural sound that was half moan and half growl. Her entire body was on fire with the knowledge that she had to have him, right here in the library, on the desk, immediately.

His hand slipped up under her gray silks, exploring upward as she angled eagerly toward him. When he reached the glorious spot between her legs, she watched as his eyes widened with joy, his arousal exciting her even further.

"Dear God, woman," he murmured into her mouth. "You're like velvet."

She gasped once more as he slid a finger inside her, warm and waiting, and cried out against his lips.

"Shh," he warned, barely holding himself together long enough to remember the house full of people.

"More," she panted, and he obliged, stroking a second finger into her body. Cordelia bucked against him as he moved back and forth, caressing the secret spot deep inside her, her breathing ragged and raw. She closed her eyes, writhing with pleasure.

"Look at me," he growled. "I want you to look at me when you come."

Her eyes popped open, wide and blue, staring into his as he moved his fingers faster, stroking her with delight, taking her to the brink of heaven.

"Cordelia," he whispered, "I want to do nothing but pleasure you. Let go for me, Cordelia."

She needed no further encouragement and whimpered as the waves of her climax swept over her, arching her back and pressing herself against his hand, slick and hot. As the orgasm subsided, she collapsed against him, shaking and shuddering. She mumbled something into his shirt.

"What was that?"

"I said," she murmured, "I need you inside me

now."

He blinked owlishly. "You've already—"

"I know. I want more." She raised her eyes to his, heavy-lidded. "Inside. Now." And then her hands tore the top button of his breeches open.

With a quiet growl, he shoved his clothing aside, and his cock sprang out, right into her waiting hand.

"Yes," she said. "Mine."

He smiled down at her, eyes ablaze. "Woman, I am unaccustomed to taking orders, but I'm occasionally willing to make an exception, under certain circumstances. This is one of them." He pushed her legs apart, cupped his hands under her bottom, and pulled her to him, thrusting inside her. She tightened herself around him, begging him to plunge deeper, harder, faster.

He grabbed her wrists, pinioning her hands on the desk beside her, holding her in place as he entered her over and over again.

Cordelia's blue eyes misted with pleasure, seeing nothing but him, wanting nothing more than to be claimed by him. "Rhys," she gasped. "Fill me up."

That was all it took. He released, muffling a roar of joy into her golden hair as he emptied himself inside her. She shuddered violently as she climaxed again, tightening around him as he exploded. He fell against her, releasing her wrists, and she cradled his head against her breast; her heart was pounding beneath the gray silk. They stayed that way for what seemed like an eternity.

As her senses returned, Cordelia smiled secretly to herself. It was no wonder the French called this moment after lovemaking *la petite mort,* the little death.

Certainly, her soul had left her body and gone to heaven; she suspected his might have done so as well.

Finally, she shifted against him. “Well. That was certainly a bright spot in what has been an otherwise dreadful day.”

“Mmmhmm,” he mumbled against her clavicle.

“We have stayed here too long,” she said softly. “There is trouble afoot.”

Aubrey stepped back abruptly. “Your sister,” he said, his voice ragged, “could find herself accused of murder.”

“What will happen to her? If, indeed, she is found to be guilty, despite a lack of clear evidence against her?” She smoothed out the silk of her skirt and straightened her necklace. Her skin was still flushed, even in the dim light of the library.

“I shall speak with Adkyns. He will wish to avoid embarrassing the Brompton family, if he wants to keep his position as magistrate,” Aubrey said. “We both know it’s unusual for someone in society to be accused of such a crime, so perhaps your sister’s status—or perhaps even her connections to the Bromptons—will be of benefit to her.” He absently rearranged Henry’s papers and books on the desk, tidying the chaos of spent passion.

“I see.” Cordelia patted down her hair without thinking. She was flustered, not just by the news of Ophelia’s earring but by how she’d spent the last half an hour. Her body heated at the memory of his touch, but she lifted her head and straightened her shoulders. “Will that be all, Mr. Aubrey?”

He did not look at her. “It will. Thank you, Mrs. Falconer.”

She left without another word.

****

The morning was gray and dismal, a mixture of sleet and rain falling on Fairfield Hall, and perfectly fitted Cordelia's disposition. She had slept poorly, dreaming restless dreams in which she chased her sister down the corridors of the Brompton house, only to find that Ophelia had vanished around each corner. No matter how quickly she ran, she could not overtake her, and Cordelia woke with a sense of frustration that she could not quite place.

Some of it, she admitted, she could blame on Aubrey. In addition to the dreams of Ophelia, there had been a few of the gentleman from Yorkshire, and although Cordelia could not quite articulate the nature of those dreams, it was extremely vexing that Rhys Aubrey had appeared in them at all. It seemed rather presumptuous of him—after all, despite the physical nature of their relationship, she did *not* intend to fall in love with him, so he had no business in her dreams—and thus she was short-tempered when the housemaid arrived to tend the fire.

"Good morning, missus," the girl whispered, a handful of wood clutched in her thin arms.

"It is not a good morning at all. It is cold and wet, the sky looks foul, and there is a dead man in the larder," Cordelia grumbled.

The girl, whose name was Amy, sniffled a bit. "Yes, missus. Everyone's very upset about things this morning. Imagine, murder here at Fairfield Hall, a respectable house!"

Cordelia stretched and pulled the blankets tighter around her. Lydia had climbed in with her in the night and stolen most of the covers. “Did you know him well? Grimm?” she asked, curious.

Amy shrugged, poking at the embers. “A bit. Handsome, he was, and friendly. Only a footman, but you’d think he was a swell, from the high words he used sommat.”

Lydia snorted daintily in her sleep and cuddled closer to Cordelia. Her warmth was comforting in the cool room. “He seemed very pleasant. I am sorry about what happened to him. It must be very hard on all of you.”

“I suppose,” the girl said.

Cordelia raised a brow. “Is it not?”

Amy shrugged again. “It’s not that, missus. To be sure, it’s hard to know that someone must’ve killed Grimm. But he was…never mind, missus, it’s not my place to say.”

Cordelia climbed out of bed, pulling the soft coverlet around herself, and moved to the hearth to warm her feet. “You may speak freely, Amy. You know that Mr. Adkyns is tasked to find out who killed Grimm, and if there is anything you can say that might shed light on the type of person he was, perhaps that will help bring out the truth.”

Amy glanced around and then shut the heavy door that led to the corridor. “You see, missus, Grimm was…he was always friendly-like, you know, but it warn’t quite real.”

“Not quite real? I don’t believe I understand.”

The girl leaned forward eagerly. “He was friendly, had the nicest manners, but you got the sense it was just for show. Like he was only being kind because he wanted something, or maybe he was really thinking wicked thoughts whilst he was saying pleasant things."

"Ah," Cordelia said. "I see. Was he like this with all the young ladies?"

"Oh, no, missus, I don't mean nuffin improper, like he'd be trifling with the maids in a dishonorable way. Not like that," Amy said. "No, it was more that he just seemed…do you know, missus, when a man tells a story and does it too much brown, as though he wants very much to be believed? On the outside, he was nice enough, and I'm sure I never saw no signs of havey-cavey business. But underneath, I think maybe he was up to something dishonest."

Cordelia studied the girl for a moment. "What sort of thing, Amy? I can't believe Lady Brompton would allow someone to remain on staff who was involved in any wrongdoing."

"Oh, I do not know at all," Amy said hastily. "Certainly, missus, I have no proof, and I've spoken out of turn."

"No, no, Amy," Cordelia said, trying to reassure the maid. "You've done nothing wrong in telling me this. If there is anything specific you can think of, anything at all, please do let me know, will you?"

Amy nodded and chewed on her lower lip thoughtfully. "Perhaps one other thing, although it may not signify."

"Go on."

"He asked me one time about Lady Brompton's jewels. I told him that those were none of my concern, as her abigail cares for them, but he asked me if I ever got leave to see them or touch them."

"I see." Cordelia felt that maybe she was, as a matter of fact, beginning to do just that. "And was this recently?"

"About a fortnight ago, missus, right after Mr. Brompton announced he was going to host a big party here at Fairfield. I didn't think Grimm was bein' smoky about it, just friendly-like." The girl kept her eyes downcast.

"Thank you, Amy. That will be all." Once she was alone—other than her sleeping daughter—Cordelia sat down at the small writing table near the window. The few times she had encountered Grimm, he had seemed polite enough—like any good servant—but she hadn't paid much attention to him. Despite her wish to feel and behave progressively, she had to admit that she noticed little about the servants. They were simply always there when needed. But what of the girl's comments that Grimm had been up to something? Could there be some merit to Amy's assessment of the footman?

She poked Lydia to wake her, finished dressing, and then made her way downstairs. The breakfast room was fully prepared, but the only people present were Mrs. Dean and Lady Brompton.

"Mother. Lady Brompton." Cordelia filled a plate with some biscuits and jam. "Did you sleep well?"

Lady Brompton made a rude noise. "Sleep well! How can you imagine we might sleep well when there's a wicked murderer loose in the countryside?"

Cordelia said nothing. Where was Ophelia? Had Mr. Adkyns decided that she was a killer? But it made no sense—Ophelia could have no reason to commit such a heinous act, Cordelia was certain. Moreover, this was her sister, who simply could not have it in her to do such a thing. And yet, Aubrey had found one of Ophelia's emerald earrings clutched in the dead man's hand.

Aubrey. Damn it all.

The mere idea of him brought a fresh round of irritation to Cordelia's mind, and she stabbed a smoked kipper viciously. Aubrey. Who did the man think he was, looking at her the way he did, making her body feel a way it had never felt, not even with Falconer, and then sneaking into her dreams like that? Then again, she was hardly some innocent girl making her debut into society. She had caused a scandal, married against her parents' wishes, traveled across the ocean and back, and was, to some degree, able to do what she wanted. The rules of propriety were far more lenient for a woman in her position than for someone like her sister, although certainly, reputations could be tarnished through association—Lady Brompton's rigid opinions were proof of that.

"Lady Brompton," she said pleasantly, startling the scowl right off the older woman's face. "I was wondering if I might beg a small favor of you."

"Really, Cordelia." Her mother frowned. "I'm certain Lady Brompton has plenty of things already on her mind."

Harriet waved her hand dismissively. "Oh, Agatha, do not fret. Mrs. Falconer, what might I do for you?"

"Well, I was wondering…oh, no. Perhaps it is too forward of me." Cordelia had the decency to blush a little, which led Lady Brompton to soften a bit further.

Aubrey and Heyward wandered in and begin helping themselves to breakfast at the sideboard.

"Mrs. Falconer, do continue." Harriet waved a fork at her.

"If you do not mind," she asked, hesitating just a

bit, "I was hoping—Ophelia told me that your jewelry collection is simply unrivaled. After so many years in Virginia…well, I must be truthful, Lady Brompton. It is sometimes an uncultured place, and it's been far too long since I saw quality English workmanship. I wondered if perhaps you might make the time to show me some of your pieces, so that I may have the privilege of admiring them."

Aubrey dropped his spoon with a clatter. "Pardon me," he muttered, but no one paid him any attention.

Cordelia's mother was clearly startled, but Harriet Brompton was delighted by the request, being a woman who enjoyed any opportunity to lord her wealth over lesser beings. "Why, Mrs. Falconer, I would not have imagined you for a lady who put much stock in fripperies like necklaces and other shiny gewgaws."

Cordelia glanced down humbly. "I think any lady enjoys pretty things, despite that we may not always have the means or opportunity to own them ourselves. And as I do hope to someday make another attachment, I fear I must re-educate myself on what is currently fashionable. I do look to you for guidance, even if I do not always show it."

Aubrey looked as though his eyes were about to pop from his skull. He stared at Cordelia, but she ignored him soundly.

"Of course, of course!" beamed Lady Brompton, patting Cordelia's hand solicitously. She shot Mrs. Dean a knowing glance. "After breakfast, we shall go upstairs, and I shall enjoy showing you my collection. Did you know, some of the pieces have been in the Brompton family since the time of Queen Elizabeth? Oh yes, indeed, they are rather magnificent, if I do say so myself."

She and Mrs. Dean excused themselves and left, and Aubrey came and sat beside Cordelia.

"What the devil are you up to?" he asked, keeping his voice low.

"I beg your pardon?"

"You know what I mean," he whispered, watching Heyward pile sausages onto his plate on the other side of the room. "All that simpering and head bobbing. I'll be damned if you've ever bowed your head to anyone in your life, and now all of a sudden you wish to look at Lady Brompton's jewels and ask her for fashion advice? You're up to something."

Heyward approached and joined them with a smile. "Mrs. Falconer. You look simply radiant."

"You are too kind, Mr. Heyward. I'm sorry, Mr. Aubrey, have you seen the magistrate this morning?"

Aubrey nodded. "He was going to interview your sister once more."

There was a sudden commotion from outside the door, and Cordelia detected both of her brothers' voices, as well as her mother's loud and hysterical sobs.

"What on earth?" She leapt to her feet, knocking her chair aside, and raced to the hallway, followed closely by Aubrey and Heyward.

Out in the corridor, Agatha Dean was wailing into a handkerchief, and Tybalt and Mercutio had Mr. Adkyns in a death grip. Ophelia stood quietly near the wall, looking as though she hoped it would open up and swallow her, and Augustus Littleberry was trying to separate the brothers Dean from the magistrate, who was turning paler by the minute.

"What in the blazes is going on out here?" roared

Rhys Aubrey. Everyone froze, in a momentary tableau of astonished confusion.

Finally, Tybalt broke the silence. “He’s arresting Ophelia!”

Mercutio pushed the magistrate against the doorjamb. “And we do not intend to let him take her away like some common criminal!”

Mrs. Dean began keening again and slid to the floor in a heap, where everyone ignored her. Heyward disappeared down the hallway, calling for Brompton.

“Tybalt, Mercutio,” said Littleberry gently, “you must let go of Mr. Adkyns. He is a magistrate, and he is doing his job. I am certain he is more than willing to listen to reason, but he will not be able to do so if you harm him.”

“He’s not taking her to jail,” Tybalt protested. “We shan’t allow it!”

“For the love of God, Tybalt!” Cordelia shouted, fed up with the lot of them. “Let go of that man, or I will get Brompton’s saber, and I swear by all that is holy, I shall run you through.”

Both of her brothers released their hold on Mr. Adkyns and stepped back, and Mercutio at least had the decency to look a little bit ashamed of himself.

“Mr. Adkyns,” Aubrey began, “are you quite all right?”

Adkyns brushed off his black suit and straightened his cravat. He was utterly terrified—a not uncommon reaction in men who were threatened by the Dean twins—and his hands shook, but his voice was steady. “I am, thank you, Mr. Aubrey. As I was attempting to explain to Miss Dean’s brothers, I believe Miss Dean herself is responsible for the death of Owen Grimm.”

This set off a fresh round of hysterics from Agatha, who clung to Ophelia's skirts, as if hoping to prevent her from being taken away in chains and irons.

"Mother, do stop this," hissed Cordelia.

"And on what evidence do you base this accusation?" Aubrey asked.

"Well, to be certain, there was blood on her dress last night, and Grimm was holding one of her earrings in his hand. That, to me, says that she likely killed him," explained Adkyns.

"Ophelia is an honorable lady from a respectable…er, from an established family," Cordelia protested. "Surely you must see that she could never do such a vile thing."

"Begging your pardon, madam," the magistrate continued, "but I don't have no evidence against anybody else but your sister."

Cordelia turned to Ophelia. "You must tell us exactly what happened."

Her sister shook her head sadly. "I cannot. I may not say, other than to give you my word that I am not the person who killed Owen Grimm."

"Aha!" exclaimed Adkyns. "Then how do you explain your earring being found on his person?"

"I cannot explain it at all," she said, looking at the floor. A single, fat teardrop rolled down her cheek and plopped to the carpet.

Heyward and Henry Brompton appeared then. "Adkyns, what is this? You cannot take my fiancée away charged with murder! It is not done, not done at all, man."

Adkyns pondered this for a minute. Although he was often a bumbler and had made some foolhardy decisions in his lifetime, he also understood from whence his livelihood came. Were he to fall out of favor with the Brompton family, he'd be fortunate to find work driving a horse cart. "Mr. Brompton, I am sensitive to your family's needs," he began. "The storm outside has gotten worse, and the roads could be nigh impassible by now. Perhaps we can allow Miss Dean to stay here at Fairfield Hall—under your supervision, of course—while the investigation is concluded. That way, there would be no hint of scandal attached to your good family name, at least not until we have some more evidence. That is—"

"That will be perfectly acceptable," interrupted Aubrey. "Won't it, Brompton? Miss Dean, if you stay here on your own recognizance, you shall be allowed the freedom of Fairfield Hall, but you must promise not to leave the property without an escort. Is that correct, Mr. Adkyns?"

The magistrate nodded, fairly certain he understood what had just been said. "That is so, indeed, Mr. Aubrey. If she stays here, all will be fine for now. No need to take her off to jail until we—yes."

"Very well," Aubrey said. "Brompton, are you satisfied?"

"I'd be more satisfied if I was not engaged to a lady accused of murder, but—"

"Brompton." There was a warning tone in Aubrey's voice, and his dark eyes flashed.

Henry sighed. "Yes. I am agreeable to this arrangement."

"Mr. Adkyns. Please undertake to complete a thorough investigation as quickly as possible, so that we may resolve this immediately."

"Yes, Mr. Aubrey. Happy to do so." Adkyns bowed deeply, doffing his tall hat, and stalked off to some other part of the house.

Once he was gone, there was silence. Finally, Ophelia broke it. "I shall retire to my room for the day," she said softly.

"Miss Dean," Henry Brompton said, "you and I must speak. Alone." Cordelia noticed that he did not call Ophelia by her given name now. Could it be that Brompton believed her sister capable of murder?

Ophelia nodded, not looking at him, and followed him down the hall.

"Come, Mother," Cordelia said with a heavy sigh. "We shall put you to bed so your nerves may recover."

Chapter Ten

The atmosphere at Fairfield Hall was a somber one that day indeed, what with the twin specters of murder and disgrace hanging over the entire place and those who dwelt within its walls. Cordelia Falconer's mood matched everyone else's, and she had little time or patience for such frivolities and useless amusements as ladies were normally expected to spend their days upon. She could not bear to sit and embroider—her skills with a needle lent themselves far better to the practical, such as stitching up shirts or a wound, rather than the decorative and ornamental—and although she loved reading very much, she could not settle her mind enough to sit down with a book.

"Lydia," she said, "there is great distress in this house today, as you have seen, and your dear grandmama seems to be taking much of this situation personally. She has taken to her bed and believes herself to be quite near death from the horror of it all. One of us, I am sorry to say, must keep her company."

Lydia's eyes were wide and pleading. "Oh, Mother, I had hoped to go for a ride on Juno this morning."

"I know, my darling, but duty calls. Besides, there is now ice forming on the paths, and it's too dangerous to take Juno out. We're all trapped inside, at least for a day or two until the storm subsides. Perhaps you can read to your grandmama from one of the books in Mr. Brompton's library."

"She'll ask me to read her something awful, like a book of sermons or lectures on proper deportment for young ladies, and it will be dull and dreary," Lydia said.

"You are, as always, correct. However, I must go endure the morning with Lady Brompton, so I feel if you read to your grandmama, your assignment will surely be the less tedious of the two." Cordelia pushed a red curl out of Lydia's face. The girl was lovely, but her hair was completely unmanageable.

"What reason would you have to spend with Lady Brompton?"

Cordelia winked. "I am privileged to sit in awe as she condescends to show me her endless jewelry collection. Did you know that some of it has been here since before Britain was even an island, or at least, such is the case to hear Lady Brompton tell it."

"I believe it possible that Lady Brompton herself has been here since before Britain was an island," Lydia said, winking back.

"Oh, hush, you. Go find a book to read to your grandmother, or I shall make you sit with Lady Brompton at dinner."

Lydia curtseyed prettily and ran off to the library.

****

The Brompton family jewels were kept, when not in use, in a locked case in Harriet Brompton's dressing room. She and her abigail, a quiet and malleable sort named Mary, were the only ones with keys in their possession. The case itself was a source of great pride to Lady Brompton, for her late husband Edmund had been given it as a gift from King George, although no one was entirely sure what Edmund had done to deserve it. Cordelia made suitably admiring noises when the ornate carved chest was presented in front of her, with some degree of struggling on Mary's part, due predominantly to both the weight of the box and the scrawniness of Mary, but also owing to the contents within.

"Now," began Lady Brompton, "I must warn you, some of these pieces are most delicate indeed. There is a filigree piece that belonged to an ancestor of Edmund's who was a lady in waiting to Queen Katherine of Aragon. It is said to have been given to her as a wedding gift by her husband, although I think we all know how unfortunately that turned out. There are also the Brompton emeralds, which have been in the family for many generations and were bestowed upon my husband's ancestor, Thomas Brompton, by the great Elizabeth herself, as thanks for his loyal service. Go on, now, Mary, we will not need you further."

The maid, as always, did as she was told and scurried from the room.

Lady Brompton turned the key and the lid popped open. "Ah, yes!" she crowed. "Here they all are, for you to see. Do not worry that you may like them too well. I am quite aware of how beautiful they are, and there is nothing wrong with liking nice things, is there?"

Cordelia blinked as the chest revealed its treasures. The Brompton jewels were indeed a sight to behold. There were, of course, the emeralds from Queen Elizabeth, along with necklaces, earrings, and rings like she had never seen. "They are…exquisite," she admitted, and she was telling the truth. "Do you wear them often?"

Lady Brompton sniffed. "Well, of course not, because that would seem ostentatious, would it not? I may wear a piece now and again, for parties or when I wish to present myself to those equal to my station, but really, I do not feel that items like this should be used every day. I am certain, living in the wilds of America, you have rarely seen any collections to rival this one?"

Cordelia shook her head. "I have not." The jewelry was truly impressive, and she couldn't help but wonder what a footman like Owen Grimm could have wanted with them. Certainly, thievery was an obvious possibility, but even a footman would have known he never could have gotten away with such a thing. The pieces were too unique, far too elaborate, for any thief to ever try selling or pawning. A footman arriving at a jeweler's with such a piece in hand would find himself clapped in irons immediately and transported without question.

"May I?" Cordelia asked.

Lady Brompton beamed with pride. "Of course, dear. Feel free to touch whatever you like, although do be careful with the filigree pieces."

Cordelia lifted a flat box which contained an emerald necklace. Each stone was set in a silver backing, and tiny diamonds glittered between the rows of green.

"Now, that one…well." Lady Brompton sighed. "I had meant for Henry to give it Ophelia to wear for the wedding—it matches the earrings, you see—but I'm rather wondering if there will even be a wedding at this point."

Cordelia raised a brow. "Lady Brompton, you

don't believe what Mr. Adkyns says about my sister, do you? You must understand, she could never hurt anyone."

The older woman glowered at her. "Mrs. Falconer, I must be honest with you, however much it may pain me to do so. I have long felt that your sister was, at best, a questionable choice for my son, due in no small part to some of your family's past history—including your own, Mrs. Falconer. Society has a long memory, as you well know."

"Lady Brompton—"

"Allow me to finish. I was willing to overlook the poor behavior of you and your brothers—please, Mrs. Falconer—because I felt that Ophelia was the only woman who could make Henry truly happy. He has held her in high regard—in affection—since they were children, and quite honestly, he's far too dull for most of the other young ladies to find appealing. Certainly, he has money and a good name, but I knew his heart lay with your sister." She took a deep breath. "However, I cannot—and will not—allow him to attach himself to a woman whose name has been associated with criminal activity. Especially the crime of murder."

"She did not kill that footman!" Cordelia burst out. "I know in my heart she did not, could not have done so!"

"Be that as it may, there are certain things that must be acknowledged. Owen's death—Grimm's death was a horrible thing, but your sister's innocence is irrelevant. She would always be shadowed by suspicion simply for her association to such a scandal. It is bad enough I've lost my best footman, but I cannot have my son marry the woman suspected of killing him—

whether she did so or not."

Cordelia stared at the emerald necklace, not truly seeing it. "And Henry? Does he share your sentiments?"

"Even his strong feelings for your sister will not be able to combat the rumors and the whispers of polite society, Mrs. Falconer. He will do what is best for the Brompton name. Sooner or later, he always does."

"I see." But in fact, Cordelia did not. If Henry truly loved Ophelia, why would he not stand beside her, no matter what? Certainly other unions had started out in far more peril than this one—her own had begun with both scandal and near penury, and yet she and Tom had still managed to have a happy marriage. Then again, they'd not had the shadow of murder above them.

"I believe that in time, you will," agreed Lady Brompton. "Now, if you will notice the settings of these emeralds, Mrs. Falconer, you will see…" She stopped abruptly.

"I'm sorry, Lady Brompton. You were saying?"

Henry's mother frowned. "The emeralds. There is something odd about them." She took the heavy necklace from Cordelia and held it up in the light, peering closely at the stones. "Ring the bell for Mary, if you please."

Cordelia did as she was asked. "It looks lovely, Lady Brompton. Is there something wrong?"

Lady Brompton pursed her lips as she inspected the necklace closely. "Yes. There is something very much wrong. Where the devil is Mary?"

Mary appeared within moments, having been lurking out in the hallway awaiting her mistress' call, as she was trained to do.

Lady Brompton frowned at her. “Mary, who has been at my jewels?”

The young woman shook her head, confused. “At your jewels, madam?”

“Yes!” Lady Brompton snapped. “Foolish girl, I am asking a simple question. Who has been into this case besides yourself?”

Mary quivered visibly. “No one, missus, not a single soul.”

“Then explain to me,” Lady Brompton said, her voice low and icy, “how my emeralds have been replaced by paste imitations?”

Cordelia and Mary gasped at the same time. “Paste!” exclaimed Cordelia. “Are you certain?”

Lady Brompton shot her a scornful look. “Am I certain? Mrs. Falconer, I have held these jewels in my hands every week since I came to Fairfield Hall as a young lady of one and twenty. I know them as well as I know my own skin. And you may rest assured that the ones I hold in my hand right now are not the Brompton emeralds at all. Mary, what have you to say for yourself?”

Mary was speechless, her mouth gaping open and closing like a fish’s. “I don’t—there is no—Madam, I swear to you I know nothing of this!”

Lady Brompton appeared as though she did not believe the maid at all, but then again, the woman did always have a scowl embedded on her face.

Cordelia took a step toward the door. “Lady Brompton, I believe we must notify Mr. Adkyns immediately. He is, after all, the magistrate, and his presence here may prove to be a valuable one.”

“Mrs. Falconer, that is an excellent idea. Please go

and fetch him. Mary, you shall stay here with me and help me examine the rest of the jewels."

Cordelia practically ran down the stairs, stopping long enough at her own room to pull on her walking boots, searching for Mr. Adkyns. Rounding a corner, she collided with Thomas Heyward, who caught her neatly in his arms, preventing them both from landing on the floor in a heap.

"Oho, Mrs. Falconer!" he exclaimed. "You are in a great hurry! Tell me, what excitement is there? Surely not another dead footman?"

"No," she said, stepping back out of his reach. "Thankfully, there are no more dead footmen, or at the very least, none of which I am presently aware. However, I must find Mr. Adkyns. Do you know where he might be?"

Heyward smiled, once again looking so like his cousin Henry. "I believe he is roaming the grounds with Mr. Aubrey. Shall I go collect them for you?"

Aubrey. Why was he taking such a keen interest in the death of Owen Grimm? He had been asking so many questions the night before, and now he had attached himself to Mr. Adkyns. "No, thank you, Mr. Heyward. I will go and find them myself." Without waiting for his reply, she dashed to the rear hall and out of doors.

The November sky was even more gloomy and gray than she had believed possible, snow falling in fat wet flakes. The terraces were already slick and slippery. Cordelia caught a hint of woodsmoke on the breeze and noted the dark clouds off in the distance.

Near the gardens, Aubrey was talking in low tones with the magistrate and Henry Brompton.

"Mr. Adkyns!" she called, waving at them as she plodded across the wet lawn.

The men turned at the sound of her voice, and Aubrey raised a brow, as though she was some exotic creature he had just discovered…or perhaps he was recalling last night in the library, when she'd been wrapped around him and moaning with pleasure.

She ignored him completely and addressed Henry and the magistrate instead. "Lady Brompton has asked for you, Mr. Adkyns. We have discovered—there is something I believe will be of great interest to you. And likely to you as well, Henry," she added.

Adkyns nodded eagerly. "I see. Yes, thank you, Mrs. Falconer. Do you know if this is something that will help us solve the riddle of the footman's death?"

She considered Amy's comments about Owen Grimm asking after his mistress' jewelry collection. "I think it *may* relate," she said slowly, "although I do not know how exactly it signifies."

He bobbed his bird-like head. "Very well, indeed, then. I shall go speak with Lady Brompton and put the matter to rest as soon as possible! Come, Mr. Brompton, let us see what discoveries your mother has…discovered!" Adkyns puffed up his chest importantly and strode toward the house with great determination. Henry bowed lightly to Cordelia and followed the magistrate, leaving her alone with Aubrey.

"You look cold," he said without preface.

"I ran outdoors in a hurry," she said. "I am going back in now and shall warm up soon enough, I believe."

"Stay a moment, if you would," he asked. Aubrey removed his long coat and draped it around her shoulders. It was warm and smelled of cloves.

"Thank you."

"You're welcome. Now, what's got you running out in the cold to find Adkyns, like a mad goose without a shawl?"

Cordelia pulled the wool coat closer around her, suppressing a shiver. "It's Lady Brompton's emerald necklace. The one that matches Ophelia's earrings."

He stood very still, his face an unreadable mask. "What about the emeralds?"

"Lady Brompton says the necklace is a fake. Not the necklace itself, but the jewels. She says the emeralds aren't hers at all, but paste glass. She knows better than anyone how they must feel, the look, the weight…" Cordelia peered up at him and saw he had gone very pale. "What is it, Mr. Aubrey?"

"Damn it," he muttered under his breath. "Damn it all. I was too late to save Grimm and too late to stop the rest of it, wasn't I?"

"Mr. Aubrey!" she exclaimed. "Whatever are you talking about? Save Grimm? No one could have saved Owen Grimm, not unless they were outside in the garden with him when he was killed. Really, you mustn't blame yourself."

He gave her a strange look. "If I don't take the blame, then there is no one else I may find fault with, Mrs. Falconer."

She shook her head. "I know you are an old friend of Henry's, and I know that you are a good person and an honorable man. Please believe me when I say I do not think you could possibly be found at fault in any of this. The individual that killed Mr. Grimm is the person on whom all the blame must be placed."

Aubrey slammed his hands onto the stone

balustrade. “You think I am a good person? An honorable man? Let me tell you something, Mrs. Falconer, and understand that I do not say this lightly or without conviction. That man, Owen Grimm, is dead partly because I came to Fairfield Hall. He is dead because he trusted me to help him when he was in trouble, and I did not do so. No, I failed him. So while your faith in me is admirable, Cordelia, it is very much misplaced,” he growled, not even looking at her.

She stood silently for a moment, until she was sure he had finished. “Well, then, Mr. Aubrey, will you not correct my false assumptions about you? You must think me a complete and utter fool. How dare you?” she said softly.

Aubrey shot her a black look. “What do you mean?”

“If I am so wrong,” Cordelia said, moving to stand beside him, “if you are in fact the terrible and dishonorable person you believe yourself to be, then tell me what it is you have done that is so horrible. If I am a sensible and intelligent person, capable of rational thought and critical thinking, then I shall be able to judge for myself whether I am wrong about you. If, in fact, you do not think me clever enough to make that judgment, then you are implicitly calling me a fool.”

“I did not mean—”

“I will not tolerate insult, Mr. Aubrey,” she said firmly. “Not of my intelligence, and certainly not by you, given our…history. What have you to say for yourself? Shall I call you out for impugning my honor, as gentlemen do when they have too much to drink and not enough sense? Must we meet in a field with pistols at sunrise, assuming the sun ever comes back out in this godforsaken country?"

He smiled a bit, despite himself. "You are no fool, Mrs. Falconer. In fact, I suspect you know exactly what you're doing. Very well. Shall we take a turn about the gardens, and I will enlighten you as to the poor quality of my character?"

"I can't think of anything I'd rather do," she said honestly, taking his arm. "I do not mind the snow, and I'm rather put out with being trapped inside all day."

They walked in silence at first, until they were out of sight of the house and reached the old Ionic temple. They ducked between its columns, into the dryness of the shelter and out of the wind. She waited for him to begin, and he soon spoke.

"Mrs. Falconer, as we've been walking I've given some thought to your challenge, and I have been weighing many things in my mind. I do wish to enlighten you as to my failings, but to do so may put you or other people in jeopardy."

"That seems overly—"

"Cordelia," he said firmly, turning her toward him. "You must understand. I value your…your friendship and your good opinion. However, I would never wish to bring you harm. You must swear to me that everything I am about to tell you shall remain confidential. You must speak of it to no one, not even your sister or your brothers. Lives—particularly your own life—could depend upon it."

A light breeze began, and the temperature dropped noticeably once more. She was in the garden temple alone with Rhys Aubrey, and he had again addressed her familiarly, although he likely didn't realize he had done so. She nodded faintly. "I swear to it, Mr.

Aubrey."

"Good. I am happy to hear it, as I expect you are a woman who keeps your word." He took a deep breath. "Owen Grimm was working for me."

"What? Whatever can you—"

He cut her off quickly. "Please, you must listen. I was sent here as an agent of the Crown. I have been investigating a ring of jewel thieves, and we had been given intelligence—from a reliable informant, no less—that Lady Brompton might soon be a victim. When I ran into Henry in London, it was not without design. I contrived to bump into him at a gentleman's club, and used our old acquaintance as a method of obtaining an invitation to Fairfield Hall," he said, running a hand through his hair as he paced back and forth.

Cordelia tried not to sputter in shock. "Jewel thieves? That's what this is about?"

"Yes," he continued, stalking about like an anxious stag. "They've struck several other old families, although no one is speaking about it, because no one wishes to admit they've been rooked. The valuable pieces are taken and replaced with false ones in the same settings. The real things are sent out of the country—France, we believe—to be sold where no one will recognize them. It takes a considerable amount of advance work to pull such a thing off. Our London agents believe they have a lead on the forger who makes the paste substitutions, but he's the low man on the ladder. Whoever is running the show has access to fine homes and rich women."

"Wait," she said. "So the leader must be a servant?"

"That's what I had originally believed," Aubrey

said, standing still at last. "It's why I sent Grimm here three months ago. We gave him good references, from people in top positions, who would vouch for him, and he'd grown up here at Fairfield, which meant he was in a position to fit right in, despite having gone off and seen a bit of the rest of the world. By God, he did make a fine first footman. But he was also investigating the staff, to see who might have had something to hide."

"The earrings!" she exclaimed. "That's why he had Ophelia's earrings! Are they fakes too?"

"They are. He was supposed to be meeting me in the garden to show some of the loose stones to me. But he went out too early, and whoever it was that killed him found him before I did."

Cordelia did not know what to say. This was all so outrageous. "And then Ophelia found him, and then Tybalt and Miss Dunlea-Boggins."

"Yes. I shall confess, when I found the earring in his hand, I initially believed it possible your sister was in fact the murderer, and perhaps Grimm had pulled it from her during a struggle. But when I observed your sister the next day, there was no sign of injury to either of her ears. The more I thought on it, the more I realized she would not have the physical strength to bludgeon a man who stood a head taller than she."

She could see her breath in the chilly air. "Then if he did not pull the earring from Ophelia's ear, he must have had it in his possession already, in some other way, when he was killed."

"It would seem that is correct, yes." Aubrey watched her, curious. "Since you've made it abundantly clear to me that you are not a fool, tell me. What are you thinking?"

She frowned. “Something does not add up. Ophelia has denied killing him, and of course I believe her. However, she’s been so reluctant to tell anyone what she was doing out here. Grimm was out here early to meet you. Ophelia said she was meeting Grimm to prevent a scandal. What could she have meant?”

Aubrey nodded. “That’s a good question, indeed, but it does explain why Grimm was out here half an hour before I was due to rendezvous with him. Could he have meant to show Ophelia that the earrings were fake, as well?”

“Mr. Aubrey,” said Cordelia, the faint glimmer of an idea beginning to form. “I just had the most awful thought.” And it was awful, far more awful than she had ever expected, although not nearly as awful as her sister going to jail—or worse, the gallows—for murder. “Ophelia has said nothing to protect herself, other than repeatedly proclaiming her own innocence. She has offered neither reason nor rationale for her presence out here. Up until this point, I had been afraid for her, because I believed she had narrowly missed being killed herself. For surely, you would agree, she must have been very near Grimm when he was murdered.”

“I would agree with that, yes.”

“What if, Mr. Aubrey,” she said slowly, “what if the reason for my sister’s lack of cooperation is not because of some guilt of her own, but that of another individual? Is it possible, sir, that she is attempting to protect someone else with her silence?” The wind picked up, and Cordelia burrowed closer into Aubrey’s coat as the sky darkened in the distance.

He guided her away from the sanctuary of the temple, their steps falling silently in the gathering snow.

"We should go back, Mrs. Falconer. Do you understand, now, why I asked you not to speak of this to anyone?"

"I do. But you did not answer my question. Is it possible my sister is protecting someone else?"

He stopped abruptly. "Anything is possible, especially when it comes to murder and greed. But who would your sister deign to protect? From what I have seen of her, she is far more concerned with herself and her social status than anything else. Who would she lie for? For Brompton? For you?"

Cordelia pulled away. "Are you making an accusation, sir?"

"No, I am not. I am simply trying to ascertain the facts of what happened to Owen Grimm, as that shall forever remain upon my head." The snow turned to sleet as they made their way back to the terraces. "But you must see, surely, that the circle of people your sister would lie for is limited at best."

She did see, and that frightened her. Cordelia pushed her wet hair from her face as the storm chased them to the doors. As she reached out for the knob, she turned to him one last time and handed him his snowy coat. "I understand you perfectly, Mr. Aubrey," she said. "And since I know very well that I myself did not kill Owen Grimm, then the person who did so must be someone very close indeed. I shall keep your secret, sir, if for no other reason than to draw out the truth."

She spun on the heel of her soaking wet boot and went inside.

Chapter Eleven

Ophelia Dean sat daintily on the window seat of her room, overlooking the snow-covered front lawns of Fairfield Hall. From here, she could see down the lane to the main road, where normally an occasional farmer drove his cart on his way to the village of Brompton, tucked behind a line of trees in the distance. Today, though, everything was blanketed in white, and the road was as silent as a tomb. The Brompton church steeple barely peeked out over the bare treetops, but just knowing it was there gave Ophelia a sense of direction.

If she married Henry—no, not if, *when* she married him—they would be wed in the chapel at Fairfield Hall. That nice Mr. Littleberry who had once wanted to marry Cordelia would perform the ceremony, and then she, Miss Ophelia Dean, daughter of an alderman and a merchant's daughter, would be the new mistress of Fairfield Hall. With that, she would become the social leader of Brompton and a large surrounding area, one that would be the envy of all her Chesham and Wycombe Heath friends, to be sure. Oh, how she would delight in inviting them out to visit her in the country! That, of course, would be how she spent her time after the London season concluded in the summertime.

Of course, there was Henry's mother to contend with. Lady Brompton would not give up her role as Fairfield's mistress without a significant fight. And now, with Mr. Adkyns naming Ophelia as a prime suspect—if not the killer—in the death of that awful footman, things could all go horribly wrong very soon.

When Cordelia came barging in, Ophelia closed the book she had been reading. “Good afternoon, sister,” she said pleasantly.

“It is not a good afternoon, not a good one at all.” Cordelia was very damp, and Ophelia frowned at her. Surely it was not polite to visit people when you might drip all over them. “Do you know why I do not believe it to be a good afternoon, Ophelia?”

Ophelia was certain there was a specific response Cordelia wanted her to give, but for the life of her couldn’t imagine what it might be. “Because it’s snowing and chilly, and we are trapped indoors?” she asked hopefully. It seemed like a sensible answer, and would have been, had she been speaking with anyone but Cordelia.

“No, Ophelia. Not because it’s snowing and chilly, although it is, and as you can see I’ve been caught out in it, so it might have been polite for you to offer me a dry robe to put on or even a spot by the fire, but I can see you are too busy to think of such trivial things. The reason it is not a good afternoon, Ophelia, is because you—my sister, a reasonably respectable, if slightly dim young lady from a decent family—have been accused of killing a man in cold blood.” She paused for a moment. “And so help me, Ophelia, I cannot fathom why you don’t understand the gravity of your own situation.”

Ophelia rose and walked to the side table, where she began rearranging a vase of dried flowers, sorting them by color and size. “Cordelia, I think it’s very good of you to be concerned for me. When I am mistress of Fairfield Hall, do know you shall always be welcome here. When Henry and I begin having children, perhaps you and Lydia might like to come visit us from time to time." She fluffed the flowers and moved the vase to the other side of the table, pleased with her work. "Honestly, I have no worries at all. I did not kill that man—what was his name?—and I am certain that all shall be well."

Cordelia stared at her in astonishment. Her sister could be facing the gallows, or at the very least transportation, and yet she was busy moving flowers around and planning visits for several years down the road. Surely, even Ophelia could not be this great a fool. Or was she, and Cordelia had simply not been around to notice it? She sank onto the sofa, at a loss for words.

"Perhaps," Ophelia continued, "Lady Brompton has her concerns about Henry and I marrying after this bit of misunderstanding, but I know that Henry shall allow his better judgment to prevail. He will not allow his mother to persuade him that he ought to set me aside. That would cause even more talk among the *ton* than the crime of the footman's death."

"And what makes you so certain that Henry will marry you, when his mother has indicated she will not brook such disobedience now? He is her only child, to be sure, and heir to the Brompton fortune, but as long as his mother lives, Henry—and you—shall be dependent upon Lady Brompton's good graces and financial support."

Ophelia smiled. "I am confident Henry shall do as I ask. His mother may threaten to cut him off without an allowance—or even threaten to make Heyward the heir, for you must be assured that possibility has crossed my mind—but I have a great deal of faith that he will never abandon me. Henry and I have held each other in high regard for many years, Cordelia. I swore long ago that someday I should be his wife, and I do not plan to let anything prevent that from taking place."

"Not even jail? Not even murder?" Cordelia snapped.

"But sister," Ophelia said sweetly, "I am not the one who murdered the footman. Perhaps I made an error in judgment and propriety in agreeing to meet him out in the gardens, but I did not kill him."

But the emerald earrings... It was time to be blunt—and possibly unkind—with Ophelia. "What did Owen Grimm know?"

Ophelia blinked. "I beg your pardon?"

"What did he know? He was meeting you in the gardens because of something to do with your earrings, Ophelia, and you may not deny that, no matter how much you may wish to, because other information has been brought to my attention." Cordelia glared at her sister, who suddenly appeared on the verge of weeping. "Did he tell you the earrings were frauds?"

Ophelia began to sniffle, and tears welled in the corners of her eyes. "He—oh, Cordelia, it's just too awful! Grimm came to me when we first arrived and said the most horrid things! He said that there was someone at Fairfield who might mean to do the family harm. He said if I gave him the earrings right before the ball, he would use them to send away the person that threatened to cause trouble! Oh, Cordie, I know it was wicked to give them to him, because Henry gave them to me, but I truly thought I could get them back later. Then, he sent me a note, asking me to meet him in the gardens, and that he would give them back to me, for he had resolved the issue with no need for me to give up my jewels." She wept into her hands and draped herself delicately across the couch.

Cordelia was astonished. "Someone wished to harm the Bromptons? Or simply steal from them? And how would the earrings help?"

"I don't know! I know nothing about stealing or fraudulent jewels!" Ophelia wailed. "Grimm told me that there was a man who had damaging information about the Bromptons, and that he would go public with it if he wasn't paid!"

"But why would this man go to Grimm—a footman—and not Henry or Lady Brompton? How on earth would a footman benefit from stopping a scandal?" Cordelia frowned. None of it made any sense.

"Cordie, I do not know. He hinted that it was something scandalous and awful, and I wanted to protect Henry, so I gave the earrings to Grimm." She sighed heavily and resumed her sobs.

Cordelia patted her sister's hair absently. If Aubrey had sent Grimm to Fairfield to investigate the alleged jewel thieves, why had Grimm used such deception to obtain the earrings from Ophelia? Could it be that he had hoped the earrings were in fact authentic, and only moved to return them upon learning they were substitutes? She took a deep breath and patted her sister's hand reassuringly. "Ophelia," she said, "you have done the right thing in telling me this. I am confident, however, that Owen Grimm was not all he appeared to be."

Ophelia blinked through damp lashes. “Do you see now why I was afraid to say anything? What if it is learned that there is a mysterious scandal attached to the Bromptons?”

“I am not certain that there is, dear. I wonder if perhaps Grimm just told you so in order to make you give him the earrings without question. Now, you must say nothing of this to anyone, other than the magistrate and Mr. Aubrey, if they are to ask.”

Ophelia swiped a hand over her tears. “Mr. Aubrey? What has he to do with this?”

“I cannot tell you, for I am sworn to confidence, but believe me when I say that Mr. Aubrey will not bring you—or the Bromptons—harm, and you may place your trust in him.”

“Thank you, sister,” Ophelia said, dabbing daintily at her eyes. “Would you like some cake?”

****

Dinner that night was a strained affair. Mr. Adkyns had returned to his home for the evening, with promises that he would be back in the morning to resume his investigation. In addition, he had several times reiterated his request that Ophelia not go anywhere, despite her having no place to really go or, for that matter, any method of traveling through the snowy roads. Everyone gathered in the large dining hall to be served, and it was a quiet meal indeed, with tension lingering in the air like the morning mist on the fields.

Mrs. Dean and Ophelia made a few half-hearted attempts to engage the others in conversation about the poor weather or plans for the Christmas holidays, but no one was very enthusiastic, and there was little to say. Thomas Heyward drank far more port than he should have, and Reverend Littleberry shot scornful glances toward Cordelia and Aubrey. Even Tybalt and Mercutio, normally jovial and enthusiastic, seemed subdued. Mercutio had gotten a letter from Bessie Venables and so was feeling down about his lot in general.

Lydia, fed up with every one of them, rose without being excused and stomped off to the library as soon as she had finished her dinner.

"Mr. Littleberry," Ophelia chirped, finally breaking the silence, "I thought perhaps we might meet this evening to discuss the details of the wedding ceremony. I should like to have flower arrangements in spring colors, even though it is wintertime. Do you think that is possible? Perhaps there are some in the conservatory that we may use."

"Er," said Mr. Littleberry. "Yes, well, I must defer to Lady Brompton on such matters as this."

Lady Brompton peered down her nose frostily at Ophelia. "Miss Dean," she said formally, "I think at this time it is unseemly for us to discuss such things as a wedding which may or may not take place."

Seeing Ophelia's look of abject shock, Cordelia wanted to climb into her wine glass.

"Why, Lady Brompton," Ophelia protested, "I do not think this is appropriate to discuss in front of others. Henry and I are going to be married, are we not, Henry?"

Henry Brompton at least had the decency to look ashamed of himself. "Ophelia, darling, I think it might be best if we postponed things, at least until this matter of the footman is settled."

Ophelia burst into tears. "But Henry, surely you

know I did not kill him? Cordelia, tell him! Tell Henry I did nothing wrong!"

"Oh!" Cordelia was taken aback. "Well, Henry, I think it is safe to say my sister did not kill Grimm. She has led me to understand that her meeting with him in the gardens was completely innocent."

Lady Brompton pounded a bony fist on the table. "Enough! I have had enough! Miss Dean, you have been accused of murder. Whether you are innocent or not is none of my concern. My concern is, as we have discussed *ad nauseum*, how your behavior reflects upon this family. My son will not—I repeat, will not—be marrying a woman whose name has been linked to something as disreputable as the murder of a servant!"

Ophelia buried her face in her hands and fled the room.

There was complete and utter silence at the table. Finally, Heyward downed the last of his wine, and said, "Well, Aunt, family gatherings have never been quite so exciting as this." With a wink at Cordelia, he slid his chair back and left.

"Mother," said Henry Brompton, "that was unkind. Surely we can find some way to delay this, so that I can marry Ophelia after all."

"Henry, you are nine and twenty years old and I am beyond caring to whom you tether yourself, but it *will not* be someone who has the stigma of criminal activity and disreputable assignations with servants connected to her name. Do I make myself clear?"

Henry nodded and poked sadly at his plate of mutton. "The engagement's already been announced."

"Well, then we shall unannounce it. I never should have let you go through with it in the first place, but did so against my better judgment," Lady Brompton snapped, spearing a turnip violently. "I am quite certain everyone who is anyone in the *ton* will understand your reasons for ending things, and no one will think the worse of you for it. Why, Lady Sackville's younger brother ended things with a girl after she danced with another gentleman four times in one night, and everyone agreed he had done the right thing."

Mercutio spoke up. "I remember that. I thought she had dropped him because he'd gotten a housemaid with child?"

"No!" Lady Brompton snapped. "That is not so at all. Lies, all of it. And besides, even if he did trifle with a servant, that sort of thing is typically overlooked in gentlemen, as you yourself are aware, I am sure. It is not so for ladies of consequence."

"Lady Brompton," said Agatha Dean as sweetly as possible, her lower lip trembling, "Ophelia is very upset and understandably so. Perhaps we might delay the…what did you call it, unannouncement? The retraction of the engagement until after the magistrate has concluded his investigation."

"I don't see any need to do so. Frankly, Mrs. Dean, I do not care if your daughter is innocent of murder. She is still not worthy of the Brompton name." She folded her napkin tidily and rose. "You are all welcome to stay here at Fairfield Hall for the remainder of your fortnight visit, although certainly if you wished to depart once the roads are clear and weather more agreeable, that would be understandable as well. However, I would not wish to rescind an invitation, for it would reflect poorly upon me as a hostess. I shall retire for the evening. Good evening. Henry, come along."

"Good heavens," said Tybalt after they had left. "That was the most spectacularly dreadful thing I've ever been a witness to."

His mother wrung her hands together, clearly agitated. "Oh, poor Ophelia. What shall we do with her? Who will want her if she is dismissed so freely by Mr. Brompton? Perhaps I should begin looking for some suitable alternative, some amiable gentleman with a quiet life in some other part of the country."

"Mother!" Cordelia said. "Really, do you have no sense of decorum at all? Ophelia is in danger of having her heart broken—and possibly going to jail on top of that, or even the gallows—and all you can think of is marrying her off to someone else where she can be quietly out of the way for the rest of her life?"

"Well, Cordie, it's not as though anyone from a decent family would have her now," her mother said. "Lady Brompton is quite right. We'll have to find Ophelia a husband from a significantly lower class, like a nice young reverend somewhere. Oh, Mr. Littleberry, understand I mean no offense by that."

"None taken at all," he said, trying to be gracious. Cordelia felt a bit sorry for him. Poor Mr. Littleberry was caught in the middle of the whole thing—it certainly wasn't his fault that Lady Brompton was a harpy or that Henry was a milquetoast who would never stand up for himself.

"Mrs. Falconer, may we speak in private?" Aubrey's voice was just low enough that no one else would hear him.

She nodded silently and excused herself. A few moments later, he followed her into the hall.

"You've spoken with your sister?" he said without preamble.

She checked the corridor to make sure they were alone and explained to him the nature of her conversation with Ophelia.

He nodded thoughtfully. "So Grimm obtained the earrings from her under the guise of holding off some sort of extortion, it sounds like. But he never mentioned this in his reports to me. This makes me question whether there was really a plot by some unknown party to damage the Bromptons' reputation, or was Grimm up to something else?"

"Indeed," Cordelia whispered. "What if Grimm was taking advantage of his role working for you and hoping to garner himself a bit of spare income on the side by taking Ophelia's earrings? Once he realized they were fakes and had been targeted by the thieves, they'd have been worthless to him, and he'd have returned them to Ophelia."

Aubrey frowned. "I don't like to think that Grimm might have been working on his own, but you raise some interesting possibilities."

"How long had you known him?" she asked, curious.

He shrugged. "Not long. He was recommended to us—grew up here at Fairfield. His mother was once a servant in the Brompton house, years ago, so he was familiar to the family. He'd been on one or two operations for us before but was mostly just in a position to gather information. Grimm blended in well with the help, obviously."

"Perhaps you might look a bit more into his background," she suggested. "For it seems to me that while Grimm was investigating your jewel thieves, he may not have been averse to a bit of dishonesty of his own."

Footsteps echoed down the corridor. Mary scampered toward them hastily, pausing to peek into each open door she passed. Cordelia leaned close to Aubrey. "That is Lady Brompton's abigail. She is the only one who has a key to the jewel chest, other than Lady Brompton herself. You must speak with her. Mary," she called softly.

Startled, the young woman dipped a curtsey when she saw Cordelia and Aubrey. "Begging pardon, Missus. I cannot find Lady Brompton's green shawl. She'll have my head if I don't find it."

"Have you a moment, my dear? This is Mr. Aubrey. He has a few questions for you."

"Oh!" Mary's face was blank. "But I already answered all the questions for Mr. Adkyns, this morning when you sent him in."

"Yes," agreed Cordelia, although she had no idea what Mary had told the magistrate. "You did, and I am certain you gave him all the information he needed. However, Mr. Aubrey has some additional questions for you. About Owen Grimm."

The young woman's nose wrinkled in mild distaste. "Ah, yes, ma'am. The footman what died at the party."

"Yes," said Mr. Aubrey. "May we speak for a few moments, once you have completed your mission? You are in no trouble, I assure you, but I must ask you some questions. I do not wish to distress Lady Brompton, as I am certain you will understand."

Mary agreed, although with some trepidation, and

vanished through a set of doors, searching for the lost shawl.

"Mr. Aubrey," Cordelia said slowly, "is it possible Mary too has been deceived by someone?"

"You mean someone may have fooled her into giving her the key to the jewel chest?" Aubrey shook his head. He gently took her elbow and steered her down the hall. "I find it doubtful. She's a loyal girl and has been with the Bromptons for ten years, since she was but thirteen years old. I can't see her risking her livelihood by giving the key to anyone else." He looked down at her, his eyes searching, as they reached the billiard room. "Mrs. Falconer, I must apologize to you once again."

Cordelia blinked. "I beg your pardon? Whatever for?"

"I feel that I may have been—this morning, when we spoke in the gardens, perhaps I was a bit too forward in my speech. Our…previous interactions notwithstanding, I addressed you overly familiarly and shared with you thoughts of a personal nature that perhaps you might not have wished to be privy to." Aubrey clearly was uncomfortable, and Cordelia stifled a laugh. He held the door for her, and she went to the table to place the cue ball.

"Mr. Aubrey," she said firmly, "there is no apology expected nor required of you. I am…in truth, I find your honesty and forthrightness refreshing."

"Do you?" He chalked his cue and took aim.

"Yes," she said truthfully. "I spent the first seventeen years of my life around people who never said what they really meant, and rarely meant what they said. Then, when I left for America—when I married

Tom, you see—I found that not everyone was like that. The people I met over there were just men and women trying to survive in a harsh place. They had no time for façade or artifice, while here in England it is a part of daily life."

There was a *thunk* as he sank the first ball.

"I finally, for the first time in my life, developed the ability to tell people what I thought, rather than what I believed they wanted to hear. It was…liberating, to say the least. Now, returning here after all this time…well, it's quite hard to get used to people like Mother and Ophelia and Lady Brompton, if you get my meaning. No one ever tells the whole truth. But you do, and I thank you for it. I value honesty immensely."

He moved closer to her, and she found herself between him and the billiard table. "Mrs. Falconer," he said hoarsely. His eyes burned into hers, and her heart pounded even more rapidly as her body reacted to him. He clearly wasn't going to move out of her way any time soon.

"Please," she whispered, searching his face. "In the garden, you addressed me as Cordelia. I wish you might do so again. As you did last night."

And then, before she knew it, his mouth was on hers, his lips warm and unyielding and tasting of wine and apples. Aubrey crushed her to him, and a soft sound escaped her throat as she responded to his kiss. His hands twined through her hair, and the pins lost their hold on her curls, but she did not care. Cordelia kissed him eagerly, not wanting to stop. His tongue parted her lips, and a shudder went through her body. He was delicious, and she wanted to take all of him in.

Abruptly, he broke away. "I apologize," he

murmured, his voice ragged as he stared at her. "Cordelia, forgive me."

She shook her head, and put a finger to his lips. "No," she said softly. "Do not say that. Do not ask for forgiveness for such a thing, because it is beautiful." She leaned into him, her eyes closed, his breath hot on her forehead. They stood in silence, his arms wrapped around her, and she pressed warm and safe into his chest.

There was a sound from the other side of the room, a gentle clearing of the throat, and they sprung apart. It was Mary, looking abashed and awkward.

"I should have knocked," she began.

"Come in, Mary," Aubrey said, his voice as authoritative as ever. "Did you find Lady Brompton's elusive green shawl?"

"I did, sir. 'Twas in the dining room, on her chair, where she insisted it could not possibly be."

"Ah. Well, I'm glad the mystery is solved." He smiled kindly, and the girl relaxed a bit. "Please, do not feel that this is a formal inquisition of any sort. I simply mean to ask you a few questions. I understand you have already spoken to Mr. Adkyns?"

"Yes, sir." Mary bobbed her head.

"What can you tell us about Owen Grimm?" Cordelia asked, trying to regain her focus.

The girl shuffled nervously. "Owen Grimm? The footman?"

Aubrey nodded. "The dead one, yes. Unless there is perhaps another Owen Grimm in the area?"

Mary shook her head. "Well, no, I don't think there is. But I do not know much of Grimm other than what I'd heard from Chibbs and Amy."

"What did Mrs. Chibbs tell you about Grimm?" Cordelia was curious. Chibbs had been at Fairfield since time began and might prove a useful source of information.

Mary fidgeted with a handkerchief. "Well, she said Grimm had grown up here, you see. His mother was a maid belowstairs, and so he'd lived here as a boy. Then he disappeared and took a post somewhere up north. When he showed back up again, Chibbs said everyone was surprised to see him."

"Why would they be surprised?" Aubrey asked. "Servants do move around sometimes, but it's not uncommon for one to come back to a previous employer for a job."

"Well, that's just it, sir. When he left—and he couldn't have been more than about fifteen—when he left, he said he'd never be back, because he had enough money and letters of reference to go off and make a new start somewhere else."

Aubrey began to pace as he worked it through. "How," he began, "would a fifteen-year-old boy have enough money to go off somewhere and be guaranteed employment?"

"And the only person who could have written him a letter of reference would have been Lady Brompton," Cordelia pointed out. "Henry's father was dead by then. But why would she have done so?"

"Mary, did Chibbs tell you anything else about Grimm? Where he got money, or where he'd gone off to?"

"No, sir, Mr. Aubrey. Just that everyone was glad when he left back then. He made the mistress uncomfortable, Chibbs said."

Aubrey bowed politely to Mary, thanked her, and sent her on her way. He racked the billiard balls again and lined up his shot, seemingly forgetting Cordelia's presence.

She moved to the sideboard and poured two glasses of wine. When she held one out to him, he blinked, startled.

"What are you thinking?" she asked.

"There's something not right. Clearly Grimm was positioned to come to Fairfield Hall by his own design, and it seems that the Crown played right into his hands by sending him to me as a potential insider to track down the real thief. But what I can't figure out is why? What was he up to? And what is Lady Brompton hiding?"

Cordelia shrugged. "Perhaps we might just ask her."

"She won't tell us anything. As you said, no one ever says what they mean, not in this circle of society. No, we're far better off speaking with people who know and see a great deal but are rarely asked about it."

She smiled. "The servants. Starting with Mrs. Chibbs." She raised a glass to him in salute.

"Indeed."

Chapter Twelve

Mrs. Chibbs had retired for bed by the time they arrived in the kitchen, as she was normally up long before the sun in order to prepare breakfast and supervise the day's feedings of the Brompton family and their guests. Despite her absence, Aubrey left a note and agreed to meet Cordelia in the kitchens first thing in the morning.

When she arrived belowstairs at sunrise, she was astonished to find Aubrey laughing and joking about with Mrs. Chibbs. She had rarely seen him truly amused, at least not unless he was entertained by someone's bad behavior, but this was a genuine laugh that stretched up into his eyes, making his face even more handsome. For a moment, she recalled the sensation of his lips on hers last night in the billiard room. Afterward, once they were done speaking with Mary, he had bid goodnight and disappeared, saying he had some sort of business to attend to. And now, here he was, drinking tea and chortling away with Mrs. Chibbs as though they were the best of friends. Wonders might never cease.

Aubrey grinned boyishly when he saw her watching them. "Good morning, Corde—Mrs. Falconer," he corrected himself, smiling warmly. "Some tea?"

"Thank you," she said warily.

He poured her a cup and then passed her a plate of tiny cakes. "You must try one of these. They're delightful. Mrs. Chibbs and I just discovered we know some of the same people," he said. "Her brother—Alan, is it?—her brother Alan works for the Earl of Derwentwater, whose holdings include Derwent Scar."

"Ah. I see." She really didn't, not at all.

Seeing her look, Aubrey sighed. "Derwent Scar is where I'm from, in Yorkshire. Alan Telford is Lord Derwentwater's groom. They're my neighbors. Or at least, my father's neighbors."

"Oh." Cordelia wasn't entirely sure how this was relevant and wondered what on earth had come over Rhys Aubrey. Had he actually just called a cake delightful?

"At any rate, prepare to be astonished by what Mrs. Chibbs here has told me."

Mrs. Chibbs nodded heartily. "That Owen Grimm was trouble enough, he was."

"I'm beginning to see that. Go on, then, Mr. Aubrey. Do enlighten me as to what you've learned."

"It would appear that our Mr. Grimm fooled a good many people. Would you like to know why he left here, six years ago, when he was fifteen?"

Mrs. Chibbs excused herself to pull some bread from the ovens, and Aubrey popped another cake in his mouth.

"I would very much like to know, yes, Mr. Aubrey," Cordelia said.

"Apparently," he said, lowering his voice, "he was asked to leave by Lady Brompton, who gave him several pounds of spending money and a glowing letter of recommendation. Her only request was that he go as far away as possible, which is how he ended up in the north country."

Cordelia frowned. "There is something very odd about all of this. If Lady Brompton did not remember a young man who had worked here six years ago, that would be one thing. However, when you told her of his death, she failed to mention he grew up here and then was paid to leave and sent away with glowing references. Why would she do such a thing?"

"According to Mrs. Chibbs," Aubrey continued, brushing crumbs from his hands, "Grimm was asked to leave because he was about to make some trouble for the Bromptons."

"What sort of trouble?"

Mrs. Chibbs snorted from her station by the ovens, and Cordelia turned to look at her.

"Go ahead, Mrs. Chibbs, do the honors," said Aubrey.

"Well," the older woman said, her hands on her stout hips, "that Owen Grimm was a problem from the beginning, but once he got older he became a real troublemaker, 'e did. Decided he was going to cause a right scandal for the Bromptons, 'less old Lady Brompton paid him off and sent 'im away."

"Yes, yes," said Cordelia, beginning to lose her patience. "He was extorting money from her. What leverage did he have against the Bromptons?"

"He claimed old Mr. Brompton was his father."

Cordelia dropped her teacup, which shattered on the floor. Shocked, she looked from Mrs. Chibbs, who seemed quite pleased with herself, to Aubrey, who merely nodded and raised his cup to her. "Henry's father? Mr. Brompton was Grimm's father?"

"Oh yes, missus. Grimm's mother was a lass named Hannah Grimm, and she was a maid belowstairs. When she got with child…well, her not having a husband, it didn't take long before she told people 'twas Mr. Brompton's baby. But 'twas all hushed up, and he gave Hannah some money, and that was it," said Mrs. Chibbs.

Cordelia nodded, realization dawning. "And Lady Brompton must have known. No wonder she was so startled when she learned it was Grimm who had been murdered."

"Oh, she knew," said Chibbs. "It's why she gave him money and sent him away. He was going to tell young Henry Brompton that he was his half brother from the other side o' the blanket."

"Of course," Cordelia said. "When he told Ophelia he could protect the family if she gave him the earrings, he was talking about himself, not some other extortionist! Mrs. Chibbs, how did Grimm get hired back on?"

Mrs. Chibbs sliced her bread neatly. "He came to see Waverly, told him he was here for the job o' first footman, and please to tell Lady Brompton he required employment. That was it."

"Where does his mother live now?" Aubrey asked.

"Oh, she's a cook for Lord and Lady Sackville now, down near Little Chepping."

"I'll need to speak with her," Aubrey said, looking at Cordelia. "If I ride down to Sackville's now, I should be back by evening at the latest. I'm hoping the roads should be passable on horseback. Tell Adkyns what we've learned."

She nodded, but caught his arm as he put on his

coat. “Mr. Aubrey—”

“It’s Rhys. You know that.”

“I—please be careful. We know that Grimm was not an honest man, but we still are no closer to finding his killer,” she whispered, looking up at him.

His dark eyes flashed in the dim kitchen, and he nodded. “It is more important for you to be careful while I am gone,” he murmured. “It is possible—no, it is most probable—that whoever murdered Grimm is here in this house. You must tell no one anything, other than Adkyns. He’s not a clever man, but he’s an honest one, and he’s the only person we know was not here the night of Grimm’s death. Even then, use your best judgment.”

“My sister—”

“No. Do not breathe a word of this to her. I will speak with Hannah Grimm, and I shall find out whether it’s true that the footman was old Brompton’s son.” He kissed her hand gently. “And you shall keep asking questions, but do so with the utmost caution. Do you feel up to the task?”

“If it means seeing my sister’s name cleared, then I am up to any task put toward me,” Cordelia said. To be sure, she meant every word of it.

****

Mr. Littleberry, who seemed more uncomfortable than usual, joined her in the breakfast room and began the meal by speaking to her of the inclement weather and the fine selection of meats on the sideboard. He chattered for several minutes while Cordelia ate her toast and jam, and they were joined by Lydia, who happily sampled each of the sausages on display.

“Mother,” she announced, “I have had enough of

staying indoors. If I have to sit embroidering and reading to Grandmama for one more instant, I shall go mad, and then our family's reputation shall be even worse than it is now. I will be committed to Bedlam, and you may be able to visit with me only on Tuesdays, and you shall have to pay tuppence to see me shrieking like a *bean sí*."

"I'll be sure to bring you some fresh fruit and a hairbrush, dear." Cordelia winked at her daughter, trying to ignore Mr. Littleberry's look of horror at such an abject display of improper behavior. "However, since you would become very bored at Bedlam, what with no books or embroidery to keep you occupied, perhaps we should devise some entertainment for you. What would you like to do, darling?"

Lydia fidgeted. "I do like riding, but I think the horses might not, with the snow. I should like to go walking for once. May we walk to the village? Waverly says the little path the servants take into Brompton should be clear enough to walk by midday."

Cordelia smiled. It would do them both some good to get out of doors and spend a bit of time away from the gloomy atmosphere of Fairfield Hall. "That would be a splendid idea! We shall indeed. Perhaps we can do some shopping in Brompton and have tea at the inn."

She had rather forgotten Mr. Littleberry was there, until he cleared his throat delicately. "Do you not think, Mrs. Falconer, that it is too far for ladies to walk? After all, it is near three miles to Brompton. And the snow! Why, it must be ankle deep at least!"

"Pooh," sniffed Lydia. "We used to walk into town all the time when we lived in Virginia, and it was at least ten miles from our home."

"It was five, darling. And no, Mr. Littleberry, I am sure we shall be fine. It looks as though the snow has finally stopped, at least for a while, and so I mean to take full advantage of it. If we take the path the servants use, it should only be a mile as the crow flies. Certainly they've been using the trail while we've sat warm and dry inside the house, so it should be good and clear by now."

"Well, then," Mr. Littleberry said importantly, "far be it for me to allow two young ladies to walk unaccompanied, while there could be danger lurking nearby. I shall escort you to Brompton."

"Oh!" cried Lydia, glancing desperately at her mother. "Surely you must have other things to do here at the house. Reverend things?"

"We could not begin to impose on you," said Cordelia at the same time, but Mr. Littleberry was resolute and insisted that he should join them on their walk to the village. After breakfast Cordelia and Lydia read their books for a while, and then changed into walking shoes and jackets and cloaks. They were forced to wait nearly an hour while Mr. Littleberry searched for his boots and then ran about packing a bag with cheese and fruit, despite their just having concluded the morning meal.

When they finally set off down the lane, it was nearly half past noon, and although the path itself was still covered in snow, and a layer of mist hung over the fields, the sun had warmed much of the air. The trees sparkled as water dripped from their bare branches, and Lydia skipped ahead, as anxious to be away from Mr. Littleberry as she was to arrive in the village of Brompton. Cordelia did not wish to appear rude to their companion and so tried to engage Mr. Littleberry in conversation of some length but of little real substance, in which he was most obliging.

There was little traffic on the path, although in the distance they could see the occasional farmer driving his sheep across the main road from one field to the next, and the day was pleasant. Cordelia might have enjoyed it more had it been silent, but Littleberry did not respond to her subtle hints quite as well as Thomas Heyward had the day they had gone riding together.

Soon, thankfully, the village of Brompton was before them. It was a typical English country town, with a collection of shops and houses surrounding a common green, and the inn itself sat near the crossroads. Cordelia hoped her smile did not betray her as she recalled the night she met Aubrey in the stables. The church and the mill sat near the river, which ran swift and high this time of year, and it seemed that many of the residents of Brompton were taking advantage of the halt in snowfall to get out of doors and get their business done before harsh weather set in for good.

Cordelia sent Mr. Littleberry off to the church to visit with his friend, the Reverend Copplewhite, and with a sigh of relief she and Lydia attended to the shops in earnest. Although Cordelia was a not a great lover of shopping as entertainment, she was sensible enough to recognize that when one needed something, visiting a store was often the only way to obtain it. It was one of life's necessary evils. Although her wardrobe and Lydia's were up to date, thanks to Mrs. Dean's insistence, there were still a few practical things she looked forward to purchasing. For example, a new comb would certainly be welcome, and perhaps a length of wool might come in handy to make a new cloak to wear on the cold days to come.

"Oh, Mother, look!" exclaimed Lydia, clutching Cordelia's hand. It was a bookstore, tucked between the milliner's shop and a tea house. "May we go in? The library at Fairfield has a great many books, but I confess, I desire something…lighter."

Cordelia laughed. "Indeed, I think we might find just the thing." Lydia was a fan of novels, particularly those in which innocent young girls found themselves at the hands of dark and dangerous rogues in gloomy, forbidding castles.

Lydia raced into the bookstore happily, and when they emerged some time later, she was pleased to have a brand-new copy of *Annabelle and the Wicked Highwayman* tucked into her basket, along with two similar titles which would have to be hidden from her grandmama inside other, more appropriate books. There was no sign of Mr. Littleberry, thankfully, so Cordelia decided it was the perfect time for them to visit the tea house for luncheon. While there, they encountered Jane and Emily Wolverton, two of the young ladies whose acquaintance Lydia had made at the engagement ball, and they all sat together, the girls chattering away like a flock of brightly colored chickens.

It was clear that they had no idea about the death of Owen Grimm, which meant word had not spread yet beyond the immediate residents of Fairfield Hall. Lady Brompton had threatened all of her staff with immediate dismissal if they so much breathed a word of the incident, and it appeared that they had been sufficiently cowed as to keep their silence. No one in the village seemed to know anything.

Or at least, so she believed, until Leticia Dunlea-Boggins walked in.

Cordelia nodded graciously to her, and in a moment, everything changed.

Leticia Dunlea-Boggins peered down her nose at Cordelia and Lydia and deliberately turned away without speaking.

The Wolverton sisters gasped in unison. While they had certainly heard of people being given the cut in public, they had never actually seen it done.

Lydia's face turned bright pink, and she leaped to her feet. Only Cordelia's restraining hand on her arm kept Lydia from hitting the back of Leticia Dunlea-Boggins's blonde head with a pretty flowered teapot.

"Sit, darling," said Cordelia, her voice cheerful. "If Miss Dunlea-Boggins does not wish to associate with us, then who are we to complain?"

"Mother," hissed Lydia, much to the astonishment of the Wolverton girls, who could not wait to tell everyone what had just happened, "she cut us on purpose. If she thinks—"

"It does not signify, Lydia, not at all. Miss Dunlea-Boggins is nothing to us." Cordelia shrugged and nibbled another frosted cake. "I confess, I am indifferent to her opinion of me, for I know nothing of her, and clearly she is someone who may not be worth knowing at all."

Emily Wolverton clapped a hand over her mouth. Surely Mrs. Falconer—who had a bit of a bad reputation, although Emily wasn't sure why because no one would tell her—had not just said that Leticia Dunlea-Boggins, daughter of a viscount and granddaughter of an earl, was not worth knowing! She bounced to her feet, pulling her sister with her. Their mother was next door trying on a new hat, and Emily was itching to share this bit of gossip with her.

"We must away," she announced.

"Good day, Miss Wolverton and Miss Wolverton," said Cordelia politely. All four of them dipped politely, and then the sisters made their rapid exit.

"How long, do you think, before all of Brompton believes we have resorted to throwing teacups and insults at the *ton*?" asked Lydia, fed up with the whole thing.

"Moments, darling. Just moments." Cordelia sighed and examined her cake. The frosting was delicious. "Well, do pick up your books and let us go back to Fairfield Hall. I shall stop and get some ribbons for Mrs. Chibbs, and then we shall be on our way." Leticia kept sneaking furtive glances in their direction, but after Cordelia waved at her cheerfully, the girl stopped turning around. They finished their tea and left, and as Cordelia stepped out of the tea house, she practically collided with Thomas Heyward, who smiled and tipped his tall hat to them.

"Why, Mrs. Falconer and Miss Falconer! I suspected I might bump into you here. Ran into Littleberry, who told me he'd walked you into town. Had I known you were making a journey into Brompton this morning, I would have been honored to accompany you myself," he said with a broad smile. Like his cousin Henry, he was a good-looking man, and Cordelia was not surprised to see a group of young ladies watching him surreptitiously from beneath their winter bonnets.

"I believe, Mr. Heyward," she said, taking his arm with a laugh, "you have some admirers."

He waved a hand dismissively. "Bah. The chits are nice enough, but most of them are more interested in my Brompton connections and whatever fortunes I may have, rather than in anything I might have to say or any sensibility of feelings. They are good enough girls, to be sure, but I have found," he said, leaning closer, "I prefer ladies closer to my own age, ladies who are certain of themselves and know exactly what it is they like."

Cordelia blinked. "Oh. Well, I certainly do hope you are able to find one who meets your expectations." This was awkward indeed. Surely his reference to women his own age didn't mean that he had set his sights on her?

"Oh, I believe I've already found one, Mrs. Falconer. In fact, I've found one very nearby."

She could not look at him. *Oh dear, this cannot possibly end well.* It would have to be nipped in the bud. "Mr. Heyward," she began, "I must say that, for myself, as a lady of a near age to you, that those of us who are certain of ourselves do indeed know exactly what it is we like. However, we also are well aware that should we find a man who is to our liking—in the sense of a potential husband, you understand—we ladies often do not hesitate to make our preferences known. It would, I should think, be a mistake for you to declare your intentions toward a lady of your own age who has not yet indicated an interest. Would you not agree?"

He stopped and smiled down at her. "I would agree most heartily, Mrs. Falconer, and would hope that such a lady might—upon learning I was interested in forming an attachment—that she might take the time to get to know me well enough that she might someday return my affections."

"Ah. I see." Cordelia was prevented from saying more by an interruption from Lydia, who had spotted a young woman with a basket full of colorful ribbons.

"Mother, look! May I select some for Mrs. Chibbs? And perhaps even one for myself as well?"

Cordelia gave her assent and busied herself in helping her daughter choose ribbons, since it gave her the opportunity to avoid further discussion with Mr. Heyward. She pointed out a lovely length of violet silk to complement Lydia's eyes and a handsome velvet piece in hunter green. "This would look so pretty on Mrs. Chibbs' dark hair, do you not think, Lydia?"

After they had purchased their ribbons, Mr. Heyward retrieved his horse from the village stables and announced that he should escort them home. By this time, Mr. Littleberry had emerged from the church, and he too joined the party. As they began to make their way back to Fairfield Hall, this time along the main road, rather than the servants' path, Cordelia turned around to see Leticia Dunlea-Boggins and the Wolverton sisters watching with undisguised envy. Cordelia bobbed her head politely and then turned away. Despite her lack of romantic inclination toward Heyward—or toward Littleberry as well, who, his hygiene notwithstanding, was considered quite a catch by the ladies of Brompton—she had no qualms whatsoever about accepting their company if it would irritate Miss Dunlea-Boggins, who clearly had decided that Cordelia was *persona non grata*.

When Fairfield Hall came back into view down the

lane, Cordelia was immensely relieved. Though Heyward and Littleberry were pleasant enough, she was tired of the habit they each had of filling any available moment of silence, and worse still, the two of them seemed to feel a constant need to one-up each other, vying for her attention. Lydia, in an unusually cheerful mood, managed to engage with Heyward on the topic of horses for a while, which did provide Cordelia some relief.

She wondered how Aubrey was getting on with Grimm's mother down at Lord Sackville's place in Chepping. Certainly, talking to Mrs. Grimm was bound to be more pleasant than fending off the dual attentions of Thomas Heyward and Augustus Littleberry. For that matter, Cordelia was to a point where jabbing herself repeatedly with a large hatpin would be more pleasant than enduring the endless bantering of the two men. They spent a good deal of time talking about themselves and enumerating their own endless qualifications, and neither seemed particularly concerned with her opinions on much of anything.

Aubrey, though, was different. He actually encouraged her to participate in conversations with him, rather than bombarding her with endless monologues. Aubrey seemed interested in her ideas—certainly about the Owen Grimm situation but also about life in general.

And the way she felt when she touched him was like nothing she had experienced in a very long time.

When she ran off in the night to marry Tom Falconer, she had been in the bloom of first love. He swept her off her feet, and having left behind all that she knew, the two of them were forced to rely on one another for everything. Their love had sustained them through poverty, a dangerous sea voyage, Cordelia's near-death during Lydia's difficult birth, and two seasons of failed crops. Through it all, at the end of the day, Tom had been the one she'd depended on, as she had been for him. She had always known when she climbed into bed each night it was with a man who loved her.

And then he was kicked by his favorite horse in a fluke of an accident one Wednesday morning, and by Saturday afternoon he was dead. The man she had spent a third of her life with was gone in the blink of an eye, and she had been alone but for Lydia. She had taken the love she had for Tom, channeled it into grief, and then, finally, set it aside so that she could get back to the business of raising her daughter and running her tobacco farm.

All of this she had done, and it never crossed her mind—not until Rhys Aubrey—that she might someday find another man she wanted to share her world with. Aubrey made her feel alive and not just when his hands and mouth were on her. Just seeing him made her more alert and vibrant, as though she had been slumbering these last five years and suddenly awakened.

"Mother. Mother, please pay attention," said Lydia, sounding annoyed.

Cordelia stopped with a sigh. She had been so lost in contemplation that she'd wandered off the side of the road and was now dragging her skirts through a large and very cold mud puddle. "Blast it all to hell," she muttered, much to the shock of Mr. Littleberry, who tried to help her through the puddle, despite her brushing his hands away. "Lydia, you may go in through the front with the gentlemen," she said. "I'm afraid my boots are unfit to enter the hall, so I shall enter by way of the kitchen." She took the packet of ribbons for Mrs. Chibbs and set off along the path to the back of the house.

Heyward tipped his hat and headed to the stables, while a bewildered Mr. Littleberry found himself escorting Lydia inside.

As her feet crunched along the stones, Cordelia glanced toward the gardens. Other than her brief walk with Aubrey, she had not been out there at all since Grimm's death. Although she could not say why, precisely, she was oddly drawn to the footpath that led into the hedges and began winding toward the spot at which he had died. Though the afternoon was growing shorter, and the sky beginning to darken a bit, Cordelia had no trouble finding the statue of Apollo that had been Owen Grimm's final resting place.

A dark stain was visible on the front corner of the pedestal, along with a bit of dark hair, and Cordelia shivered. Despite the snow of the past day, the statue had clearly made contact with Grimm's head, which had hit the marble base as he fell. Prior to that, someone had delivered a killing blow that had destroyed the side of his face—but who?

She stood for several moments thinking. The shadows in the garden grew longer, but she did not return yet to the house. There was something, she felt sure, that she was missing.

And then she remembered. Ophelia had said the statue of Apollo was looking a bit "topple-y." Stepping back, she surveyed Apollo critically. To be sure, one of the statue's winged sandals appeared as though it had detached itself somewhat from the pedestal. With a frown, she drew closer and examined the spot where Apollo's foot should be resting, careful not to touch the rust-colored stain just a few inches away. There was a hole in the underside of Apollo's sandal.

And there was something in that hole.

Crouching down, Cordelia peered up at the opening and saw a small piece of rough material. She slid two fingers into the hole and was just able to pinch the fabric between them. Although it held fast at first, with a few tugs she was able to free the object from its hiding spot. After a quick glance around the gardens to make sure she was truly alone, she carefully unrolled the fabric.

Even in the dim light, she could make out the seven green stones.

With a gasp, Cordelia quickly wrapped the emeralds back up, tucked the pouch into her basket with Mrs. Chibbs' ribbons, and made for the house without looking back. She hoped Aubrey would return from Little Chepping sooner rather than later.

****

Once in her room, Cordelia locked the door behind her. She would have to hide Lady Brompton's emeralds until she could give them to Rhys Aubrey. How, though, had they come to be hidden in the statue? Had the jewel thieves placed them there for safekeeping until the emeralds could be sent to London, and Owen Grimm attempted to retrieve them when he was killed? Or had Grimm himself tucked them up into the hollow space in Apollo's foot? None of it made any sense, and the entire situation made Cordelia seethe with rage because it was her own sister being blamed for the footman's death. Worse, it was her sister who refused to exonerate herself by telling the truth.

But what to do with the gems? There was a vase of dried flowers sitting on the writing table. Without a moment's hesitation, she pulled the flowers out in a single stroke and dropped the pouch into the vase. She was just fluffing the still-bright dahlias when there was a tapping at the door.

It was Tybalt. "What are you up to?" he said with no preface.

"I'm certain I have no idea what you mean." Cordelia tried not to sound too frosty, but the effort was wasted.

"You've been skulking around the gardens. I was coming back from the stables with Heyward, and we saw you scurrying in through the lower doors." He strolled in and made himself at home in the chair by the fireplace. "You kept looking around like you were afraid someone might see you. So, I shall ask again. What are you up to, Cordie?"

"Tybalt, I can't tell you everything, I simply can't. However, suffice it to say that Owen Grimm was not the honest and loyal footman he pretended to be. In fact, he may have been a very unpleasant man altogether, which could be why he was killed."

Tybalt grabbed the poker and jabbed at the burning logs. "Does this have anything to do with Aubrey's note?"

She froze. "Aubrey's note?"

"Yes, a courier arrived while you were in the village, with a note from Aubrey. Did you not read it?"

Sure enough, there was a folded letter waiting on the writing desk, propped neatly on a small silver tray.

"Bloody hell," she muttered. Quickly she unfolded it and read it.

"Dear Mrs. Falconer, please be advised that I shall be delayed at Chepping overnight and will not return to Fairfield Hall until the morning. I have had a very interesting conversation with Mrs. G. and believe that I may have an inkling as to who is responsible for all that has happened. While I realize the temptation you must be feeling to ask questions and investigate matters at Fairfield in my absence, I strongly urge you to be careful and do not place yourself or your sister in any further danger with your explorations. Yours, R. Aubrey."

Well, then. Aubrey was clearly on to something. But certainly, he had no idea of her discovery, and she smiled with some satisfaction to think of his reaction when she showed him the emeralds the next morning.

"So," Tybalt pressed, "what are you and Aubrey doing? He's racing off to Chepping like a bat out of hell, you're slinking about behind the hedgerows, and now you're getting letters from him. I've seen the way you look at him, too."

"Tybalt, there is nothing untoward. And if there were, what of it? He is a…friend and wished to let me know he would be delayed until tomorrow."

"Not to put too fine a point on it, Cordie, but I've known him as long as you have, and I do not see any notes on silver trays waiting in *my* room." Tybalt raised an eyebrow at her. "He does seem rather fond of you."

"Stop it," she said. "Right now."

"And clearly you're fond of him as well," her brother continued, with a wiggle of his brows.

"For the love of all that is holy, Tybalt, you must

stop this at once." He said nothing, and at last she sighed. "Yes. I am very fond of him indeed."

"Thought so. It shows on your face when he walks into a room."

"Oh, Tybalt, you mustn't say anything to anyone. I've only known him a week. I can't help that I find myself drawn to him. He's so…he's quite different, isn't he?"

He shrugged. "Cordie, when you came back to England several weeks ago, Mother was certain you'd be some miserable grieving widow who had to be petted and coddled and then finally tucked away in a corner somewhere to grow old alone. Although she'll never admit this herself, I suspect she was more than a bit relieved to find you healthy and happy and moving on with your life after Falconer's death. You're a grown woman. You have money and land—despite it being a bit unfashionable for ladies to have either—and you can live wherever you wish, without being forced to depend upon our parent and her good graces. Should you choose to marry again, you can marry whomever you like." He paused. "I rather envy you."

Cordelia sat beside him. "You poor dear. Has Mother been making her *Tybalt Must Marry* noises again?"

"Not lately, thank God, because she's had Ophelia to keep her busy. But once Ophelia is married—or considering current circumstances, banished back to Wycombe Heath with the rest of us reprobates—then Mother will find herself once again on the marital warpath and force me to call with her upon boring young ladies and their harpy mothers. I'll spend endless hours commenting on the weather, discussing musical performances I didn't actually attend, and observing how all of the best people of society are here in the room and isn't it lovely. All so that our dear mother can rest assured that someday the Dean line shall continue down a legitimate path for yet another generation."

Cordelia felt a bit sorry for him, but her brother was making this into far more of a tragedy than it truly was. "Tybalt, it's somewhat hard for me to empathize. While Mother may hound you at this point about marrying and having children, at least you have some measure of security, as our father's heir. The rest of us must make advantageous marriages—or, as in my case, land investments—or we will end up paupers at the mercy of others. It's why Mother is so eager for Ophelia to marry Henry Brompton—because if Ophelia marries Henry, then Mother can rest easily, knowing Ophelia has a decent future. And poor Mercutio…."

"Poor Mercutio? What of him?"

"Well, he loves Bessie Venables. She may be the daughter of a blacksmith and a bit coarse around the edges, but he loves her. And he'll never be able to marry her, because then he'll have nothing at all other than what little Father bequeathed him in his will. Oh, dear. Mercutio might actually have to work for a living to support Bessie and the children. Now that I think of it," she said, "you and I have things rather easy. I married a poor man who at least loved me, and you shall marry a dull girl who guarantees you an heir, which makes your inheritance secure."

Tybalt snorted and stared into the fire. "We're not so far removed from work, if you'll recall. Grandfather made his money by investing in ships. I'm certain that took some degree of effort."

"And what would you or Mercutio know about how to invest anything, other than wagering on horses or speculating in some sort of land scheme? No, neither of you has ever lifted a finger. And that," she said firmly, "is why neither of you shall ever be really happy. Your lives center on drinking and gaming and heaven knows what else, and you've never done a day's work in your lives. But you both know that all good things must come to an end, and eventually you'll have to do your duty and marry well, whether it pleases you or not. You'll have an amiable and moderately pretty wife, as well as your inheritance, and you'll be simply miserable from the boredom."

"Well," her brother said lightly, "not all of us can elope with the servants, can we? At any rate, you still haven't told me what you and Aubrey are plotting."

"And I shan't," Cordelia said with a smile. "Sworn to secrecy, dear Tybalt."

"Very well. In that case, I shall see you at dinner. You might want to go see our sister. Ophelia's been locked in her room crying all day. While normally I would not care a fig, I believe Henry is a bit concerned."

Henry certainly ought to be concerned. Because if Henry truly ended the engagement, as his mother insisted he do, then Ophelia would be brokenhearted, and Cordelia would have to do something about it. She wasn't sure what that something would be, but in her imagination, it involved several sharp pointy objects, with Henry on the receiving end. "Perhaps I shall go speak with her, then," she said. "I might be of some comfort to her."

Tybalt was horrified. "Now I know beyond doubt

that you are up to something. You have never tried to comfort Ophelia in your life. In fact, I believe your typical response to her weeping has always been that she must put her chin up and stop gibbering."

Cordelia smiled as she made for the door. "Yes. Well, that is comforting to some of us."

Chapter Thirteen

As Tybalt had predicted, Ophelia was sobbing into her handkerchief and had been doing so all day. Being Ophelia, she was weeping quite prettily, finding sufficient misery to produce tears yet not so many that they might render her complexion swollen and blotchy, should Henry Brompton or anyone else of importance condescend to visit her. This degree of balance was something Ophelia had developed after many years of practice, having learned fairly early on in life that her mother would only pity her so far, and that once Ophelia's face was pink or puffy, Mrs. Dean lost interest in patting and consoling her. Thus, crying was always performed with a certain level of decorum.

"Cordelia," she said softly. "It is so good of you to call on me."

"I'm hardly calling on you, dear. You're two doors away from me, and you've been shut in here all day. It is time for you to dress for dinner and come downstairs." Cordelia used the same no-nonsense tone with Ophelia that she had employed when Lydia was five years old.

"Oh, but I cannot," Ophelia said, and draped herself across the bed, an arm resting over her forehead. "Lady Brompton is so vicious, and she has made it clear I shall never call her mother-in-law, despite it being the one thing I have wished for since I was a child of ten."

Cordelia blinked. "You've thought of Lady Brompton since you were ten?"

"That's not what I mean, Cordie. I mean ever since I was a child of ten, I have known I should marry Henry Brompton. And now his mother hopes to ruin it all, and while I do so wish to be obedient, I must stand my ground on this matter. I shall remain here at Fairfield Hall as Henry's fiancée," she said determinedly, not even looking at Cordelia. "And once I tell Henry the truth, he will understand that he cannot send me away, whether his mother objects or not."

Cordelia frowned. "The truth? Ophelia, you indicated that you had already been telling the truth when you denied any untoward involvement with Owen Grimm."

Ophelia pushed her face into a red velvet pillow. "Not about that," she said, muffled.

Cordelia sat on the bed beside her. "What, then? If you know something about Grimm's murder, you must tell me. I cannot help you if you are not forthcoming." Indeed, she must learn as much as possible here at Fairfield while Aubrey was off scampering about the countryside.

"I shan't," Ophelia said with a sob, and this time, it was real. Great, racking sobs from deep within her soul came pouring out into the pillow, and all Cordelia could do was hold her and wait for it to pass.

When Ophelia had finished, Cordelia got the washbasin and a soft cloth and began wiping her sister's face down. "Here," she instructed. "Lie back with the cloth on your face. It's nice and cool, and will help your skin look better at dinner. I know how important such things are to you."

"Thank you." Ophelia hiccoughed.

"Now," Cordelia said gently, "I know this will be difficult for you, my dear, but you must tell me what you know. I have been working with Mr. Aubrey, you see. He is an agent of the Crown and was sent here to make certain inquiries, unbeknownst to the Bromptons. If there is some way you can shed light on the death of Owen Grimm, you must tell me at once."

Her sister was shocked. "An agent of the Crown? Whatever for?"

Cordelia waved a hand. "Do not worry. I am certain it has nothing to do with Henry. Now, what has happened?"

"Oh, but you see, Cordie, it has *all* to do with Henry!" Ophelia sobbed anew.

"What has to do with Henry?" Now Cordelia was thoroughly baffled.

"Henry! In the garden that night!" her sister whispered.

"In the…Ophelia, what are you saying?"

"When I went out there to meet Grimm." Ophelia took a deep breath. "He had asked me to meet him by the statue of Apollo, and when I got there, I saw him lying on the ground. I didn't—I didn't realize he was dead at first, until I got right up next to him, you see. That was how I got the blood on my skirts."

"Why didn't you scream or cry out for help?" Cordelia demanded. "Instead, you came rushing back to the terrace, pretending all was well."

"Because of Henry," Ophelia said sadly. "I saw him in the darkness, running away from Grimm's body. It was Henry, Cordelia. Henry Brompton, my fiancé, killed Owen Grimm."

Cordelia sank into the pillows. "Oh, Ophelia." She felt her heart ripping in half, not just for her sister, but for Henry as well. What could have driven her childhood friend to murder? More importantly, how had she not known, not sensed that Henry was a killer? Now, suddenly, everything was divided into two parts of life—the part in which Henry Brompton had been her friend, and her sister's fiancé, and the part in which he was a cold-blooded murderer.

"Ophelia," she said, trying to hide the shaking in her voice. "My dear, are you certain? You saw him do it?"

"Grimm was already on the ground when I came up the path. I saw Henry from behind, as he slipped away, heading the other direction." Ophelia sniffled. "He must have heard me approaching, and then escaped. Of course, it was dark enough that he likely did not see me. I have not told him, you see."

"Told him? You haven't told him you saw him there?" Cordelia was astonished. If she thought a man she loved had killed someone, she'd have confronted him on the spot, and as loudly as possible.

"I didn't want to say anything," Ophelia said. Her eyes were red rimmed and puffy, and no cold compresses would make the swelling go away before dinner. "I know Grimm was only a servant, but what if Henry were to be arrested? Then he'd be ruined, and I'd never get to marry him!"

"If I understand you correctly," Cordelia said as realization dawned, "you said nothing in order to protect Henry from ruining his own reputation and going to jail. Now that you yourself have been accused, you're going to tell him that you saw him that night, and thus prevent him from breaking the engagement. Because after all, if he breaks the engagement, you no longer have any reason to protect him." She pulled away from Ophelia and moved to the window.

"Oh, Cordie, I knew you'd understand. I'm sure it's awfully wicked of me to behave this way, but I do love him, and I know we could make each other happy if he'd just get out from under his mother's influence."

Cordelia said nothing and simply stared through the damp glass out at the lane. It was nearly dark now, and the snow had returned once again, with a vengeance. It would be nothing short of a miracle if Rhys Aubrey were able to ride back from Chepping in the morning. And now that she knew who had killed Owen Grimm, she had to tell Adkyns, and Henry would be arrested just as Ophelia feared. But why would Henry have done such a thing? Had he known about the stories of Grimm's parentage?

"Ophelia," she said, trying to keep her voice even. "What could have driven Henry to kill one of his family's loyal servants?"

Ophelia shrugged. "I don't know, although I suppose it does not really signify. Perhaps Grimm was impertinent or rude to Henry, and Henry just lost his temper."

"Dear sister, we have known Henry Brompton these past twenty years, and when have you ever seen him lose his temper at anything? You could not have chosen a more mild-mannered gentleman to fall in love with. No," she said. There was still some piece of the puzzle that she was missing. "Something is not quite right about this. Ophelia, stay in your room and say nothing to anyone, particularly about Aubrey's work for the Crown. I shall tell everyone at dinner that you are indisposed. I'm certain they will all understand and pity you greatly, which I know you like very much. Lock the door behind me, and let no one in other than myself or the maid."

Ophelia sat up, brightening a bit. "Oh, Cordie, have you thought of a way to help Henry?"

"Not exactly. Lie down and get some rest. I shall return later. Again, do not allow anyone into this room, do you understand?"

****

Cordelia dressed for dinner and then asked Waverly to convey to the others that both she and her sister were ill. Perhaps, she told the butler, she might join the rest of the party later. That would give her a good two hours in which to explore and collect what evidence she might need. At half past eight, when she was certain everyone was down in the dining hall, she crept out of her room.

Fairfield Hall was constructed in the shape of an H. As in most houses of its status, the lower floor was given over to the kitchens and storage areas, as well as some of the servants' quarters. The second floor was where the family dined, danced, read, welcomed guests, and generally socialized. The uppermost level, however, was where the Brompton family's private rooms were, along with the dozen or so guest rooms and suites that came in quite handy when entertaining for a fortnight-long party.

The family's apartments were located in the east wing, while Cordelia and the other guests were assigned rooms on the western wing of the H and the center corridor. As Cordelia slipped through her door, she glanced about to make sure she was alone. The hall was dark and quiet, and shadows flickered eerily in the soft glow of the single candle she carried. If this were one of Lydia's novels, a spectral monk might come gliding by at any moment. However, there were no ghostly apparitions or anything else present in the hallway other than a large gray and white cat, and Cordelia progressed to Henry's room unmolested.

Once within the room, she locked the door behind her, taking a quick inventory of the room's layout. Henry's room was ornate—fine chairs were by the hearth, several paintings (including one of Lady Brompton herself) adorned the walls, and the bed was a fairly large structure with posts and curtains, looking as though it were at least a century old. All of the furniture was heavy, dark, and masculine, which Cordelia found an odd paradox, given Henry's mild-mannered demeanor.

She examined the writing desk to see if there were any telltale sacks of jewels lying within—for though it might be ridiculous, it would certainly wrap things up neatly—but found nothing. A few scraps of badly composed poetry paying homage to Ophelia littered the top of the desk, and after reading one or two awkward couplets and feeling vaguely nauseous, Cordelia moved on to the heavy oak wardrobe.

Henry's shirts had been neatly pressed and folded by his valet and stacked tidily within. She set the candle on a small table and then began examining the shirts, but was unable to see anything out of the ordinary. His coats, all of which were of the finest material and the latest style, formed a precision line organized by color, hung on rails toward the right side of the cupboard. She frowned, thinking Henry seemed very fond of dull colors like tan and brown. In fact, the only bright color she'd seen him in lately was blue, and that was the night of the ball. She paused.

One of Henry's blue coats was out of place.

Within the wardrobe, the coats were lined up and sorted. Five tan coats, four brown ones, two blue coats with an empty rail between them, and a pair of black woolen ones.

And then there was a third blue coat, at the very end.

Carefully, she lifted the coat out of the wardrobe to study it in the dim candlelight. It was a bit wrinkled, as though it had been shoved in hastily, rather than with loving care by the valet.

And on the cuff of the left sleeve was a dark, dry stain.

Cordelia stifled a gasp and lifted the candle to get a better look. The rust-colored blotch was nearly black, appearing evil and malevolent in the flickering light. In addition to the stain at the cuff, there was a telltale bit of spatter farther up the sleeve and even a fleck or two on the collar. Whoever had put the coat in here had clearly been in a hurry.

And Cordelia, for the life of her, could not think as to why Henry would do such a thing. If Grimm's killer had intended to stop him from telling the truth about his parentage, how did the jewels tie in? And if he was killed because of the jewels, why would Henry have been involved? Henry Brompton certainly had no need to steal the precious gemstones of society's grand families.

Something did not make sense, and she could not quite put her finger on it.

Putting the coat back in the wardrobe as she had found it, she blew out the candle and slipped out of the room.

****

Everyone else—other than Ophelia, of course—was still at dinner when she joined them at the table.

"Are you feeling better, Mrs. Falconer?" Littleberry asked, pulling out a chair for her.

"I am, thank you, Mr. Littleberry. Perhaps I just needed a short rest," she said. Conversation was less than animated, and Henry's behavior was particularly sullen this evening.

Thomas Heyward, who had clearly been into the port already, leaned in close to Cordelia. "Mrs. Falconer, you look stunning this evening."

"Thank you." Cordelia inched her chair back a bit, but Heyward was persistent.

"I must ask," he said in a low voice, "have you had opportunity to give any thought to our conversation of this afternoon?"

She speared a piece of meat with her fork. "To be perfectly frank, Mr. Heyward, I have not given it any thought at all. Do try the duck, it's lovely."

"Please," he murmured.

Cordelia glanced around, hoping she was the only one able to hear Heyward making such a spectacle of them both.

"You and I could marry," he continued, to her horror. "I don't have much money, other than what my aunt condescends to give me, but I've got respectability and a good name. If we are being frank right now, those are two things that you are rather lacking at present."

She scowled at him. "While you may have respectability and a name, you certainly cannot be said to have good manners or a civil tongue. Unlike you, I have plenty of money and do not need to depend on the charity of an unkind and controlling aunt to support my bad habits. So, Mr. Heyward, the answer to your question is an emphatic and unequivocal *no*."

The room was suddenly silent, and Cordelia froze for a moment. There had been, as is wont to happen occasionally during a dinner party, a general lull in the conversation, so that everyone sitting nearby, through their own lack of speech, was able to hear Cordelia's. Her mother and Mr. Littleberry were looking at her with undisguised shock, while her brothers and Lydia were trying desperately—and mostly unsuccessfully—to cover laughter.

Lady Brompton banged on the table with her soup spoon. "What are you saying down there, Mrs. Falconer? Thomas? What's going on over there?"

"Nothing, Aunt." Heyward raised his glass to Lady Brompton. "All is quite well over here. Is it not, Mrs. Falconer?"

"Splendid," she agreed with a forced smile. As much as she had started to dislike Heyward, there was no need to further embarrass him at the table. A few moments later, she began to reconsider this charity when his hand lightly brushed against her thigh. The second time it happened, she deliberately jabbed his knuckles with her fork.

He shot her a hurt look. "Mrs. Falconer, whatever has gotten into you?" he whispered with a sly smile.

She rose to excuse herself and leaned close to his

ear. "Do not presume to touch me again, Mr. Heyward. In fact, please do not speak to me if it can at all be avoided."

The gentlemen all bowed goodnight to her, and as she left the dining room, there was the scrape of a chair and soft running footsteps. Lydia appeared behind her. "What is it, Mother? You look unwell."

"On the contrary, Lydia," she said, steering her daughter down the corridor. "I am fine enough, but I fear that we have all been greatly misled, particularly your aunt Ophelia. Come upstairs with me now."

"What is it?" Lydia followed her as she hastily made her way up the stairs.

"I need you to stand guard for me."

Lydia stopped in midstep. "Stand guard? Mother, what on earth are you doing?"

Cordelia took her by the hand and pulled her along. "There is not a moment to lose. Come here." She propelled Lydia down the hallway into the east wing and finally came to a stop near a door. She opened it quietly and stepped into the room. "Lydia, listen to me. I need you to stand in this doorway and keep an eye on the hallway. If you see anyone—anyone at all—you must step into the room with me and then hide under the bed. Do you understand?"

Lydia shook her head. "No. What is happening?"

"I must search the room, and I must be quick about it. They will finish dinner soon, and then we may be out of time. Come, Lydia. Now."

Lydia followed her mother into the room and closed the door nearly all the way, leaving just enough of a crack so that she could see out to the main stairs. Cordelia headed straight for the wardrobe and flung it open.

"Whose room is this, Mother?" Lydia whispered, but Cordelia ignored her.

Unlike the neat and ordered precision of Henry Brompton's room, this wardrobe was arranged haphazardly—clearly by a man who had no valet to take care of him, nor any sense of organization of his own. Coats were a jumble, and a few wrinkled shirts lay in the bottom of the wardrobe where they had been casually tossed.

The shirts.

Cordelia dug through the pile until she found what she had been looking for. A white silk shirt, with a dark stain around the very edge on the cuff of the left sleeve. "Got you," she said aloud.

"Not entirely," came a voice from the other side of the room.

Chapter Fourteen

She whirled about, and there was Thomas Heyward, one arm casually around Lydia's neck.

"Mother?" Lydia asked, her voice steady.

"Lydia, all will be well. Mr. Heyward is not going to hurt you, are you, Mr. Heyward?"

He smiled but did not release Lydia from his grasp. "Well, that depends, Mrs. Falconer. But please, let us not stand on ceremony. You should call me Thomas, and I may call you Cordelia. How does that sound?"

"As you wish," she said pleasantly.

"Now," he said, pointing to the shirt in her hand. "What brings you here to rummage about in my wardrobe? Clearly you think you have found something of great import."

"Ah." Cordelia examined the sleeve. "Well, yes, you see, Thomas, I have been very concerned about my sister, for she truly believes that it was Henry who murdered Owen Grimm the other night. However, she was willing to marry him nonetheless, because like him—and you—she is greatly concerned with station and status."

Heyward burst out laughing. "Henry? My cousin could barely squash an insect, let alone kill a man! And what reason would he have for killing Grimm anyway? That's ludicrous."

She nodded. "Well, that's what I thought, you see.

I found Henry's blue jacket in his wardrobe earlier, with a bloodstain that corresponds to this one. However, it seemed out of place. In fact, the whole thing seemed off—I tried and could not think of a single reason for Henry to kill the man. Even the notion of Grimm's parentage just didn't seem like a good enough motive for murder."

Heyward shook his head. "His parentage? That had nothing to do with Henry."

"Oh." Cordelia frowned, trying to add things up. "Henry's father wasn't Grimm's father?"

Lydia squirmed a bit, and Heyward squeezed his arm around her tighter. "Stop fidgeting, dear. Henry's father? Hardly! I don't think anyone knew who got Grimm's mother with child—possibly not even the girl herself. My aunt was smart enough to send her away, but the servants—and likely everyone else—still assumed that it was old Brompton who'd put a bun in that oven. Owen Grimm was likely just the son of some itinerant tinker."

Lydia had stopped wriggling, and Cordelia smiled at her. "Lydia, you're doing just fine. Mr. Heyward—Thomas—I am so very sorry that you feel you've been somehow wronged, but I am certain that your killing Mr. Grimm was an accident. He must have simply fallen and hit his head on the statue of Apollo. That poor boy."

"No!" he barked. "Poor boy, indeed! He had found out about a…poor investment I made and was threatening to tell my aunt Brompton. It would have ruined me permanently—I'd have never got another cent from her!"

"What sort of investment, Thomas?" she pried.

"You know I've been looking for new investment opportunities myself."

He softened a bit. "It wasn't exactly an investment. It was…there's a group of men in London, you see. They buy jewels and replace them with replicas. Then when you've got the money, you can buy the real ones back. I had so many gambling debts that I thought it might be a good way to loan myself some money."

"How many people did you take jewels from?"

"Just a few families," he said earnestly, "and not from anyone who needed them. I'm always forced to attend these house parties, you see, where the women are wearing necklaces and earrings that are just dripping with fortune…I just needed a little bit here and there. So I worked with these men in London to replace the real jewels with the paste copies."

Cordelia tried her best to look sympathetic. "Oh, Thomas. What you must have gone through. And with your aunt having so much money and keeping you on such a tight allowance…no wonder you felt compelled to do this." She shook her head sadly. "And that Grimm. How awful of him to try to blackmail you. Of course you had to stop him."

"Precisely!" he crowed. "I knew you'd understand, Cordelia. You and I are actually a great deal alike, did you know that?"

At Lydia's expression of horror, Cordelia stepped closer.

Heyward moved back toward the door, pulling Lydia with him. "Not so close, Cordelia."

"I'm sorry, I'm sorry," she said hastily. "I just…I think it is possible that I misjudged you, Thomas. You're far more clever than I ever realized or gave you credit for. I do apologize for underestimating you." He seemed mollified by this, so she continued. "Would you terribly mind releasing Lydia? She seems anxious, and I believe you and I can clear up any misunderstanding between us if she is not in your way."

Heyward's eyes narrowed. "You know, Cordelia, I rather don't think so. You see, you're not the only one who questions people's motivations. You wondered what reason Henry could have had to kill Grimm, and you were correct in realizing that he had none. Likewise, I'm wondering what reason you could have for suddenly deciding you wish to be my friend after all. And I am seeing none."

Cordelia sighed and cast her eyes down. "You're right, Thomas, of course. I don't like you. I don't wish to be your friend. And I can't think of anything I'd enjoy better than seeing you go to jail, both for killing that footman and for stealing jewels from your own family and friends."

He laughed heartily. "Well, at least now we're being truthful with one another."

"Not entirely," she said.

"What do you mean?"

Cordelia held her breath. She would have one chance, and one chance only, to get Lydia away from him. "This shirt. Do you see the problem?"

"Cordelia, quit speaking in riddles. It's a shirt. It has blood on it. The blood is Grimm's, the shirt is mine. What more do you want?"

She met his eyes. "I want you to get away from my daughter." Before he could respond, she flung the shirt directly at his face and then launched herself at him, knocking him to the floor.

Lydia sprang away, flung the door open wide, and shrieked at the top of her lungs.

****

When Rhys Aubrey arrived at Fairfield Hall, he was greeted at the door by Waverly, who directed him into the dining room. Lady Brompton was in her typical vile mood, Henry was staring gloomily at his plate and moving his vegetables around without actually eating them, and Mrs. Dean was lecturing everyone under her breath. Mr. Littleberry chatted pleasantly with Mercutio and Tybalt.

"Excuse me," Aubrey said. "Where is Mrs. Falconer?"

"Who knows?" replied Tybalt. "She wasn't feeling well, and then she joined us for a bit, and left before the cake was served. Lydia and Heyward are with her somewhere, I believe."

He froze. "Thank you. Tybalt, would you and your brother come along with me, please? As well as you, Henry. I have something I must speak with you about that cannot wait."

The men grumbled but rose and followed him into the corridor.

"Please, do not ask questions, for I shall explain later. I have reason to suspect Mrs. Falconer could be in great danger."

"What?" exploded the twins in unison.

"If she is indeed with Mr. Heyward, she could be in peril. I am reasonably certain that he is the killer of Owen Grimm."

"Good heavens," said Henry. "Why would Thomas kill one of my footman?"

"It is a very long story," Aubrey said, "and we

have no time. We must find Mrs. Falconer and Lydia."

They split up then, Tybalt pairing up with Henry Brompton to search the lower levels of the house, and Mercutio accompanying Aubrey to the upper wings. When they reached the top of the stairs, Aubrey put a finger to his lips. Muffled voices came from a room down the hall.

Aubrey pulled a pistol from somewhere inside his coat. Quietly and efficiently, he removed a pouch from his pocket and proceeded to pour powder down the pistol's barrel, stuff a paper wad inside, and then drop a ball in behind it. He handed it to Mercutio and then repeated the process with a second pistol. "Have you shot one of these before?"

Mercutio shook his head. "Not at a person."

"In that case, don't stand behind me with that. Just hold it in case I need a second shot," Aubrey whispered as they approached the door.

Suddenly, there was a loud thump from inside the room, and the door flung open to reveal a disheveled Lydia. When she saw a startled Aubrey and Mercutio pointing pistols at her, she did what any sensible fourteen-year-old girl would do.

She shrieked at the top of her lungs.

In one swift move, Aubrey reached out and pulled Lydia from the room, passing her to her uncle. He pushed the door aside and found, much to his astonishment, Cordelia sitting on Thomas Heyward's chest. One of Heyward's arms was pinned up under Cordelia's knee, and there was a white shirt wrapped around his neck and clutched tightly in Cordelia's left hand.

"You. Will. Not. Touch. My. Child." Each word

was punctuated with a harsh slap across Heyward's face, and he was trying to protect himself with his one free arm.

Aubrey cleared his throat and lowered his pistol. "Cordelia?"

"He was going to hurt Lydia," she growled. Her hair was in disarray, her face pink, and her blue eyes glittered with rage.

"Cordelia, get off him. Lydia is safe, and so are you. He can't hurt you," he said softly. "I won't let him. I won't let him hurt either of you. I promise."

With a whimper, she stood and stepped away from Heyward. He bore scratches on his face from the rings she wore, Cordelia noticed with satisfaction.

"Get up," Aubrey ordered. Heyward rose to his feet. He brushed himself off and glared at Cordelia.

"You realize, don't you, that this is all your word against mine," he said. "No one will ever believe anything you say about this."

"Lydia heard it all as well," she reminded him.

Heyward scowled at her. "It doesn't matter, Cordelia. No jury would ever find me guilty. Not when the dead man was a simple footman trying to blackmail his master, and I'm a respectable gentleman."

Cordelia laughed softly. "Oh, Thomas. You are many things indeed. But respectable will never be one of them."

In the blink of an eye, he lunged at her, and a cracking sound rang out.

Heyward's eyes widened, and he toppled against her, knocking her into the wall. Without another sound, he folded to the floor, and a stain widened on the front of his coat, blooming like a soft red flower.

Cordelia turned her gaze to Aubrey, expecting to see the pistol smoking, but he still held it at his side. Instead, it was Mercutio, standing in the doorway, lowering his gun, as Lydia peered around from behind his back.

Aubrey moved to her, and she slid into his arms, not caring who saw or what they might think.

****

Later that evening, the two of them sat in the library together, sipping claret.

"I didn't think you'd be back until the morning," she admitted.

"I hadn't planned to originally. But once Mrs. Grimm told me the truth, I knew who our killer was. And I knew it wasn't Henry."

She frowned. "What could Mrs. Grimm have said to make you think that? Surely she couldn't have known Heyward was her son's killer."

Aubrey swirled the sherry in his glass. "It turns out that Henry's father wasn't Grimm's father at all."

Cordelia nodded. "Really? Who was it then? Heyward seemed to think it was some tinker."

He shook his head. "No. It was another servant, a groom who is now at Lord Sackville's place."

"Imagine! But why did the staff think it was old Mr. Brompton who'd gotten her with child?"

Aubrey shrugged. "When Hannah Grimm found herself with child, Lady Brompton asked her point-blank who the father was. Hannah told her, and the old lady threw her out. Everyone just sort of assumed it was Mr. Brompton that had gotten the girl in trouble, and Hannah Grimm herself wasn't around to correct the misunderstanding. When her boy got old enough, he came here looking for work and must have heard the servants talking. He got it into his head that Brompton was his father, which was why he was trying to blackmail Ophelia into giving him the earrings."

"And Heyward must have heard those rumors as well and thought to take advantage of them by threatening to expose that Grimm was in fact Henry's half brother."

"Right. But since I had asked Grimm to keep an eye out for fake jewels, he knew right off the bat that Ophelia's earrings were imitations. He must have figured out that Heyward was the one behind the thefts and decided to blackmail him over that as well. It was a double cross. He was playing both sides, you see," Aubrey finished.

"So Grimm was to meet you to turn over the fake jewels and reveal Heyward's involvement to you, but instead Heyward, wearing Henry's coat, got there first and killed him."

Aubrey raised his glass to her. "Exactly. I had Waverly go out and search the gardens, and he found a heavy branch with blood on the end, hidden in some bushes. But how did *you* know it was Heyward, and not Henry, as Ophelia believed?"

Cordelia moved to the window and peered out into the darkness. Fat white flakes drifted against the window. "For some reason, he decided that I was the woman with whom he wanted to form an attachment. Why are you laughing? I'm not that awful. At any rate, he'd had a bit much to drink at dinner, and when I jabbed his knuckles—well, he had scratches and a bruise on his left hand. And all I could think was that this was the piece of the puzzle I'd been missing all along. That it wasn't Henry at all; it was Heyward wearing Henry's coat who had killed Grimm. I went upstairs to search his room and had Lydia stand guard, but he must have come up the servants' stairs and surprised her before she could warn me."

He nodded. "It makes sense, given what we now know of Heyward's thought process, does it not? If he married you, you would provide him with a source of income to cover his gambling debts, and he could provide you with the respectability that the Bromptons clearly feel you lack."

She shuddered. "Ugh. Can you imagine being on such a tight leash to this family?"

Aubrey joined her at the window. "I suspect that's why he got involved with the jewel thieves. It would be easy for a man like Heyward to have access to jewels that most people wouldn't even notice missing, or at the very least would not notice if they were replaced with paste glass. It would be easy money for very little trouble or effort." He put a hand on her shoulder. "Cordelia. That is enough about Heyward."

She shook her head. "Please, do not."

"You must hear me. I have little to offer you. I am the second son of a Yorkshire viscount and have made what little money I have as an agent of the Crown. It is unlikely that I will ever inherit my father's estate, as my brother has several sons. Despite all of these shortcomings, I want—more than anything—to be with you. And you must know I am not speaking of the sham engagement we discussed just a few days ago."

"Aubrey," she said, but he interrupted her.

"I would travel to the ends of the earth to be with you, Cordelia. Can you not see that? From the moment

I laid eyes on you, I knew you were the woman I need to spend my life with. And I must believe that you feel something for me as well."

She turned into him. "Mr. Aubrey—Rhys. Once my sister has married Henry Brompton, I shall take Lydia and return to Virginia. I have realized these past few weeks that I have no wish to stay in England any longer. My home is in America, on my tobacco farm."

"The night in the stables, then? All of this, everything we've said and felt? None of it has meant anything?" he asked, storm clouds brewing in his eyes.

"It was never supposed to mean anything," she whispered. "You were a stranger, and I wanted a diversion with someone I would never see again. I know that makes me wicked, but I could not help it."

"And the night in the library?"

"Please, Aubrey. Do not make this harder for me than it is already," she said. Cordelia was holding herself together but only just.

He nodded. "Cordelia, have you made up your mind, truly? You are determined to leave?"

"I must. England has not been my home for a very long time, and yet I did not realize that until I came back here. I shall sail once spring returns." She could not meet his gaze.

"Very well," he said, taking her hand in his. "Then that gives me three months in which to change your mind."

Chapter Fifteen

Two sturdy horses drew a cart up the hillside. The road was rocky, yet stable, and the horses had no trouble navigating the angles and turns of the ridge. Although the journey was slow, the passengers in the cart did not mind. The man at the reins, a well-dressed and handsome sort, took the opportunity to enjoy the scenery. It was early autumn, and the countryside was awash in color—blazing reds and oranges and yellows dotted the mountains, as though God himself had laid a cheerfully colored blanket across the countryside. The smell of woodsmoke lingered in the air, for the nights were now cold enough to warrant a fire in every hearth, and at many of the nearby farms, meat was being smoked and put away for the coming long winter.

As they rounded a bend, the woman beside him exclaimed, "Why, that must be it! Over there!" She pointed at a sprawling red farmhouse, sitting a half mile or so away, right in the center of a pasture. Even from this distance, they could make out the barns, the stables, and the men working in the fields. It was a busy time of year indeed.

When they finally approached the farmhouse, a lean red-headed girl came running down the lane, shoeless, waving. She held her skirts up out of the puddles, leaping easily over the few spots of mud that remained from the morning's rain. "Uncle Mercutio!"

she called, racing up to the cart. "You've come at last!"

"Lydia!" Mercutio Dean leaped from his seat and swept his niece into his arms. In the half year since he'd seen her, she seemed to have grown several inches. He hugged her tightly. "My sister is well?"

She nodded. "Mother is more than well. She is excruciatingly happy." Lydia grinned as she suddenly noticed the other occupants of the cart. "And you must be my new Aunt Bessie!"

The woman smiled back and nodded. Bessie Venables—no, she was now Bessie Dean—had been uncertain as to how she would be received by her new husband's family in America, but if Lydia was any indicator, it appeared that Bessie had little to fear. "It's a pleasure to meet you, Miss Falconer."

"Oh, please," the girl laughed. "It's Lydia. We're family, are we not? Besides, we're not much on formality around here, you'll come to find."

Mercutio drove the cart up the lane, with Lydia bouncing along beside them, admiring the children and pointing out the sights. "Those fields over there are where we've got tobacco in this year. Next year, we'll rotate wheat and corn through, although right now those are planted in the south fields. Oh, goodness—watch out, the pigs seem to have gotten loose again."

A pair of fat sows ran across the lane, chased by a young man with a stick.

Lydia waved to him. "Hello, Duncan! This is my Uncle Mercutio come to stay—please, try to catch them before Juliette gets into the garden again!"

As they approached the house, Cordelia stepped out onto the wide front porch, wiping her hands on her apron. "Mercutio!" She walked up to the cart and held out her arms to her brother in greeting. "I am so very glad to see you all. Bessie," she said with a warm and genuine smile. "I am happy to welcome you to our home. I'm baking pies in your honor, so I do hope you like apples. Now, hand me that baby, and you and the rest of the children come join me in the kitchen."

Bessie passed a fat infant to her new sister-in-law and hoisted a toddler down to the ground. The oldest child, a sturdy and serious boy of about five years in age, extended a hand to Lydia. "Are we cousins now? Are we to stay here with you in Virginia?"

"Yes, for as long as you wish," she said, reaching out to help him from the cart. "Would you like that?"

"Very much," he said. "You have a big house."

"We do," she said with a wink. "And we have chickens. Do you like chickens?"

He nodded. "I had a chicken in England. Mama named her Agatha."

"Well, Jonathan, I shall give you a chicken of your very own, and you may call her Agatha too, if you should like." Lydia grinned, thinking about her grandmother's reaction if Agatha Dean ever learned there was poultry named in her honor.

****

That evening, after the children had been sent out to play, full of pie and fresh sausage, Cordelia sat on the front porch with her brother. "How is Tybalt?"

Mercutio sighed. "That's the other bit of news. He's to marry Letitia Dunlea-Boggins."

"Good God," said Cordelia. "I shall send them my regards and best wishes, but I am not returning to England for another wedding any time soon."

He laughed. "I do not blame you. Besides, I think

you and I are probably not invited. What with your habit of making scandalous attachments, and me marrying Bessie—"

"She's good for you, Merc. I like her very much."

"Cordie, when I married her—well, Mother said I should lose my annual allowance. Tybalt gets it all, and I have nothing but a few pounds I've saved up from betting on horses and sitting at gaming tables. Thank God Bessie doesn't mind. She's used to being poor, even if I'm not." He sighed and squinted at the lush and abundant fields.

Cordelia pointed down the hillside, where the sun was setting in the west. "Look over there, Merc. It's so much land and so rich and beautiful. It brings me such joy to be back here once more."

"I can tell. You never would have been content to remain in England."

"No." She shook her head. "It's not my home. This is. Here, in Virginia with Lydia and my husband. Look! There he is now."

Sure enough, Rhys Aubrey was making his way up the path in the fading light. As she had expected, he had a doe slung over his shoulders, as well as the bonus of a pair of wild turkeys in his hand. "Mercutio! Welcome, brother," he called out, holding up a bird in greeting. "I've been harvesting dinner off your land for you."

Mercutio blinked. "Off my land?"

Aubrey winked at Cordelia. "I suppose I'd best stop talking now and let you tell him your news." He kissed his wife long and deeply and then pulled away. "I'll take these out back. Turkey for dinner tomorrow."

"Lovely," she said, watching him with undisguised admiration. After nearly a year, he still set her heart pounding every time she saw his face. Cordelia turned back to her brother. "Yes. Well, you see the apple orchard over there? On the western slope?"

Mercutio nodded.

"Beyond that," she continued, "there is a stream full of fish, and on the other side of that is a parcel of about two hundred acres. Up until recently, it belonged to an elderly Scot named MacFarlane and his wife. They died this past summer—both of them quite old, and within a week of one another. At any rate, their children have decided they don't want to remain in Virginia any longer. They're striking out for the west, heading to the frontier in Kentucky. So I bought some of the MacFarlane land. The hunting's quite good, there's timber, the soil is healthy, and there's a small cabin up on the ridge. Not a bad place for someone to get their start if they wished to make a life for themselves and their family," she mused. "Not bad at all."

"I see," said her brother. "And if someone wished to purchase that land from you, they might need to save up a substantial sum."

"Oh, it's not for sale," she said matter-of-factly. "Not yet. However, I've decided I might lease it to you for a few years. That way, you can develop an understanding of farming life here in America. You can decide whether this is the right place for you or not. If not, then you can head back to England—or wherever you and Bessie decide to go—and I'll still have my land. If you choose to stay and make a life for yourself here…well, then we'll talk about you purchasing it from me. In, say, five years or so, I'll sell it to you—if you're interested, of course—for the amount I paid for it this summer, minus what you shall pay me in leasing fees. Does that sound fair enough?"

Mercutio made a strange noise in his throat. "It…yes. Yes, it does, Cordie. Thank you."

She reached out and took his hand, giving it a squeeze. "You're my brother. That's what family does, you know."

He nodded. "I had forgotten."

She smiled in the fading light. "So had I."

****

Late that night, once everyone was tucked away for the evening, with the children piled into Lydia's bed, and Mercutio and Bessie bunked down in the parlor, Cordelia sat at her bedroom window and brushed her hair, the moonlight washing over her, pale and silver.

"It's good to have them here," she said absently.

"It is. They're good people, and Mercutio is far more like you than anyone else in the family," Aubrey said. "You should write Ophelia, and see how she's getting on as mistress of Fairfield Hall."

Cordelia snorted. "I'm sure she's battling for the role every day with that old harpy Lady Brompton. I don't especially care how Ophelia is getting on, and I'm sure she is even less interested about how you and I are faring."

He nodded. "That is probably true."

"You know," she continued, "I don't know which troubles me more. That my sister was willing to marry a man she believed to be a killer just to retain her status, or that the same man refused to stand up for her when she was the one being accused."

"They're very much alike," he agreed. He came up behind her, taking the brush, and began running it down her long hair. “You’ve got a tangle.”

“Yes. Well, Merc’s baby was pulling on it. I’m lucky I have any hair left at all,” she said, relaxing at his touch.

“I’m glad we’re here,” he said suddenly, and it was true. At first, he’d been unsure about living in the house she had made with her first husband, and then he had come to realize that as long as he was with Cordelia, he was home, no matter where they might be. He moved her hair from the side of her neck and kissed her soft skin.

Cordelia shuddered a bit. “Good God, Aubrey. You know what that does to me.”

He murmured in assent, but did not stop. She closed her eyes and leaned back into him, feeling his lips on her neck, his tongue tracing gentle swirls beneath her ear.

She thought for a moment of the first time he’d touched her, more than a year ago. Cordelia laughed softly.

He paused, glancing up at her. “You’re clearly pleased about something.”

“I am, because I’ve realized how very fortunate I am to have found you. You were willing to cross the ocean and come to this brand-new place with me, and make this your home.”

Aubrey smiled back at her. “Cordelia. Did I not swear to you I would travel to the ends of the earth to be with you?”

She wrapped herself around him once more as he kissed his way down her body, joyous in the knowledge that as long as Rhys Aubrey drew breath, she would never again be alone.

Indeed, as long as the two of them were together, she was home.

A word about the author...

Patti Wigington is the author of several Amazon Top 100 books on witchcraft, but fiction holds a magical place in her heart. She fell in love with the past as a child and has a Bachelor's Degree in History.

Patti loves a good historical romance, especially if there are elements of mystery and suspense thrown in between dances and duels. She is fascinated by the Regency period and colonial America, and regularly wishes she could host an afternoon tea chat with Jane Austen and Alexander Hamilton.

Patti lives in Ohio with a pair of college students, a vast collection of books and Tarot cards, and a very large dog.

http://pattiwigington.com

Thank you for purchasing
this publication of The Wild Rose Press, Inc.

For questions or more information
contact us at
info@thewildrosepress.com.

The Wild Rose Press, Inc.
www.thewildrosepress.com

www.ingramcontent.com/pod-product-compliance
Lightning Source LLC
LaVergne TN
LVHW050619100826
845148LV00011B/1655